Tower of Jacob

D. A. Brattain

To Mike,
Thanks again for
the great hospitality!
D. A. Brattain
7-25-07

Outskirts Press, Inc.
Denver, Colorado

Tower of Jacob

v5.0

Outskirts Press
http://www.outskirtspress.com

ISBN-13: 978-1-4327-0349-3

Printed in the United States of America

Dedicated to my loving wife Jennifer
who allowed me the freedom to fly,
my son Chris and daughter Katie
who are my greatest joy and to Joyce
who was always there for me…

Chapter 1

The carrier slipped through the waves, emerging from the morning mist like a silent grey ghost. An eerie steel mystery that pitched and rolled in the open ocean it's flight deck like a section of highway overpass broken off and adrift on the sea. It was hard to see from a distance, its form so monotone against the vapor rising from the waves that one might question whether it was there at all.

He could see it though and its crew, shuttling about, oblivious to the rocking waves and the ship underneath them. He was dreaming, or half awake and emerging from what had been a dream. He could feel himself drifting, thinking of things beyond oceans and the electro-mechanical environment of the carrier, of the dissonant ring of rock tunes, laughter and the chatter, the lean tough looks, the practiced phrases. It was good to be away from those things, away from the stinking bars and holes where conversations were reduced to the clanking jingle of pinball chatter, speaking not to him, but through him, the dead eyes staring through an alcoholic haze and smiles worn deep into faces, tired from so much smiling. He was glad to be away from there, away from them.

He glanced over at his wallet, lying on the small desktop next to his bunk. He wanted to be sure that it was still there. He remembered them, could feel the desperate pressure of small hands, spindly rough hands from farms and villages and their bodies pressing against him, pleading for his attention, his money and for him to move quickly as there were other customers waiting their turn in the darkness. He was away from there now. He was sleeping it off.

It was good to be away from there, he thought, I will not drink anymore for a while. I will stay on the ship and fly the missions and go home. I won't go back there.

His thoughts of penitence were interrupted by the sounds coming from several decks above him, the hard sounds of metal on metal, the mechanics of the heavy ship, the artificial air blowing through the lower decks, and the smell of oil, jet fuel, paint and sweat. Soon he would be dressed, up the stairs and out onto the flight deck. The wind would be blowing hard from bow to stern, and the crews would be moving to their support personnel, climbing into cockpits and getting strapped in.

His mind drifted over the scene. The ship already pointed into the wind and jet engines coming to life, the deck swarming with yellow, green, red, purple shirted crewmen all moving in quick choreography to the rhythm of flight operations. The Air Boss up above on the flight operations control deck, barking out instructions over a phone that seemed glued to his hand, controlling their movements in an effort to get aircraft off the deck and into the air.

The time came and he moved up the gantry and out

onto the deck with the other crews. In deliberate, orderly movements, he climbed into the F-4 Phantom and with the aid of the support crew, buckled in. They were well seasoned to carrier operations and without a second thought, tightened restraints, ran through checklists, got clearance to start engines and follow the directions of the deck and launch crewmen who waved them into successive positions over the catapults.

He looked to one side and could see the second F-4 waiting to launch next to him, the pilot and his "six", his navigator.

He felt at ease with the situation and the knowledge that something was coming back to him. That a life that heretofore had been out of the grasp of his memory was returning to fill in the gaps of his consciousness.

In position now, the two planes straining against the launch arms of the catapult hooked to their nose gear. With blast shields raised behind them he raised a thumb and a quick return salute to the launch crewman.

Almost immediately, he was pressed into the back of the seat by the sudden force of the catapult and the thousands of pounds of thrust generated by the two engines in full afterburner.

Zero to airborne in less than three seconds he quickly shifted his mind from the deck to the aircraft and focused his attention ever further ahead of it as both Phantoms gained altitude and speed, quickly joining with one another as leader and wingman.

Switching radio frequencies, he could see the other aircraft join up with them on their port side and familiar radio transmissions rang out in his helmet.

"Alpha-1, turn heading 060 and climb to flight level 15..."

"Roger, Con, 060 and 15."

He turned to the work in the cockpit, the general housekeeping, checking headings, altitude, and radar and weapon systems as the coastline closed rapidly on the horizon. He could make out the deep greens and browns of the coast a pencil thin line of sand that met a deep aqua and indigo to white. There was the hilly jungle beyond and the contrast of the land between a clear blue sky and the blue and white sea below.

He had been there many times before, he thought. It was always a beautiful place when viewed from altitude. He was aware of the beauty below his wings and that he carried the seeds of destruction and death. He felt the familiar anxiety, wanted to stop, to go no further.

"Alpha-1, we have you over the coast. Your feet are dry."

"Roger Con, we are with you at 1 5 heading 060."

"Alpha-1, turn to heading 040, altitude at your discretion. Fire support on grid coordinates, Baker 4 at 200 yards from smoke."

"Roger, con 040 to Baker 4."

"OK, stay close. We'll go down to 500 when we're inside 10 miles." He barked out in rapid staccato, routine instructions he had given a hundred times before.

"Roger." a voice responded.

The twin phantoms closed on the target at over 600 miles an hour. Within minutes they had reached the shore, climbed to 15,000 feet and were moving to the target. The planes seemed suspended over the sweating tangle of jungle and rice fields below. As they approached it, both planes nosed over gained airspeed and lost altitude. They leveled to 500 feet. At this altitude the relative speed of the aircraft rapidly became apparent and the trees, hills and the landscape rushed past them as they screamed over the countryside toward the objective.

"I got smoke at 11 o'clock."

"That's it."

"O.K. drop down to the deck and lay down some fire."

His wingman replied with two quick clicks on his mike.

The two aircraft rolled over in turn and closed on the smoke that marked the target below. Closing on the ground, he could see the details of the treetops filling his windscreen. Now very close to the ground and at the beginning of the run, a calm, business like voice called out.

"Armed…on the target… Ready… Bombs away…"

The napalm canisters fell free from both aircraft and after skipping once or twice over the ground, exploded into a huge ball of fire and black smoke. The flames saturated the target below and unleashed a huge burning inferno of gelatinous fuel, vegetation and human flesh. The aircraft turned sharply and rolled in a wide arc about the target.

"Let's give them one more pass."

He reflected quickly, he wanted to be sure, he thought. The thought bit at his nerves suddenly with a kind of uncertainty, an anxiety that cannot be described. It was elusive, there and gone before he had time to consider it. He hesitated for a moment, glanced at his hand on the stick, then over again at his wingman.

He wanted to be sure...

Without hesitation, both aircraft turned again to the target area and began the low level run to drop their ordinance. This time they came in closer to the ground. He could feel the machinery of a rapid-fire machinegun canister as he let loose a strafing burst into the jungle canopy below, peppering the area with 50 caliber rounds not aiming at anything specifically but chewing up the jungle growth. He was so low that he thought that he could smell the smoke from the burning napalm fire below and the cordite from the rounds as a steady stream of spent cartridges poured out of the gun pod underneath him. Then he felt the pressure in his seat as he turned sharply to starboard and climbed in an effort to get out of the target area.

He was breathing heavily through his oxygen mask.

"Con this is Alpha-1, request a return vector." he said, knowing where the carrier was but also wanting the extra insurance.

"Roger Alpha-1, turn 240..."

"Roger, 240."

Then as the two planes turned for the open sea and home and began to climb to safety, he caught a series of rapid muzzle flashes and tracers coming from a small clearing just ahead off their port side. The flashes looked different than those he had seen in the past on other missions. They seemed to be coming from somewhere behind them.

"We have ground fire." the voice again called to him in a controlled tone.

"Roger, I see it. Looks like it's off our six! You get any bogies on…"

Almost immediately they flew into a hail of large caliber rounds. Suddenly he felt successive shudders under his seat like a jackhammer working its way down the fuselage. Then a sudden shriek, barked in a panic stricken voice into his headset.

"I'm hit! I'm hit, Jesus!"

"You've got smoke, and lots of hydraulic fluid leaking!" A voice called out to him, his wingman reporting from alongside.

At the same moment he could see the panel in front of him light up with pressure and fire warning lights. The audible alarms rang in nervous protest and mixed with panic stricken voices as the fire rapidly poured smoke into the cockpit.

"Con Alpha-1! Mayday! Mayday!" He fought the stick with both hands as the steady loss of hydraulic pressure stiffened it and made the plane nearly impossible to control.

"Back off! I'm losing it!"

"Time to go!" There was no response from the back seat. His navigator had taken a round through the seat and lay limp behind him.

As the plane shook ever harder and began to nose over on its way toward the ground, he quickly blew both canopies, reached over and behind his head for the ejection handle and without hesitation pulled it forward.

He was immediately thrown clear of the aircraft and was sent spiraling end over end past the tail of the burning plane. The deafening rush of the wind past him subsided when the canopy blew off and the ejection system fired and the seat made several rotations skyward. Below him the phantom snapped over and rolled into the jungle floor where it exploded in a ball of fire. Within a few rotations, he felt the seat fall away. It all happened so fast that there was no time to slow down, no time to prepare, his airspeed was high, too high to eject safely. The parachute deployed behind him and jerked his legs out in front of him, then once filled it slowed and righted its self. He hung helplessly, swinging in the harness as the morass of jungle vines and trees raced up to meet him.

He had ejected at the last possible moment and was on the edge of the envelope of survivability for such an escape. He could feel himself hit the ground with a sudden thud, missing the larger branches of the trees, tangling his chute. The impact knocked him senseless and he lay there in the tangled brush of the jungle floor, covered in sweat, hydraulic fluid and jet fuel.

He lay there for several moments; his body racked with pain. Semi-conscious and disoriented he tried to direct his body to wake up and to stand and to fight the terrible nausea that was welling up from the pit of his stomach.

It will pass if you just lie still; think of something else, it will go away. If you just lie still for a moment the sickness will subside and you will be able to move, he thought his mind spinning out of control, his heart beat pounding in his temples. He could feel himself slipping into shock. He could feel the earth and the reality around him slipping in and out of his consciousness. Each beat of his heart, each breath brought on another wave of panic and nausea. He fought the urge to vomit, and tried to control his breathing.

I cannot let them hear me, he thought.

He could make out the murmuring of voices in the distance, though he could not understand what was being said. As the shuffling grew closer, his hope was that his camouflage parachute, entangled in the vines and trees would not be seen. He lay there in silence, swallowing down the bile in his throat. Slowly the noise and talk subsided. He could feel pain in his lower back and a cold numbness in his left leg. Within moments, he could feel the throbbing of the wound and thc onslaught of a raging headache pounding in his skull. Unable to get up, he rolled over on his stomach, and tried to crawl along a ridge. He could feel himself partially paralyzed, unable to move through the slippery undergrowth of the jungle without pulling himself along with his arms, kicking with one leg, dragging the other as he slid along on his stomach. He wanted to crawl down the side of the ridge into a hollow to a low creek bed. He struggled down letting the slick muddy side of the ridge take him to the bottom of the hollow.

Exhausted, he rolled over onto his back and looked up at the sky. He laid there as a quiet mist drifted into the creek bed and enveloped him in darkness. He could hear the howling and taunting of creatures out hunting in the cover of the jungle darkness and feel the bites of hundreds of mosquitoes who were attracted to him by the carbon dioxide in his breath. He was too weak to fight them off, too weak… He would let them have their way with him.

He thought of them, searching, like the groping hands in his pockets, the quick and efficient hunting for wounded prey in the undergrowth. The curtain of mist closed over him. He found it harder and harder to hear the voices. Blood pounded in his temples. He could feel himself slipping away, slipping into unconsciousness. The voices grew faint. The creatures would soon be upon him. In the last moment, the moment between life and death the light of the sky shown down through the treetops above him. Slender fingers of light that touched him there in the darkness of the jungle floor.

He looked up toward the sky. He thought that he could hear it, a lonely rasping sound that droned overhead, the sound of a rotary engine drifting with the wind.

Chapter 2

The sky was like slate and the cold wind of Autumn blew field trash into swirling clouds that drifted like ghosts across the road below. As if suddenly awakened from a dream he was there, drifting with the wind. Confused, he snapped up startled by the moment and struggled to get his bearings, to make sense of the thoughts that had come to life in his mind. The biting cold of the early fall morning streamed over him, the wind penetrated his jeans and leather jacket and chilled him to numbness. He looked down and flexed a gloved hand that had become stiff from holding the control stick in the biting cold. He looked out at the ground below, over an empty strip of roadway that stretched out in a narrow black band to the horizon.

The aircraft, an old Stearman biplane rumbled under him, its engine growling in a low throaty conversation with the wind that blasted his face and buffeted his hair. It closed his eyes in tired slits that watered and protested against the wind as he peered anxiously over the cowling and back behind the wings in search of a landmark.

At first, he wondered if the entire notion was but a

dream. He felt that he had been over this road for a long time and that he had drifted over it many times before. He tried to take some inventory, to remember who he was and where he was at the moment but could not get a clear picture of it in his mind. There was little that he could remember and the past slipped in and out of focus like the words to a song or a face or name of a casual acquaintance, overheard in passing or given so quickly that it cannot be remembered.

How long had he been up there searching the ground below? He did not know.

It seemed that he had taken the plane on an impulse. In the middle of the night, he had taken the keys from the hook in an unnamed hanger on some small patch of flat grass and crumbling concrete, dragged it out onto the tarmac and flown away.

He could feel the sting of his cut lip and the swollen mouse under his eye. He could not remember how he had gotten them but there was a sense of anxiety at the thought of them. He felt that he had been compelled to do these things, to take the plane and to run. He had not taken this road as an option but out of necessity.

He consciously breathed in the rushing air and could feel its icy cold and smell the farms lying quietly below him. Dew had settled over them now and the morning mist moved like a ghost as it drifted over the open fields. The morning sun was laboring to melt away the ghosts and he could see only glimpses of the sullen emptiness of the fallow patchwork that passed underneath him. He looked down and could make out only brief, seductive glimpses of the earth below through the ethereal wisps of clouds that hugged the ground.

Pulling the zipper of his jacket up to his throat, he

pinned the stick between his knees momentarily and rubbed his gloved hands together in an attempt to warm them. As he did this, his thoughts turned instinctively to the state of the airframe under him, its sounds of seeping compression and the protests of cables, canvas, and wood that resonated with the weariness of many miles.

He glanced down at the fuel gauge and eased the throttle back with his left hand. He took the stick again and began to think pensively about the low fog that clung to the ground below.

It is a siren's call to pilots, he thought, luring them ever lower to a field. It is a dangerous illusion, to permit one's self to go down to a very low altitude and to be lured in then suddenly trapped in a milky labyrinth of zero visibility without reference to attitude, position or the runway, flying blind as the earth rushes up to meet you.

He thought about the others, nameless, faceless pilots. Men he had see in his mind but now could not remember. They had encountered moments in the fog. Some had suffered the dire consequences of their missteps. He had learned from them, learned that while most of the dangers of flying and weather could be anticipated and avoided, there remained the unpredictable and sudden changes of fortune that could result in an incident that remained in the pilot's mind for life. It was a deep and lasting memory that linked reflexes to senses and married instinct with reason to control fear. It was a lesson that must be learned if one had any chance of survival.

He knew that the only answer was to quickly add power and climb out of the fog, that the tops of these grounded clouds were very low and that disaster could only be avoided by climbing over them, and then with patient waiting or a quick decision, move on to an alternate field and find the safety of the ground.

He knew these things. He had learned what all experienced pilots knew and carried with him, the same faith in the pressure sensitive instruments, the spinning gyros and reason that allowed them to make the transition from the visual to the abstract without concern.

He knew this and knew too that there were others who for reasons of fear, disbelief or a false faith in their own senses relied solely on their ability to pick out visual references on the ground to orient themselves and in doing so panicked and stalled. For them the desire to cling to the reality of their senses and to get back on the ground was so great that they became overwhelmed and flew back into the runway or simply gave up and froze at the controls.

He thought about the inexperienced, eager encounters with this situation and those who had departed from airfields under these conditions. He could remember them as if he had been them. He imagined the seconds following take-off, when in the first 50 feet or so they could see nothing at all and in a struggling climb frantically pulled up too steep in a panic stricken effort to escape the claustrophobic and disorienting embrace of the mist billowing around them.

He thought that he had heard it said that it was no coincidence that the approach lights at the end of a runway were most often formed in the shape of a cross. It was a faith that transcended the physical and natural phenomenon of the world, the principals of lift, thrust, drag, weight and balance and the other truths of aviation.

He visualized the distant images of logbooks and thousands of hours, flying. The aircraft talked to him and he began to recount its life and reconcile it with his own. It came to him in a long series of landings, of long sleepless nights in chairs in flight offices or in hangars, or under a wing. The airplane sang on and on to him through its whistling cables and rumbling exhaust. The song and the memories settled his anxiety as the aircraft moved on through the growing clouds.

Then the thoughts turned to other things. He thought of a satchel beneath his seat and the fragment of a memory came to him.

The money, he thought and with the thought, he leaned over quickly and tried to reach under the seat to find the bag, one hand searching the other trying to control the aircraft. He could feel the bag under him. He grabbed it and tugged at it slightly. He could feel its weight and was suddenly reassured. He felt good now. The cold melted away and he relaxed in the seat. His mind struggled to remember.

Okay boy! Don't get excited now. Try to remember. Where the hell are you supposed to be going? He thought in an effort to reconstruct what had happened.

He struggled to remember as the propeller cut a swath through the blackening sky and pressed forward through the mist. He could not remember any more. The memories of the recent past were dark shadows that drifted like storm clouds in the distance. He resolved to let the plane take him as far as it would go. It was a stupid, careless thing to do. He knew that. It was the sort of thing that ran against the faith.

It came to him as one of an entire volume of old facts that all pilots knew. The book of experience that separated the guys who stayed alive from the faithless multitude who for a while are able to bluff their way through and fool themselves into believing that they're too good to follow the truth. They tempted fate and for a while enjoyed a measure of success with half truths and unfinished details, but eventually the absolute finality of all that they had done and failed to do would come for them at some point and that they would be forced to confront the unconquerable and unforgiving truths of both time and gravity. It would come for them at a moment least expected, to pull away the veneer and reveal the lies and weaknesses in frantic, panicked epithets.

No one gets out alive, he thought. It seemed that it was something some old man had once said to him. He thought about the words for a moment. There was nothing anyone could do except run, run hard and fast and stay ahead of it for as long as possible. He knew this. That eventually he would hesitate, make a fateful slip and the dark rider would come for him too.

"Not today." He said to himself as he struggled with the idea in an effort to force it out of the moment and wished that he could continue drifting unconscious as before. But the thought and the emotion stayed with him as if it had been written into his mind, painted by some unseen hand. A naked fear would have its grip on him at some point, come for him and try to overwhelm him, force the controls from his hands and leave him to spin hopelessly into the ground. Uncertainty and indecision were fearful places, he thought, filled with unseen dangers where all pilots walked with an ungainly swagger under a veil of thin bravado. They were open, exposed places of impotence and frustration that shed an unyielding light of self-doubt and cast shadows that became etched in an open logbook of missteps and miscalculations that stared back as cold entries of dates and destinations, routes and duration. He felt that he was in a desperate race now, a race to avoid the inevitable. The anxiety grew again as he realized that he was in fact lost and adrift, aimlessly wandering without a flight plan. He could not determine if he was putting distance between himself and some pursuer or if he were on a direct collision course with it.

He flew on and the fog that had been only a morning mist began to gain ground and grow with the wind into a rough chop. He looked out over the cowling at the huge bowl of open fields and could see the phantom clouds growing and shading the ground in ever-larger blisters of white and grey.

He glanced down at the fuel gauge again and could see that he would need to find some place to set down. Someplace where he could get a tank full of gas, something to eat then press on. He tried to maintain a safe altitude but continued to drop further under a rapidly deteriorating layer of clouds that had grown into a line of gray black nimbus marching toward him on the horizon. He could not avoid thinking about the clouds and of storms and the wind and weather that continued to change. He drifted down further, coaxing the controls in an effort to avoid being blinded. He tapped the fuel gauge and felt small pellets of freezing rain as he met the edge of the storm.

The blackening clouds came at him almost in an instant with unrelenting waves rolling in an angry torrent of wind and sleet that assaulted him as he flew on. He thought for a moment about the possibility of turning round to a heading in the opposite direction. Where would he go? What was there over that horizon? He did not know and in spite of his own reason and better judgment his stubborn will let the tug of the biting propeller push him on into the building storm.

He repositioned an old pair of earphones down tight over his head and tuned his ADF radio in an attempt to get a bearing. Flipping through the AM selector, he drifted through a screeching wail of reverberation and the faint but fervent diatribe of AM radio signals. Between stations, drifting through the bleeding signals of far off stations, the ghost voices drifted in and out like howls and shrieks of electro-static demons tormented and trapped in the ionosphere. He struggled with the stick and the selector franticly as panic began to overtake him. Then it came in a booming voice flooding the airwaves with weary gospel music that poured in over the radio. A low baritone sang out over the background choir.

"What a friend we have in Jesus..." the words sang out loud and clear, trailing off at the end with a piano, then the well-practiced harangue of a radio evangelist poured out words that drifted in and out with a loud staccato as the signal picket-fenced its way through the air.

The ice pellets and gusting grew in intensity. He looked down at the chart clipped to a metal board he had strapped to his thigh and fought with the controls to turn toward the signal. He had no idea of his location relative to the faint glimpses of the road just below and ahead of him. He took a quick glance at his compass heading and moved a finger up the chart in a desperate attempt to locate the roadway somewhere in its folds.

Then suddenly, it presented itself on the chart, the symbol for a small radio station antenna that appeared to be consistent with the swinging needle of the direction finder.

"OK, Now where the hell to land?" he yelled to himself as the buffeting of the wind and the growing assault of rain and sleet continued to grow in ferocity. It matched his growing anxiety to a point that almost exceeded his limits of control. He was flying right into the beast and would soon be swallowed up in its belly, he thought.

"Not today!" he yelled at the top of his lungs, the words burning into him with stubborn determination as the radio screeched ever louder and the preacher's bombast reached a fevered pitch in the howling storm.

With every passing second the engine gulped fuel sucking the tanks dry. He fought on frantically dividing his attention between the chart and the rolling and pitching of the aircraft, looking again and again at the water stained chart for someplace to land. Then, suddenly, in an instant he could see it.

There, next to the antenna…

A small magenta circle, an airfield appeared. It was almost on top of the antenna symbol. He'd almost missed it. It sat there, nothing more than a small stain, a slight spot on the map. He struggled to look through the wet stinging in his eyes. He could make it out. It was in near perfect alignment with his heading.

He peered through the cloud and freezing rain, and could just make it out, a small asphalt strip bouncing up and down through the whirling propeller. It stood there, just a few hangers and a small cinder block building and a black stripe of broken asphalt weaving up and down through the sheets of pouring rain.

At that moment, almost on queue the engine began to protest and lose power. He knew he had run the tanks dry as the engine sputtered and then went silent.

The preacher's voice loud, and clear above the rushing wind and ticking sounds of ice pellets blared forth buzzing the receiver and the earphones as he passed,

"Welcome brothers and sisters! Welcome to the feast of our lord, Jesus Christ! We are as lost sheep, crying out in the darkness of sin and wickedness but the Lord, brother; the Lord has come to find us, to save us from our selves!"

The big bulk of the radial engine bore its way through the wind and the free spinning propeller, sapped the last of his precious airspeed and altitude.

"Your pastor in Christ, the Rev. Creflo Spooner is here, bringing the message of the Lord to all of you out there on the farm radio network…Welcome and now ya' all listen as we bring the sounds of Henry Morgan and the Morgan Quartet, sing' in that ole time gospel favorite, You've Got To Walk That Lonesome Valley…!" The pounding of a rickety old piano, plinked out chords and a weary foursome sang out over the crackling hiss of static. It rang out in a mocking cacophony of sound blasting through the headphones as he approached.

He was on the proper heading, close but loosing altitude fast. The end of the old asphalt strip now became clear through the rain and haze. He trimmed, and kicked at the rudders to use the wind and to maintain his glide as the gusts fought him for control of the now dying beast.

"Damn!" He jerked back in the seat, pulled hard and kicked right rudder as the ghostly grey steel structure of a radio antenna suddenly came into view through the billowing veil of cloud. It loomed large like a lone sentinel, guarding the airstrip and blocking his glide path.

The aircraft lurched and banked in a sloppy sideslip as the radio blared and the hair on his neck stood up from the electricity of the static hum. The radio's needle swung about wildly as he passed within feet of the structure and rapidly closed with the ground below.

"I'm just going to make it. Don't get greedy…Hold the nose… Don't stall it!" He coached himself, as he passed over the end of the strip and made his flare to land.

"Not today… Damnit…!"

The Stearman hit hard and the runway already slick with rain and sleet caused it to slip and turn into the quartering gusts. A sudden gust blew the plane dangerously close to the side of the runway as he struggled to dip a wing and hold his position over the centerline. He bounced, touched down again and began to slide. Another gust and the tail spun around and the plane, swapped ends, slid off the side of the runway and onto the grass, then with another gust the tail rose up and the plane cut a muddy swath through the infield as it bounced and slid through the soggy turf.

He held onto the stick and clutched the edge of the cockpit sliding, bouncing then rolling as the aircraft rolled itself into a heap of twisted canvas and wire then finally came to rest with its nose buried in the mud near the end of the runway.

"Yes brothers and sisters, Creflo Spooner here, with a message about your future… Have you made your plan to meet our Lord today? Are you ready? Have you made peace with our Lord and Savior? Friends are you s-a-v-e-d, saved?" the radio voice blared out at him above the din of the wind and rain sapping the battery.

He shut off the power and sat hunched forward against the instrument panel for several minutes. All he could hear was the wind on the stretched canvas and the steady creak of the rudder as it bounced back and forth against the gusts like a loose storm shutter.

He sat there mentally checking his condition, getting his head adjusted to the lack of movement and his situation. Convinced that he was alive and able to move, he climbed out of the cockpit and pulling the collar of his jacket up to cover his face, struggled in the rain to walk around the aircraft to survey the damage.

The Stearman was a design that had been built before the Second World War and was used by the Army Air Corps for training new pilots. A sturdy, well-built aircraft, it was intended to take punishment and the rough handling that would come at the hands of ham fisted neophytes. His had clearly seen this and more. Years of service and thousands of hours had worn the airframe thin with age and abuse. He crouched down in front of the nose. The open engine had dug its way into the mud and the lower cylinders were semi-buried and hissing moisture. The propeller was broken with a large piece missing and the canvas on one wing was torn and exposed ribs stuck out from it like a gaping wound. The lower half of the fuselage was bent upward at a right angle to the line of the aircraft, like a broken leg.

He quickly pulled his bag from the cockpit and looked around for one of the buildings that he had seen from the air. He peered through the pouring rain and saw a cinder blockhouse. It sat in dreary quiet detachment in front of a grass and hardtop tarmac. He ran toward it through the pelting ice and rain to the front door and ducked inside.

The small room was inauspicious and like so many other small fields that rose up in his jumbled memory had all of the trappings. A large freestanding radio sat next to a window that looked out onto the runway. It was tuned to the same evangelical station and was playing in loud clear tones; its insides amass with glowing tubes warm from the current running through them.

Wood paneled walls were covered with old sepia and black and white photos of pilots, planes, some autographed and others with words of thanks. A coffee pot sizzled quietly next to a small grill and a counter and stools lined one side of the room. Pie sat under glass on the counter along with ketchup bottles, salt and peppershakers and worn paper menus.

On the other side of the room, old worn chairs, a sofa, side tables littered with old charts, magazines and a coffee table worn from the heels of countless boots and shoes sat in a forlorn arrangement around an old oil stove.

"Anybody here...?"

He asked as he dropped his bags on one of the worn chairs, pulled his fingers through his hair and wiped the rain from his face.

No answer. He stood around in uneasy solitude then slid off his wet jacket threw it on a stool and began to poke around the counter. He reached behind it for a coffee cup then filled from the pot. He reached for a paper napkin grabbed several slices of pie and stretched out on the broken down sofa, eating. He pulled off his wet boots and after a time the warmth from an oil heater slowly drew him into a deep sleep.

He drifted off, his head on the arm of the sofa, his stocking feet on the other arm. Resting as he knew he had done a hundred times before in hangars or in an airport lounge in some forgotten little town.

The confusion of his situation melted away with the drone of the radio and the low tick of an old wall clock, its seconds drifting by in slow methodical beats. It seemed to be keeping time with his pulse as he drifted away to an alabaster landscape of wind and cloud. He drifted away in the dream and a heavy sleep crept upon him.

He drifted away unable to hear the sound of another aircraft, high overhead. It too was fighting the heaving thunderstorm, its dark shadow weaving through the angry clouds.

"Not today", he said to himself. His last words before he drifted off to sleep.

Chapter 3

She came to him in a dream. He looked down upon her like a devoted voyeur as she slept. He had no desire to disturb her but only to watch over her, to take in the full composition of her beauty.

If there ever were angels, if they ever existed, he knew that she must be one. She laid in perfect silence a Wyeth in the dripping, heavy tropical heat. Her bedroom was white, cool, with a quiet calm and only the whisper of perfumed breezes that shifted the long sheer curtains that drifted in through the half open windows.

She was peaceful in her privacy. Her body unclothed lay in quiet repose, her olive skin soft against the white linens. She lay over them, and let the wisps of breeze wash over her. She laid very still, her face in childlike sleep, her lips smiling in innocent pleasure. Large soft down pillows and billowing sheets of white linen lay under her like the wings of an angel at rest. Her hair a jet black stream of shining strands lay about her head and small impish ringlets of black onyx adorned her crown dancing lightly as the wafts of air flowed over her.

Quietly, a Victrola unwound in the corner playing a

soothing nocturne filling the room with a melody. A song came forth from it, the words, scratchy with the wear of the old Bakelite disk sang in sad French. Though he could not understand the words, he thought it sounded forlorn, somber, a song of lost love.

He looked down upon her his heart filled with love and desire and slowly her eyes opened in half sleep and she turned to meet his gaze. She smiled a slow calm, inviting smile that greeted him with a knowing look of happiness and contentment. Her gifts were many and she presented them to him in calm satisfaction, every delicate feature, every movement, every sigh of breath from her rose up to greet him. He reached down to her; his hand touched her cheek his lips lowering to her, hers to his in a single innocent, loving kiss.

He woke with a start, momentarily unsure where he was. He could feel something warm and wet on his face and sat up suddenly. He focused through his sleepy haze to see a one-eyed mongrel dog licking the remains of pie filling from his face.

"Hey, hey... Get down!" The old dog backed up and sat by the sofa, looked back at him through a single eyed stare, licking his chops and wagging his tail furiously.

It was clear that the animal had been in an accident. He had lost his right eye and his entire right front leg. He sat there, totally without any concern over his disability, and seemed more interested in his newfound benefactor with pie filling on his mouth.

The young man wiped his face with a shirtsleeve as he slowly roused himself. He shoved the dog off of the couch and looked at his watch. It had stopped. He had been sleeping but he did not know for how long. He got up from the couch, slowly and gingerly walked to the window holding his head in his hand, a headache pounding, pushing at his eye sockets. He looked out in an effort to see the wreck of his aircraft but saw nothing. It had been removed from the infield and was nowhere to be seen. The weather was still blowing hard.

"So how's you're head!" A stocky well-worn elderly black man in dungarees, work boots and an old olive, oilcloth jacket appeared suddenly as if from nowhere and waddled past him. He took off his gloves and reached for the coffee pot behind the counter.

"Yeah, sorry but…"

"No, no! That's all right boy. You're here now, out of the rain. You just take it easy there and rest for a while…"

"Took care of your aircraft" the old man said as he poured a cup of coffee.

"My plane, yeah where is it?" the young man asked as he took the cup from the old man.

"Towed it to the hangar… It's pretty banged up. Looks like it's going to need a new wing spar, prop, fuselage rebuild and some other work. You made quite an entrance I'll say that."

The young man thought for a moment and could feel a hint of resentment rise in him.

"Yeah well, I wouldn't have had a problem if that radio antenna hadn't been there!"

The old man continued to waddle about undeterred by his words.

"Yes sir got a lot of old battle scars on her. Noticed your tanks were dry. Antenna did that too I suppose?" he said as he continued to rifle through items under the counter, speaking as if to himself, in a tone worn from repeating.

He looked to be at least seventy, maybe older, with the quiet confidence of a man who had seen much more than he cared to remember. He moved about in a tired bony frame, covered with leathery dark skin well worn with hard work and exposure to the elements. His eyes were dark, hawk like and were encased in a large closely shaven face and head, the skin dark brown and gleaming with perspiration.

The dog hobbled over to him and begged for a treat. The old man took something from his pocket and threw it to the mongrel then pointed carelessly after it as it trotted off into the corner chomping on the tidbit with delight.

"Sorry bout the dog, Son. Ole Hop, too nosey for his own good. Got too close to a spinning prop... Odd thing, he don't usually take to strangers."

The young man rubbed his eyes and sighed then winced slightly from the painful knot that had developed on the crown of his head.

"Where the hell am I?"

"Well my boy you can be certain that you ain't in hell, and just in case you're interested you ain't in heaven neither."

"Then where am I?"

"Well I'd just say from the looks of that airplane you're lost."

The young man tried again to remember where he was going. He struggled to fit it into the scrambled mix of images searching for something that made some sense.

The old man retrieved another coffee cup and poured, "So…?"

"So what…?" The boy replied.

"You get lost boy?

"Lost?" he thought, "Yeah I'm afraid I'm lost…"

"You should have turned around when you saw that storm coming. Where you headed?" The old man asked.

He thought for a moment and wondered what would happen if he unloaded his story or at least what he could remember of it. He remembered the bag and the money then noticed a phone in the corner and struggled to think of someone he could call.

"Listen, what's the chance of getting a ride somewhere? Is there a town out this way?"

"Not one close, anyhow the weather's too bad to travel."

The old man bent down behind the counter again, continuing to look for something then stood up.

"Listen I'm in a hurry, would you mind giving me a lift?" the young man said as he reached for his pack.

"Maybe when this lets up some… Where did you say you were headed?"

"I'm not sure. I mean, the crash, I can't seem to remember."

"No fuel. Tanks run dry…" The old man said this in the matter of fact questioning tone half under his breath with a head shaking resignation that had come from years of experience.

"Can I use the phone?"

"Nope..."

"Look, I got enough money to cover the gas or a call, if that's what you're worried about?"

"Money's got nothing to do with it son, you just can't use the phone. It's only for incoming calls."

"What the hell are you talking about Pop?" the boy said. He started to make his way to the corner when a sudden anxiety welled up inside of him.

"I got to get out of here." He said as he lurched forward then stumbled back on his heels.

The old man reached under the counter again, "Looks like you got a good bump there. Here." He tossed him an ice bag he had been filling from behind the counter, "Put that on it."

"I have to go..." the young man insisted.

"Look sonny, its like I said, nobody makes outgoing calls from here."

The old man reached over and picked up the receiver, "Tell you what though; I'll make an exception in your case. I'll even dial the number for you. You just tell me the number and I'll make the call. How's that sound?"

The boy stood in silence as the old man waited patiently for the number.

"Well? What's the number son?"

"I…I can't seem to remember…"

"Well now." the old man said with satisfaction.

"Yeah, its like I told you son, folks don't make outgoing calls from here." He chuckled quietly to himself as he returned the handset to the receiver.

"So what's so funny?" the young man responded, frustrated with his failed attempt to remember.

"No, no nothing son..." The old man returned to his place behind the counter.

"What is this? I don't get it."

The boy walked over to the phone, holding the ice pack to his head. He picked up the receiver.

"There's no dial tone here? What's with the phone?"

"Like I said boy, no outgoing calls..." the old man cackled with laughter, the dog barked in response as if to join in.

"O.K. Fine, Pop! How much for the pie...?" The boy said, slamming the ice pack down on the counter.

The old man recovered from his laugh then responded

in a more serious tone, "It's like I said boy, money's got nothing to do with it. Here you are and here's where you're going to stay, for a while at least."

"I pay my own way old man, you just tell me how much. I got plenty of money to cover it."

The old man looked at him for a moment and sighed with a knowing resolution as if he had been through the same argument many times before.

"Alright, alright, calm down… Lemme see here…" He waddled over to the end of the counter, took out a pad and a pencil from his shirt pocket and wetting the pencil tip on his tongue figured under his breath. He pushed at the paper for a moment then frowned slightly and self-consciously pulled a pair of reading glasses from his pocket, put them on his nose and looked up at the young man.

"Look there is no need for you to leave right now boy. At least until you figure out who you are and where you're trying to go."

Through the confusion of the situation, the young man felt that he was right, but he was unwilling to let go of the desire however confusing and unreasonable, to leave, to get away.

"How much?" the young man asked.

The old man sighed in resignation.

"Well. Let's see two slices of pie, salvage recovery of the aircraft, hanger rental, labor… Looks to me like 50 bucks…"

"Fifty bucks? You've got to be kidding?"

"Nope, Fifty bucks, ah would you like to check my math? Never been real good with arithmetic, folks used to say, Gabe, I don't know how you get by; you couldn't add two and two if your life depended on it!"

"Look, here…" The boy reached for the satchel

containing the money and pulled out a wad of bills.

"Take it." He pulled out a handful from the roll and pushed it to the old man.

"Now if it's not too much trouble, I'd like that ride to town."

"Sorry kid, I can't risk the truck in this storm."

"Look, I have to get out of here. I'll pay more when we get to a town, now let's go!"

"Sonny, I told you, I have no need for it… Why are you in such a big hurry to leave? You should stay for a while. You in some kind of trouble?"

"That's none of your damn business!"

The young man grew tepid and frustrated with his situation and the memories that he could not lay his hands on. It was as if he had fallen between a dream and reality. His head ached with fatigue and the painful bump throbbed. Then as he reached around in the satchel, he felt the cold sharp edges of something deep in the recesses of the bag. His hand emerged holding a beat up, semi-automatic pistol.

"O.K., I don't know what's going on but I'm leaving. Now you go get that truck and bring it round. You hear?"

"Afraid I can't help you son." The old man continued to work behind the counter, oblivious to the weapon that was pointed nervously in his direction.

"I don't have time to argue. Don't try me old man. I'm not going to ask you again."

The old man stood up and looked at the gun then at the boy. His gaze was quiet and calm, without fear or concern.

"Look at you! You fly in here, wreck that plane on my runway, and eat my pie…" He shook his head and turned his back as he spoke. "Now you pull a pistol on me and start making demands. I'm tryin to help you son. You best give that thing to me now and settle yourself down."

The boy stood there in disbelief, beside himself with anger and fear. He knew he was in a standoff, the old man's hawk eyes staring down at him, looking through his veiled threats. He knows I'm bluffing; I can't shoot this old coot, he thought.

"Take the damn thing!" He tossed the gun on the table in front of the couch and worked his way to his feet pulling on his boots.

"Which way to town?" he barked out impatiently as he pulled on his jacket, grabbed his bag and turned to walk out the door. Hop got up and hobbled along laboring on his three legs in an effort to follow him.

"Like I said, ain't no town close by. You shouldn't go out in that storm boy. You ain't fit for it. You're just gonna get yourself lost is all."

The young man turned, zipping his jacket, "Yeah well, I'll take my chances out there. And keep that gimpy mutt away from me!" He slammed the door then turned and walked off into the night, the three-legged dog following close behind.

His anger and frustration moved him in cold determination down the lonely country road. The wind continued to blow in icy gusts and sheets of rain continued to fall soaking him through to his skin.

He walked past the radio station, a lone cold cinder block hut and a grey aerial, its superstructure standing alone in mute silence. It stood over him like a ladder to the sky its uppermost portion obscured by clouds.

He cursed as he looked up at it letting the rain wash down his face. Its signal had brought him here. He had been lured to it, he thought. It had directed him down to the field, to pass within yards of wrapping his airplane around it.

A large cross, outlined in cobalt blue neon tubes buzzed on the side of the building as he walked past. The backlight of the burning sign, reflected white from the pealing paint on the wall and cast a reflected shadow along the road for several yards. He could feel the static electric hum of the aerial and transmitter. He looked directly upward as he passed under the antenna. The rain fell on him in a continuous barrage of large heavy drops that soaked his face and hair.

He looked back at the dog that trailed behind him in the darkness as he walked. He could hear the animal panting and struggling to keep up with him through the wind and rain. He thought to picked up a rock and hurl it at him.

"Get away from me Damnit!" He yelled back at the dog.

The animal moved up behind him and sat, looking up at him, its single eye glowing with the reflected light from the neon sign, its tongue hanging out of one side of its mouth. The young man turned and resumed his pace and the dog continued behind him undaunted by the threats and the rain.

"This cannot be happening…You don't just wake up in a storm, crash land in the middle of nowhere and end up on some god forsaken road with a one-eyed dog!" the young man argued with himself as he walked on through the pouring rain.

There was no sign of life. No houses or towns. He walked on through the rain with no change in the scenery, no traffic. Just open flat fields, barbed wire fence and telephone poles standing at even paces in the small icy drifts that had accumulated along the roadside.

He was cold, tired and smoldering with anger at his confusion and the situation.

"There's got to be a town, a house, something around here. Damn sticks!" he said to himself as he scanned the horizon for a water tower. A reflex that all pilots learned. Look for the water tower, that's where the town is.

Hours passed, the anger and frustration began to fade and a creeping anxiety began to build in his stomach.

Like the drifting sands of an endless desert the land lay open to him in waves of grass as he plodded along in the darkness. The slow cadence of his footsteps and the tapping of dog's claws played out a syncopated beat, tapping out a rhythm on the open pavement. Each puddle of water underfoot resonated in his boots, pleaded with him to think. It was like the first few notes of a melody that he could not remember, close in his mind but just out of his grasp.

Hours passed and the wind's progress thinned the precipitation and heavy cloud cover. After a time the clouds parted to reveal a glowing blue-white moon hanging alone over him. Occasionally obscured by wafts of inky blackness blown over the night sky its shining light followed him. He could see that there appeared no end. It seemed that in spite of his footsteps he had made very little progress from the tower that stood off in the distance.

Suddenly he heard a low droning sound, an aircraft throttling down and flying slow overhead. He looked up for it, peering into the dark night sky, illuminated by the moon's shining light. He could not see it. It's sound grew louder and then a dark image, only several hundred feet above the ground circled in tight turns off in the distance. He thought for a moment about how he might follow it, that maybe it was circling over some sign that would lead him to civilization.

Then his attention was directed to something on the road ahead of him. His eyes sharpened as a small form appeared in the middle of the roadway off in the distance. Hop looked up at it and barking with excitement scampered past him toward it. The young man's walk broke into a jog and the two of them covered what seemed to be several hundred yards without closing on the image. His anxiety grew as he increased his gait to a full run. Hop, plodded along furiously to keep up. In spite of his effort he could not gain ground on the form. He felt a desperate need to reach it. To find someone else lost on the road. He did not want to continue to walk alone. Finally he stopped and bent over his hands on his knees, gasping for air. Hop had stopped as well and sat there in front of him, panting heavily.

"Hey, who ever you are. I'm lost! I'm not going to hurt you. I just need to figure out where I am!" The figure made no move but stood still in the middle of the road.

"Look, I'm lost and I need some help! Is there a house or a town around here close by?" He began walking again toward the form that drifted along just at the edge of his vision.

"This is nuts." He said to himself as he struggled to make out the image and began to shout another sentence in its direction when a voice came up from the distance. It was the frightened voice of a small child, a little boy, lost in the darkness.

"Are you my Daddy?" the voice quivered with the cold as he called out.

"No, I'm lost; I'm not going to hurt you. Please stay there and we can go and find him. OK?" He started walking toward the figure again.

"OK..." the voice called back. He could see that the form remained still in his gaze and that he was closing on it. As he approached he could see that the figure was that of a little boy, maybe 8 or 9 years old. He was a young innocent looking child, blonde short cropped hair, thin and frail; his face was smeared with dirt and tears, his shirt torn and one shoe missing from a dirty white sock on his foot. He clutched a small toy plane in one hand and the remains of a dirty, torn blanket in the other one. He could see that the child was soaking wet from head to toe, his matted hair stuck to his forehead as he stood shivering in the cold.

"Are you alright kid? What happened? Where are your folks?" He suspected that the child was in shock that, maybe he had been the victim of an auto accident or some other situation. He lowered himself on one knee in front of him to look at his face more closely. The boy smiled at him brightly and lowered his hand and patted Hop on the head.

"Hi. What happened to your funny dog?"

"Where are your folks? Were you in an accident? Are they back there along the road?" the young man asked the questions, his mind spinning with the thought of the boy's face and of something that he should know but did not.

"Mommy got tired and went to sleep."

"Tell me, where's your folks?"

"I told you, she's sleeping."

"Where are they sleeping? Show me where."

"I can't." The boy began to shake harder in the cold and looked at him, frightened.

"Why not, are you lost?"

"I have to go now." the little boy said as he looked up at the dark shadow of an aircraft that now loomed high above them.

"What do you mean, you have to go? Where are your folks?"

"My Mommy will wake up soon, and I have to go home."

"Take me to her." He was hopeful that in spite of the shock that the boy might be able to direct him to someone who could help.

"You can't come!" the little boy called out as he wheeled about and began running toward the circling plane, "You can't come! You can't come!" He sang this in a mocking taunting way as he ran down the road holding the toy plane in his hand, flying it along as he ran after the form his blanket billowing out behind him like the wings of a cherub.

"No, Wait!" The young man leapt after him in an effort to grasp an arm but was unable to take more than a few steps before the child disappeared into the night.

He began to look around for someone who might be there. He tried calling out then trotted in the direction of the boy and looked up and down for some sign of another person. Within a few moments, the droning of the aircraft engine grew silent and he could see the distant glow of headlights.

The truck passed him then stopped momentarily and then slowly backed up next to him. The occupant reached down from the driver's side and rolled down the side window that was fogged over with condensation. The old man stuck his head out the window. His voice rang out over the idling motor with a twinkle of delight.

"Well, looks like the weather's calmed down some... What do you say, son? Should we give it another go?"

His tone had changed from the gruff old man that he had encountered hours before. His voice was congenial, friendly, as if he were going to ask a favor.

The young man's head was splitting, his mind numb by all that had transpired. He quickly turned to the vision of the child in an effort to get the old man's help.

"Did you see the kid, that little boy? Look there's a little child, a boy, some kid, his folks; I think there's been an accident!"

"No time for that now boy. Get in!"

The young man was stunned, "What do you mean? Somebody could be dying out there! I'm telling you there's been an accident!"

The old man cracked open the driver's side door turned and called Hop who ambled up onto the running board and into the cab. "Look son, I ain't got time to explain right now, hurry and get in. I need your help…" he said, impatiently.

The young man rounded the front of the truck and slid in beside him on the passenger's side. Hop had managed to jump up into the seat and sat there proudly between them.

"What the hell is this? What's go' in on?"

"Look, don't ask questions…I'll explain when we get there."

The old man looked down at his watch the hands glowing green in the darkness.

"What the hell are you talking about?"

"No time, just close the door…"

The old man nervously fumbled with the gearshift lever and jammed the truck into reverse then forward, spinning tires and throwing up gravel as they sped off into the night.

Chapter 4

They drove in silence and time seemed to stretch forward without measure. They made their way along, twisting and turning through the lonely countryside. The road shifted from pavement to gravel to deeply worn paths cut by tractor tires that meandered through open fields of twisted corn stalks and small clusters of old oaks and spruce trees.

Darkness filled the space around the cab and the weak light of the headlights threw spindly shadows about as they weaved in and out of the ruts and potholes.

The old man seemed preoccupied with his destination. He provided no apology, no sign of understanding or empathy regarding the child.

The young man finally overwhelmed with the silence spoke up.

"Okay, okay, I get it..." he said, in an effort to convince himself.

Hop who was snoozing on the seat between them stood up looking, panting in anticipation of a treat that might emerge at any moment from one of their pockets.

"This is some sort of a dream! I mean it's got to be.

Neither of you are real! This is a dream and you, that kid on the road and this mangy footstool are all a part of it!"

The old man released the wheel with one hand and without taking his eyes off of the road, held it out across the seat to him.

"I'm Gabriel, though most folks call me Gabe."

"Who might you be son?"

The boy was startled with the question and struggled to remember. My name, I don't know my name, I can't remember…, he thought.

The old man gave him a moment then spoke up.

"I'll tell you what. Let's say I call you Jacob, I mean can't go round calling you sonny or boy all the time."

The young man was startled at the notion that he could not remember his own name, and that the old man had decided to choose one for him.

How would he know me? Know my name?

"How the hell do you know who I am? Doesn't it bother you that you're just a character of my own screwed up imagination?"

"No not really. I knew a gal once, thought she was a Russian princess…I figure as long as I know who I am, ever body else is entitled to their own identity. As for you, oh that I can't say… Maybe we can talk about it some more later when we get this other business attended to."

Jacob sat back in the seat and Gabe continued to drive silently, intently peering through the windshield as they bounced around in the darkness.

"Am I supposed to know what's going on here?"

"Don't know… Suppose that's up to you?"

"What makes you think that we know each other or that I should know where we're going?"

"Don't know that I do really? As for names well, you look like someone I knew once. His name was Jacob. You don't seem to know your own name so there you go…"

"Yeah but…"

The old man cut him off.

"Well your's or not, it won't matter any to the other guy. Believe me he don't need it."

Gradually Gabe slowed the truck to a crawl and shut the headlights off, driving with his eyes peering over the steering wheel, probing the darkness.

"What are you doing? You're going to hit a tree or get us stuck out here."

"Quiet!" he whispered, agitated as he concentrated on the darkness in front of them.

"Yeah, this is it, I'm sure it is…" He stopped, turned off the engine and they sat in silence in a small clearing nestled in the middle of a large group of trees, well back off of the road.

"What? What is it?"

"Shush! Listen…" he whispered.

"I don't hear a damn thing…"

"Keep yer mouth shut and listen!"

As they sat there in the silence, Jacob strained to hear something. He could hear nothing but the rustling of gusts through the trees above. They sat there in the darkness as the seconds rolled into minutes.

"Look, I don't get it? What the hell are we doing out here?"

Gabe mumbled to himself, "Must be off by an hour or so. That's got to be it, we're early, and we'll have to wait him out."

"Wait who out?"

"Look you just sit there and keep listening."

"You listen, I'm tired. I'm going to get some sleep."

"Suit yer self, but if I were you I'd want to be awake for this."

Over the course of an hour they sat near the clearing. Jacob tried to manage a nap but frustrated with the drafty cab, his wet clothes and Gabe's continued vigil he only managed to drift off for a moment or two. He looked down at his watch then took it off and shook it in an effort to get the hands moving.

"Damn this watch… O.K.", He sighed, I don't know about you but…"

"Be quiet! There, listen!"

He didn't hear it at first. It was more like a feeling, a tingling that one gets just before someone creeps up on them from behind. A sense that something is there out of sight, approaching you, you feel the slight pang of panic, the fear in knowing that it is there but it comes too quickly, before the adrenaline has had time to signal your limbs to flee.

Then suddenly, Jacob could hear it; the muffled whine of an aircraft engine, approaching them, the sound of its rumbling growing with every moment. He could tell by the sound that it was not the engine of a commercial or private plane but that of a powerful piston engine, massive, intended to carry a heavy airframe at great speed.

He looked over at Gabe, staring into the darkness, listening with a transfixed intensity almost hypnotized by the sound.

Then it passed and within a moment, another sound; a whine like iron cannon shells whistling through the wind. They screamed down, diving like two heavy arrows flying furiously toward an unseen target.

Gabe suddenly looked over at Jacob and stared through him in a reflective gaze. Then with a single word, drew forward the dream of a ghost.

"Merlin!" the word came forth from Gabe's lips like an "Amen" at the end of a prayer. A single word that flooded him suddenly with a mind full of fragmented memories that flashed before him like a movie flickering fast in front of his eyes, a switch that turned on a small piece of something that had happened, distant, far off in the fog, a vibrating image in black and white celluloid, an image from the gun camera as the tracers raced to their target.

He struggled to make the connection but in an instant, was interrupted by a blinding flood of white light as Gabe switched on the headlights. The beams bathed an open field that lay out in front of them from their position in the woods. There was nothing to be seen but the brown and grey of field grass and the inky blackness of the void beyond the glow of the headlights.

Jacob almost turned to speak to the old man when suddenly; he caught the flash of two aircraft as they screamed past them in a low pass over the open clearing. They were too fast for him to make out their silhouettes in the darkness, but it didn't matter. He knew what they were. He knew, but like a dream the meaning of it and why they were familiar to him lay beyond his comprehension.

"Jesus Christ! It's a Mustang!" he called out as the plane passed through the light of the headlights.

He could hear the engine of one of them labor slightly as the aircraft pulled up and began its turn for another pass. His mouth opened in stunned disbelief as once more, in a matter of seconds, the ghost passed, this time alone the other aircraft trailing off as if it had broken off its pursuit, its engines drifting into the distance. The lone ghost now passed within yards of their headlights, no more then four or five feet above the ground.

"There he is!" Gabe blurted out the words and laughed in delirious delight as the sleek form of the fighter screamed past.

"Jesus! That guy must be nuts!"

"Nope!" Gabe whispered sternly, "He's lost!" He swung open the door to the truck and clambered around to open the tailgate.

"What are you doing?"

"We have to help him down!"

"What do you mean? There's no way he can land that here! He'll rip the landing gear off!"

"He's not going to have a choice." Gabe moved quickly and grabbed one of a dozen smudge pots he had piled up in the truck bed and handed it to him.

"Take these and follow me!"

They worked quickly as the ghost continued to make pass after pass over the field.

Jacob looked up for the other forms in the dark sky overhead, trying to follow the sound of what seemed to be other aircraft that were circling off in the distance.

"Don't worry bout them, they're gone..." Gabe called, as the laboring aircraft passed and turned again. He turned his attention quickly to the remaining aircraft. "Why doesn't he just wait it out, I mean it will be light soon? He can't be that far from the field?"

"That will be too late..." Gabe yelled over his shoulder as he trotted along in parallel with him lining up the pots on the ground, fumbling about in the darkness.

They lit them as they worked and laid out dotted lines of flame as they quickly marched off steps in an effort to outline a makeshift runway in the broken field. With the pots lined up and burning, they quickly returned to the truck.

"We're going to need this chain. Get it untangled." He tossed the mass of tow chain to Jacob and ushered him into the back. We'll stay out of the way until he's down!" Gabe's last words came as a loud yell as the plane once more roared past them.

Then, the aircraft engine labored for a final time and bellowed a crackling cough as it struggled to gulp a few remaining drops of fuel. It sputtered to a stop, and then dead silence followed by the low whine of air over the airframe as it dove on the glowing pots.

Jacob could hear the sickening thud of the tail wheel hitting the dirt, several strikes, then a cacophony of sliding, shearing aluminum, crumpling and tearing with every bounce and skid over the rutted field. Then silence.

Gabe had already started the truck and slammed it into gear. They bounced frantically out over the clearing, over the ruts and rocks toward the general direction of the crash.

They both emerged from the cab and Jacob ran to the smoldering hulk. His face glowed in the dim panel lights burning low in the darkness of the cockpit. He reached in to slide the open canopy back, searching for the master switch. The air was heavy with the perfume from vestiges of aviation gas leaking from the wing tanks. Like a solid mass its odor washed thick over him as he slipped on the wing's surface.

Gabe yelled to him, "Look around, he must have been thrown clear!" Jacob shifted his thoughts to the pilot. He must have been thrown clear! He was far too low to bail out?

He yelled to Gabe, "There's still gas leaking out of that wing! Stay the hell back!" He yelled again as several remaining sparks leapt from the cockpit console. He turned to look for Gabe but could see only the remaining light of the smudge pots that flickered on in the silence. Only there a moment before, Gabe was suddenly nowhere to be seen.

The truck sat there quietly bathing the now broken airframe with its headlights. Jacob reached into the cockpit, found the master switch and toggled it to the off position, then walked around the wrecked airframe. He peered out into the darkness in an effort to see him.

"Hey Old Man! Where the hell are you?" he called out as he walked around it inspecting what he could in the darkness.

Overcome with anger and frustration, he yelled out,

"That's great! That's just great!"

He stood there in the approaching dawn, angry with himself for getting in the truck and for letting himself get entangled in the situation. He thought for a moment about taking the truck, about driving off in the darkness. He opened the door to the truck and looked for the keys.

"Damn it!" he cursed himself for not having paid closer attention to where they were going and to the old man.

"He took the damn keys with him!" He grumbled as he kicked at a fragment of aluminum lying nearby.

He sat down on one broken wing of the airframe to wait. He reached for a cigarette, then remembered the fuel and decided against it.

In the quiet stillness of the approaching dawn the sun began to move up on the horizon revealing the colors of the surrounding fields. Its light brought forth a single orange shaft that illuminated the shining twisted skin of the wreck and shown down on Jacob like a single eye opening from sleep. As the light began to bring out the details he could see the full extent of the damage.

The wings were dug into the earth; the massive propeller was twisted and bent. A large breach in the fuselage showed signs that the airframe appeared to have dug itself into the earth some time ago. Weeds and other growth protruded out from the airframe's gaping belly. It became clear to him that whatever it was that he had seen the night before; this wreck could not have been it. At the same time however, he was haunted by thoughts of it and of something that connected him to it. He peered again into the cockpit, the instruments and controls worn from countless revolutions and handling. It seemed to him that each faded dial and scratched out placard was like a familiar piece of him. He reached in and placed his hand on the stick. It felt as if his grasp instinctively wound round the handle, his index finger and thumb aligned to actuate the guns. The marks of wear fitted to his hand.

Wonder if this thing is armed? The thought came to him and he quickly pulled his hand away. Even though it looked like it had been there for some time and any sign of life long gone, he decided not to test them.

Then he noticed something. It flashed in the sunlight as he moved to step away from the open canopy. It lay on the floor of the cockpit, a small rectangle of stained white paper. He reached down and picked it up from between several twisted cables. He stood there, and inspected it. It was a photograph, dimmed and washed out from many hours of sunlight and elements that had made their way into the cockpit. He spit on the tail of his shirt and carefully used it to wipe the grime from the picture. Slowly an image emerged.

It's her! He thought to himself. The figure in his dreams, the beautiful angel looked back at him in the faded sepia photograph. There were slight differences, the print dress, the hair pulled back. But even with these it was clear to him. He held it closer in an effort to find a name, a date something to tell him who she was, something that might help him remember her. He wiped the back of the picture carefully peering through the layers of dirt. Then it too emerged from the lower corner of the paper,

'To my Jacob, I love you, your angel…' Before he could think, the photo dropped from his hand in a sudden gust and was carried off into the grass beyond the wreck.

Franticly he climbed down the wing and ran over to it, digging through the weeds to find the photo.

He managed to recover it and was slipping it into his shirt pocket when he heard the rustle of tall grass and Gabe approaching him.

"We're too late…" The old man said.

"Yeah I'd say years too late from the looks of this wreck." Jacob replied nervously, still thinking about the photo and what it all meant.

"Look around… There may be foot prints, maybe a blood trail." Gabe said as he bent over nervously and began searching the ground, brushing by the long weeds, scanning the ground.

"It looks like this plane's been here for some time. Whoever we were supposed to help is long gone now."

"Look around…Look, here! Here it's an impression in the ground." Gabe began to wander off a few yards from the wreckage.

"Looks like he was able to get out in time." He said.

"There's no way! He was too low to bail out! Besides, the plane came in on its belly. If he had jumped it would have nosed in." Jacob said this surprised that he would have knowledge of what would happen if the Mustang's flight controls were left unattended and the aircraft's response to such a situation.

Gabe began walking an invisible line that he had plotted over the ground. "Look here's the boot prints! He got out here, then probably rolled, then stood up and started walking in that direction." He pointed off into a direction away from where they stood then began marching off in the general direction of his comments in an attempt to pick up the phantom trail.

"Are you nuts? There's no boot prints, no pilot! This junk has been here for years!" Jacob said, raising his voice in frustration with the old man's apparent delusions.

Gabe ignored his pleas and continued to bark out orders entranced by the invisible markings on the ground.

"You pull the truck in here, boy. Get the chain and pull the wreck out of the mud then use the winch and start loading it into the back."

"Are you kidding? There's no way I can get all of this in the back of that pickup! Even with a winch this thing has to be over a ton!"

"Make a couple of trips… If you get started now you should be able to get the wings, the engine and the rest of it back to the shop by breakfast. There are tools at the shop and some pry bars. Bring those when you come back."

"Where are you going?" Jacob called back to him.

"I'm going off to find him. You keep at it and I'll meet you back at the hangar by the time you get the first load on the truck." With this, Gabe left him there and moved off into the high weeds in search of the pilot.

"Wait a minute! I don't know how to get back! How will I find the airfield?" He called after Gabe who had once again disappeared into the weeds.

Gabe's voice called back calmly from a distant pile of tangled brush, "Just follow the tire tracks back to the road. You'll find it. I'll be there directly."

Jacob stood alone with the wreck in the early dawn, tired, confused, with half images and things hastily remembered then forgotten in an instant. He considered giving in to the situation, resigning himself to playing it out, to see what lay at the end. There was something in the picture, something with the girl that had to be pieced together. Right now, it was all he had. There were no phone numbers, no names or towns to run to. His only reality was that which was revealing it's self to him now.

Jacob reached into his shirt pocket and pulled out the picture and a wrinkled cigarette. He smiled slightly in resignation as he looked down at the old derelict rusting at his feet and at the girl from his dream. He lit the end of his smoke with a match and tossed the smoldering punk down next to the rubble, no longer concerned that there would be any fuel to worry about, then walked to the truck to sort through the tools that he would need.

Chapter 5

Jacob made several trips to the site of the wreck. He did not know why he was doing it. His head still pounded with pain in the growing light of the sun as he worked with the odd collection of tools that he had managed to pull together.

He cut away at the derelict in an effort to break it into manageable pieces that he could fit into the bed of the pickup. He had managed to get the wings and fuselage pulled apart loaded and trundled back to the airfield. It was rough going, pulling the massive pieces onto the truck under the protests of a tired wench and the worn out truck motor that had been rigged up to drag the heavy pieces of junk up onto the bed.

He had gotten lost several times during his first trip to the airfield taking several side roads in an effort to get some lay of the land around him and possibly find a way out. After several changes in direction and failed attempts to get beyond the road to a town he managed to re-trace Gabe's tracks from the night before.

Now nearly exhausted and frustrated with the prospect of being stuck in the middle of nowhere, he worked with what remained of the engine and propeller. He pried them loose from the earth and hoisted them along with the remaining metal skin, control cables and the entrails of the cockpit onto the back of the truck.

The work had given him time alone, to think, to try to sort things out. He had worked the problem over in his mind for the better part of the day and made his way toward the airfield mulling over the best possible answer that he could come up with.

I must have intended to land at that old field all along, he thought. That has to be it; I was never lost at all...But why? He could not come up with an explanation.

I'm supposed to be here. If I hadn't hit my head on the console when the Stearman nosed over, I'd know that.

As for the boy, he had developed a theory as well and surmised that both he and the image of the plane were also the result of the blow to his head.

This junk has been here for years. If it had not been for the picture of the girl, the whole thing would've made sense.

Then it occurred to him, the old man called me Jacob? He called me that. I didn't tell him that? It may not be my name at all? That's it. He's just some old nut who's pulled you into something!

Damnit, this makes no sense. He shook his head and cursed himself for not being able to explain it all away.

His clothes were covered with dirt and grime, his face tired with sweat. It had taken hours to get the whole thing disassembled, loaded and hauled. With each trip the sun rose higher in the sky. He looked up at it now, and thought about how cold it was even though the sun was shining. He was grateful for the fact that the rain had stopped but cursed the soaked boots and clothes that clung to his aching body as he guided the truck down a path and out onto the roadway toward the airfield.

He estimated that it was now close to midday and as he drove on, his attention turned to the old man and his search for the pilot. The whole situation seemed so pointless, so out of place.

Boy, that old guy really knows how to play one once he has it hooked! What an idiot! He cursed to himself. He could not understand why he had agreed to go with the old man, to come to this place, and recover the pieces of junk strewn around him on the ground. He could not understand why he had gone with him. He felt compelled to go, as if it were something he had to do, and yet his last bit of reason held a nagging uncertainty and he found himself still questioning the girl's image and her presence in his mind as he drove out on to the pavement of the road and made his way to the airfield.

The events seemed out of place with the rusting carcass that he had worked for hours to dislodge from its resting place. Weeds that had grown round the openings in the fuselage and the rusted parts and the engine showed the signs of deterioration of a machine that had not turned over in decades.

But it was there. I did see it flying! He struggled with the notion and remembered the glint of its shining fuselage and the sound of the screaming engines of the other aircraft rip through the silence of the night sky.

Hell! There was no way he could have made it out of the crash alive. And yet, that old man was determined, almost obsessed with finding him. The body shouldn't have been far from the crash site? There's no way in hell this wreck was in the air the night before. I'm losing it. Maybe that's it? Maybe I've lost my mind? Maybe I'm in a hospital someplace?

As he pulled up to the hanger, he could see Gabe, still dressed in his work clothes from the night before, sifting deliberately through the pile of rubble.

"How the hell did you get back here? Did you find anyone?" Jacob asked as he climbed out of the cab.

"Nope. He'll turn up." Gabe didn't look up. "Did you get everything?"

"Yeah I think so, I looked around and I didn't see anything left. Hey I'm not so sure that anyone will turn up."

Gabe ignored his comments. "You're sure?" Gabe looked at him, as a father would look at a child who had told a lie.

Jacob thought about the picture in his pocket.

"Yeah, I'm sure, I got everything."

"Good. We've got to get it all, can't leave anything behind."

Jacob responded in an effort to sell the lie further "Look, It's all there Pop. But if you want I'll go back and take another look around. Is there something that you're looking for?"

He noticed that Gabe carefully pulled each piece of sheet metal, wire and part from the pile and inspected them carefully. He was sorting pieces, placing them into separate piles and organizing the remains in an effort to take an inventory.

"No, I'll do it myself. You don't need to bother with it. You've done enough. I'll take it from here."

"You want me to help you sort through this?"

"No I'll do it. You just get the rest of the engine off the truck. I'll get everything into the hanger."

"What are you going to do with all of this junk?"

"Put it back together." Gabe said as if he were surprised by Jacob's question.

"What the hell for? It's a total loss. There's no way this thing will ever fly again. Nobody's going to want the parts."

Gabe stopped sorting and looked up at him. "Oh it will fly again. It's got to."

"And why is that?"

Gabe looked up at him for a moment then went back to his work.

Jacob threw his hands up in exasperation, "Here we go. I swear to God, what did I do to end up out here in the middle of nowhere with a lunatic?"

"I don't have time to explain it all to you. You just get that engine down off the truck and leave me to my work now. I've got a lot to do." Gabe said calmly as he leaned over a large piece of one wing.

Jacob untied the rope holding the remains of the engine to the truck bed, rigged the winch and worked the assembly onto the edge of the bed. He then backed the truck up to the door of the hangar and under Gabe's direction pulled it off onto the concrete floor at the foot of the door of the hangar.

"You sure you don't want me to help you with this?"

"No I do not… You've done enough already." Gabe was adamant.

"And do not go poking around in this hangar. Understand?" He pointed to the hangar door as he talked and looked at him with a stern warning.

"Hey? What the hell is that supposed to mean? I just thought I could help."

Gabe's attention was returned to inspecting a wing section, fingering several holes and mumbling to himself.

"Well, if you'd been more careful in the first place I wouldn't have to go to all this trouble."

"What? Are you nuts Pop? I thought you said you

needed my help, so I helped!"

"Yeah well, you're making things a lot more difficult than they need to be, that's for sure." Gabe lifted a piece of aluminum skin to eye level then slipped his index finger into a small hole that he had found. He stole a glance at Jacob as he did this in an effort to get his attention.

"Hey wait a minute, what are those?" Jacob drew closer.

"What do they look like?" Gabe responded, his brow furled and his expression fixed in anticipation of Jacob's answer.

Jacob could see several rough lines of holes that made their way across what looked like the upper half of the wing. Each hole was about the size of a dime, the edges turned inward like punch marks along the metal skin. Some of the holes had corresponding exit wounds of similar size on the opposing wing surface, these with jagged punctures that belied the nature of the damage.

Not certain how he knew, Jacob instinctively responded to the question, "Looks like 50 caliber."

"Close but not quite Son. More like 13 millimeter machine gun rounds."

Jacob stopped at the thought.

"Now wait a minute! You're not suggesting that this wreck was shot down out there?" Jacob's face grew in intensity and Gabe could see from the look on his face that the wheels were turning inside his head.

"What do you think Son? I mean you said it, this wreck has been in that field for years!"

"So what are you saying then?"

"Not saying anything, just that we got a pile of old airplane parts here, some bullet holes in one wing that's all." Gabe looked off toward the diner.

"Well I think I got a full day's work out of you. Go

get cleaned up and get some rest."

Gabe disappeared into the hangar with the piece of perforated aluminum tucked under one arm without another word.

Jacob stood there stunned. There had been no explanation, no answers, just an old man who only hours before had needed his help, but now acted as though he was in the way.

He walked to the diner, Hop following along behind. He found the shower stall in a back room and stripped off his clothes. The warm water felt good and he let it run over his head and neck and languished in the warmth, letting it sooth his tired muscles and wash the grime and sweat away. It was the first shower he could remember in a long time. He tried to think of the last time he had one.

He thought about this, the words and the images that came to him the night before. It seemed clear to him that the answers would not come to him directly. There was a stack of fresh clothes that Gabe had laid out for him and he pulled on some clean overalls and walked out to check on his progress.

Suppose I should be thankful for small favors, he thought as he pulled together the last button on a fresh shirt. The old man had been a step ahead of him.

It was late in the day now but he was surprised to see no sign of the piles of rubble that had been in front of the hangar only an hour or so before. He could hear the sound of machine tools and hammer blows against metal parts, grinding metal against metal, the whirring of machines. He struggled to look into one of the painted over windows but could not make out anything.

Finally he gave up and moved over to an old picnic table that sat forlorn under an elderly apple tree a few yards from the hangar. He lit a cigarette and sat there, listening and smoking while the machines worked away feverishly inside the hangar.

It didn't seem possible that he was in there doing all of the work alone. It had only been the two of them and the dog? He thought. He considered this as he drew the smoke from the glowing cigarette, holding it between his thumb and middle finger, sucking in the smoke, allowing it to sink deep into his lungs. The smoldering tip produced a thin line of blue haze that rose up through the limbs of the tree and after a moment, drew his attention upward to the branches and leaves that danced almost imperceptibly in the stillness of the late afternoon.

Hop had trotted over and lay in the grass at his feet. The dog moved from time to time only to look up at him with a casual glance that left him thinking that this was something that was routine.

He could not place the memory or the exact circumstances but he was certain that whatever was in that hangar, held the key to his questions.

The sun was warm on his face and the breeze drifted in waves of calm rustling rhythms, like a slowly advancing tide, the rustling of the leaves like the low rush of waves against an oncoming giant.

A giant of steel and heavy machinery buzzed in his mind and came forward from the sounds emanating from the hangar. He felt himself adrift in the sea of breeze as he dozed in the sun. He could smell the scent of the apples that lay on the ground. The sweet smell of cider from the over ripe fruit brought to him other images. They were images of the small boy on the road, of a time long ago and a summer of little boys in youthful innocence and play, far from the long contrails that stretched out on the horizon marking the distance traveled.

In his drifting, he thought he heard the laughter of the little boy coming from the tree overhead. He thought for an instant that the boy's voice sang out from the limbs above, singing with the spontaneous lilt that only a child can know. It occurred to him that no man could know this when in the end he finally becomes a man. Joy is something different then, something more elusive. It occurred to him that a man must work hard to find the joy in things.

A large apple slipped from its bond to the tree and fell to the table top with a sudden thud that snapped Jacob to return to his present situation.

Hop whined a bit, as if he feared that he might be left alone. Jacob looked down at the dog then, noticed that the sounds from the hangar had gone silent.

Gabe emerged, covered with oil and a fine dust of ground metal fragments that peppered his face and bald head.

"Well, Mr. Wright, how's it going in there? Still going to try and piece that thing together?" Jacob called out. Gabe said nothing and walked slowly past him to the diner.

Jacob jumped up from the table and followed him matching him stride for stride.

"I'll tell you if you are, you're in for some work, my friend. That airframe took a hell of a lot of hours and a whole factory of engineers and machinery to put together. Hell the engine alone is a damn jigsaw puzzle of screws and parts, half of which are so old and rotten...You'll have to fabricate sections of the fuselage, send off for parts and gaskets. It'll take several good mechanics a couple of years to put that museum piece back in order."

He followed the old man as he pled his case, trying to keep up with him and argued the futility of his solo effort in an attempt to get a chance to get into the hangar and find some answers.

Gabe moved behind the counter ignoring Jacob's comments and began washing his hands and arms, then his face and bald head in the sink his dark brown skin like chocolate under the water. He took a long drink from a tin cup that sat at the sink and wiped the moisture from his hands with a towel.

"Why do you care what an old man does?" he asked in a tone that suggested that he knew that Jacob was concerned that he might find something in the twisted metal that he did not want revealed.

"You act like you're scared of something."

"What do you mean? I don't know a thing about any of this. I'm just saying that you're wasting your time."

Gabe looked at him through the mirror in front of the sink. "You'd be surprised what one man can do."

Gabe looked down at him, then the counter, as if he had expected to hear this, "So you want to stay? You want to see what I've got in that hangar?"

"Well I think I can spare the time, I can put things together, I know how to fly just about anything that can make its way into this cornfield though I don't know why I'd want to. Besides it doesn't look like you have a lot of other takers jumping up to lend a hand."

Gabe looked up at him, "Tell me son, why would you want to hang around this place?"

Jacob thought again about the picture of the girl and the images from the night before.

"What do you mean? I don't know, I haven't thought about it much? I don't know why I'm here in the first place or why I'm even having this conversation with you? Look, I'll stay on for a while, help you get some work done, and then when my plane is fixed, I'll leave. Whatta ya say?"

Gabe called over to Hop.

"Yesterday he couldn't wait to leave; now all of a sudden he wants to stay?"

He looked again at Jacob, "So what do you want?"

Before he could think about the question a response leapt from his lips.

"To live, that's important, being alive." He tried to catch himself but couldn't.

Gabe shook his head, "Livings only part of it. What do you really want?"

"Hell, I don't know? Look I'm offering to help, that's all. I'm trying to figure this out and get the hell out of here."

The old man took another drink from the cup and looked down at the counter as if dissatisfied with the answer, "No you're not. You're asking for help…"

"This is bullshit. Forget it!"

"Yeah friend, I think you're off course." Gabe said.

Jacob was caught off guard tried to defend the words though they had not been his own.

"What is with this? I can get along fine on my own."

"Who said it had anything to do with you?" Gabe hesitated and looked away as if he had inadvertently revealed something important.

"Well, like I said, it's none of your concern."

"I think it is. As a matter of fact, I think you know why I'm here and you just don't want me to know!"

Gabe walked toward the door, "You're wrong there. I want you to know." The old man looked at him now, as if he was waiting for him to have some revelation and realize the answer.

Jacob stood there puzzled by the whole conversation.

"It's like I said son, it's about what you want that's important. Tell you what, you think about this some more. Look around see if anything hits you."

Jacob now convinced that the old man was leading him down a path that he was not prepared for returned his attention to the situation.

"I need to go check out the Stearman. If you don't mind, I'll probably need to borrow some tool…"

The old man cut him off, "Aircraft's locked up in the hangar. Like I said, can't let you in there."

"What is this? I still own it!"

"Oh really...? Well I own the facility and that hangar is off limits to everyone but me."

"What the hell are you doing in there?"

Gabe grinned and slapped his cap on his head. He turned from Jacob's protests and walked out to the distant hangar with Hop hot on his heels.

He thought he could easily push his way past the old man, break the lock and go inside. But even though it was possible, he was unable to bring himself to do it. While he was sure that the answers were in there, answers to who he was and why he was there, he was overcome with the fear of what might be on the other side of the hangar door and what knowing the answers might mean. He was certain that he would need the old man's help to put everything together and make sense of the situation.

Almost on queue, the radio in the diner came on with a crackling hum that brought to life a faint four-part harmony of gospel music. He listened to the music as it strained to come through the weak static and the innocent, blue-collar voices that intertwined the melody and the words to the beat of a base fiddle and guitar. He could imagine their faces, rough, weather worn and tired, their voices belying their efforts to cover over the anguish and pain of years of hard labor and misfortune. They were not as much singing as praying aloud.

In some ways, he thought that he was a lot like them, down to his last bit of pocket change, placing it all on the only thing that remained. They sang the tired strains with a weary faith as if they were prepared to accept yet again another disappointment, adrift, clinging to some last bit of flotsam in a sea of uncertainty. The empty strains clutched at the faint hope of relief, rest and something more beyond the empty fields and barren storefronts of dead farms and dying rural towns.

He stood in the doorway of the diner and listened to them singing. He could feel his heart sinking with them; the irony of the words and the sound of their desperate voices drew him down. He prayed that his reality, in whatever form it would take would not be like theirs and that the answers to his questions would amount to something more than he suspected they would.

He would bide his time. There would be an opening somewhere that he could take advantage of, he thought. It always came down to that, an opening in the clouds that would allow him to break out and find his way down.

Chapter 6

Gabe walked off toward an incoming plane that was taxing up to him waiting to be directed to a position to be parked on the field.

Jacob could make out the model and recognized it as an old Aero-tractor. It is an odd looking beast of an airplane, he thought as it made its way down and taxied toward them, a bold yellow monstrosity with a low square wing, slats for slow flying and a powerful rotary engine built on a strong tubular airframe that can take hours of abuse at the hands of its pilot. It's a workhorse, designed and built to spend its entire useful life making endless circling low passes over farm fields and orchards, spraying chemical pesticides.

It's a dangerous job crop dusting. There's a narrow season for the work and when the work comes, 'dusters' work hours on end without sleep or meals in an effort to get in as much of it as possible before the lean fall and winter sets in and the bills pile up.

The plane rolled up to him its engine coughing in protest, its exhaust manifold burned up with rust crackling with heat as the airframe shuddered to a stop.

The pilot popped up from a hunched over position in front of the instrument panel and climbed out into the mid afternoon sun with the deliberate movements of an ambulatory patient recovering from a painful injury. He was tired looking and incredibly thin, a near skeleton of a man, his denim overalls and tee shirt hanging from him like a loose sack. He was as tan and dark as tobacco and the deep-set sockets of his eyes were worn with fatigue.

"Where the hell am I?" he called to Jacob in tired resignation, his slow drawl all but eating up the words as he spoke. He pulled a crumpled pack of cigarettes from his pocket, tugged one out, lit it with a match and leaned back against the fuselage of the plane, cigarette dangling from his lower lip as he looked around and rubbed the dust from a crop of grey brown hair on his head. He was covered with a fine chemical spray of insecticide, dirt, oil specks and dust that had managed to work their way into the cockpit over the many hours of endless flight. It had collected in the cabin and it was obvious that he had probably ingested a sizable amount over the course of his work.

"Don't ask…" Jacob piped up impishly still thinking about the previous night. He made his way over to the plane following Gabe's lead and put the chocks under the wheels.

He realized that the man didn't catch the joke and smiled, "Well don't worry bout it right now friend. Where ya headed?"

"Florida I think?"

Jacob chuckled knowingly and interjected, "Well I can tell you, you're definitely not in Florida."

"Oh… That ain't good…" the man groaned as he pulled a hard drag on the cigarette and slowly walked around the wing to open the fuel cap.

"Hey friend…! Think that's such a good idea?" Jacob said as he took a quick step to one side of the wing.

"Whatddya mean?"

"The cigarette…open fuel tank…" Jacob replied as the man unscrewed the cap and leaned over the opening, cigarette dangling.

"Probably not…" he responded in a matter fact tone and looked over at Jacob then took a hard drag on the butt as he leaned in closer over the opening.

"You got gas around here?"

Gabe responded, "Sure. Listen you look a little tired to me. How bout some coffee and a sandwich…?"

"Why that's a fine idea friend, I could use a bite." the man replied, his tired voice slowly rolling the words along as he inspected the leading edge of a wing and poked his head under it to look at a tire.

"Suppose I should get that tire looked at too…" He mumbled to himself.

At about the same moment a Beech Eighteen landed and taxied in a quick, efficient line then parked in front of the hangar where the three of them were standing.

The plane was in showroom form, impeccably maintained its bright skin shining in the sun. A small bald man in a white wrinkled short-sleeved shirt and thin black tie emerged from the side door and clambered down the wing to meet Gabe as he approached.

"Who's the mechanic here?" the little man barked as he put his hands on his paunchy hips and looked at Gabe with a horn rimmed bespectacled glare. The man stared through the glasses in spite of a defiant right eye that wandered independently from the left. He turned his head when he spoke like someone who expected to be slapped in the face at any moment.

In an automatic, seemingly rehearsed voice Gabe answered him slowly, "I am… What's the problem?"

Jacob was surprised at how suddenly the old man had become a distant, businesslike stranger to this fellow. He had fallen into the kind of speech that rural folks make when confronted by the pretense projected by strangers who impose money and position and a world too important for rural life on them.

"What's the problem…What…what's the problem?" the little man retorted in disbelief.

He immediately jumped to his well-rehearsed, confrontational tone, grabbing his horn-rims from his face and wiping them with a handkerchief nervously.

"Didn't you hear that left engine as I was coming in? Jesus Christ, what kind of facility is this? The engine was running so rough I could hardly keep it flying!"

"Really…?"

"Yeah really, take a look at it will you. I haven't got all day and I have to be in Chicago by this evening!"

"If you give me a minute I'll finish up here and take care of you." Gabe responded coolly.

"Damnit, I haven't got time to wait."

He turned to the duster who was leaning like a tired question mark against the wing of the tractor. The little man seeing an opportunity to press his point spoke to him.

"Look, I'm sure you can understand, you look like a sensible fellow, I have to make that appointment. You let me in ahead of you and well, well what can I do for you?"

The duster scratched the dust on his forehead, almost confused with the decision that he was now confronted with.

"Well I'm a little short on cash…Say you cover my gas?"

"I suppose..." the little man grumbled impatiently, "Have your boy fill him up while you work on my plane and I will cover it." He said to Gabe.

"Say, you know that tire there, is pretty worn too, would ya mind throw'in in a replacement?" the duster said, as he stood there smoking the remains of the cigarette and scratching himself sheepishly.

"What? You want a tire too?" the little man argued, impatient and clearly agitated.

"That is if ya don't mind?"

"OK, OK give him the tire too!" The little man ordered as he walked past them toward the diner. Jacob followed eager to see what would come of the stranger.

The man looked about inspecting the room and shook his head.

"What a dump." His tone and nervousness set Hop up from his doze on the floor. He looked at them then yawned and scratched in disinterest.

Without asking the man reached over the counter, grabbed the phone and began dialing.

"What the hell is wrong with the phones around here? I've got to call my client and I can't get this Goddamn phone to work!" The man continued, clicking the receiver and pacing the length of the phone cord up and down the counter.

"It doesn't take outgoing calls." Jacob said in a quiet resigned tone.

The man looked at Jacob with a questioning glance then ignoring him went back to fiddling with the phone.

"Can I get you anything while you wait?" Jacob asked.

"What? No, no just tell your boss to get that aircraft fixed...!"

Jacob decided that he would leave the man to his pacing and looked out the window. He could see that Gabe had entered a covered service port a few hundred yards away. He walked out to the shelter and could see him sifting through old coffee cans and boxes of spare parts, tools and odds and ends looking for something. He seemed to move with quiet confidence among the tools and junk like a man who always has some answer, some solution to the problem hidden in his collection and merely needed a moment to remember where the necessary item was. He returned with a length of cable, some tools and a spark plug and hunched over the open cowling of the left engine. It seemed remarkable to Jacob that this little man in his white starched shirt and tie had picked out this small airfield amidst all of the open cornfields to stop.

The man clearly frustrated with the situation stormed out of the diner and paced about outside as Gabe worked slowly on the problem and the duster leaned casually against the plane like a tired old farmhand.

Used to getting his way the little man kicked at the ground in frustration while Gabe quietly worked away in silence. After some time, he realized that he could not get the situation to resolution any quicker and decided to make small talk in order to fill the silence that was obviously too much for him to bear.

There is an unsettling humor that sometimes makes its way into a pilot's conversations. Jacob hadn't thought about it much until then. He considered it a kind of carry over from the stories heard from other pilots or mechanics who spent their lives piecing together lost rivets and sheet metal remains of others' missteps. They were stories that were told, retold, changed and exaggerated to fit some situation either real or fictitious. They described an incident, a fatality, a crash, collision or near miss with the elements.

Jacob reasoned that Gabe was probably good for a number of these tales. He thought too that this gift was at times a point of consternation for a waiting customer who would be standing over him impatiently while he had his head down in an engine or under a cockpit seat with his hand reaching out for a tool.

Gabe handed Jacob a wrench as the little man spoke.

"Look, I ah, well, I'm glad I found your field here when I did. Damn near collided with another guy trying to land here I think. Didn't get his tail number or what he was flying. Damn fool sprang up from out of nowhere."

Gabe didn't respond, but kept working.

The little man continued, "You know I heard about an accident that happened up north not long ago."

"Clean this up will ya son?" Gabe seemed to take the beginning of the story as a queue and stood there with the little man and the duster and listened intently to his story, a story that he and half the pilots in history had heard countless times before.

"I heard that a guy was killed up in Chicago some time back." The man started, nervously, almost afraid to let down his guard. He took off his glasses and began wiping the lenses again with the handkerchief.

"No kid din, did he end up in the lake?" Gabe asked, reeling the little man in with his interest.

"Well, yeah come to think of it?" the man laughed sheepishly, "Crashed up around Meig's Field. Bad accident too, killed him, his wife and a little boy." he spoke in macabre satisfaction, full of himself at recounting the incident, setting himself above the error made by the anonymous pilot in the story.

"How'd it happen?"

"I heard that the guy was late for some meeting. Wife and his son wanted to do some shopping so he took them along. Anyway, the guy I talked to said that this guy was in a hurry, he didn't think he checked his fuel before they took off, got lost, lost track of time, ran out of gas lost an engine something like that. Can you believe it?"

Gabe looked intently into the man's eyes, "You don't say? Did you know him?"

The man stared back in near embarrassment then answered in a tone of nervous denial. "No…No… I didn't know the man…"

"How bout his wife or the kid…?"

"No. Damnit, I just heard about it that's all!" the little man answered impatiently.

Gabe turned and looked at Jacob, his face drawn with a look of sadness and disappointment at the man's answer.

Then Gabe spoke up suddenly, his words laced with a twinkling lilt as he chained a story on to this incident in a conscious effort to change the tone of the conversation.

"Ya know it's funny but that reminds me of something that happened a few years ago. A guy wanted to take his fiancée up for a little sightseeing. He came by and wanted to rent a cub for an hour or so. He was checked out in it, had a bunch of hours and so I said sure. Then I got a call a couple of hours later from the sheriff."

The duster drew a long drag on his cigarette, then looked up at the sky and blew it out and turned a glance and a quick knowing wink to Jacob as if he knew how Gabe's tale would turn out.

"Yeah…?" The little man was visibly still very

nervous but somewhat relieved by Gabe's change in direction.

"Yeah. Seems the guy decided to land in a field near a little romantic spot of trees. After a while they decided to go but the guy couldn't get the engine started and decided to hand prop the plane. Well anyhow this guy had his girl sit behind the stick and showed her how to work the controls, fuel, ignition; you know just enough to hold the plane down once he got the engine started."

"Yeah, what happened?"

"Well, when he pulled the prop through, he slipped on a cow pie and fell clear, the engine kicked in and the cub started rolling down the field bounc'in over ruts and rocks." Gabe continued the story now prancing about, his arms extended in illustration.

"It finally got airborne and took off headed for Chicago with her at the controls."

"You're kidding?" the man laughed nervously.

"Nope... The guy walked a couple miles to the nearest farm house called the sheriff; we set out for Chicago hoping to find her."

Then Gabe paused and looked in on Jacob, who sat helplessly, entangled in his work. Gabe handed him another tool without breaking stride. He waited until the man could hold back no more.

"Well what the hell happened? Did you find her?"

"Oh yeah…"

"Well?"

"She never made it to Chicago."

"Well, OK what happened to her?" the man asked anxiously.

"Last I heard she married some guy in Gary."

The duster laughed coughing out a puff of smoke,

"Still can't help it, I'll bet I heard that one a hundred times." He laughed harder and coughed in tired spasms.

The little man laughed self-consciously, realizing that he had been sucked into a story that any line boy or mechanic had probably heard a dozen times before. He pulled the handkerchief from his pocket again and this time mopped his bald head nervously.

Jacob emerged from the cowling.

"All done..."

The little man snapped back to the business at hand and replaced his glasses in an effort to return himself to his character.

"So, what do I owe you?"

Gabe dispensed with the paper and pencil exercise.

"Ignition wire and a plug, say 5 bucks, twenty for the gas in the tractor and a tire let's say forty dollars even."

"Alright…" The man fished for his wallet and took out a fifty-dollar bill.

Gabe took the bill and turned to walk to the diner.

"Where are you going?"

"To get your change…"

"Look, keep it, I have to go, I have got to get to Chicago." The man looked at Gabe, nervous, fearful and almost overcome with the desire to escape, to get away. He clambered into the cockpit and slid open a side window as Gabe took a step toward it.

"Now let me ask, do you need fuel?" The question seemed odd in the way that Gabe had asked it. His tone was consoling, fatherly.

"No…No." the man replied, nervously rushing through his checklist.

"You're sure?" Gabe repeated.

"Damnit, I'm sure and I'm in a hurry. I've got to get

to that meeting in Chicago!"

"Listen, now son..." Gabe's tone was calm and clear as if trying to give the little man an opportunity to correct himself, "If you need anything, anything at all, you know how to get back here and I want you to know you're welcome any time."

The man looked at him, again fearful, anxious and nervously fiddling with the knobs and levers in the cockpit, "I doubt I'll be back this way..."

Gabe and the man paused and looked at each other, their gaze held together in a bond, a knowing that the man did not want to realize and that Gabe could only make known to him if he were to admit it himself and recognize where he was.

For a moment it seemed that the man would accept his situation, his fate but then in an instant as if snapped from a trance, he quickly slid the window shut and started the engines. The wind of the whirling propellers kicked up dust as he quickly swung round and taxied to the runway, then without a single pause, he applied power, and rushed down the runway, lifted off and disappeared into the late afternoon sky.

Gabe turned to the service bay to return the tools and unused parts, Jacob followed after him.

"What the hell was that all about?"

"What do you mean?"

"I mean that whole thing about the fuel, the 'If you ever need anything' and all that?"

Gabe stopped and looked at Jacob in a way that suggested that he too should somehow know the answer to his own question.

"He'll be back." Gabe said with a sigh as he slid the tools in a tray.

"That makes no sense. You're telling me that that guy came down here on purpose? Down to this old, worn out airstrip just to bitch and complain? And that he'll be back?"

Gabe didn't answer but continued to clean up.

"This is nuts!" Jacob protested, "Look the guy had a problem with his engine and found his way down here. Of course he was able to avoid that damn radio tower otherwise he'd probably still be here pacing the floor and wringing his hands! I mean there's no mystery to that. It's coincidence plain and simple."

Gabe walked over to a coffee can and dropped a few remaining screws into it.

"He comes here every now and then. He gets tired you see. He needs to come down for a while. I try to help him but he's too stubborn, won't listen. He tells me the same story and I let him tell it."

"What the hell are you talking about? You say he's been here before? He acted like he'd never seen you before. He just said that he wasn't coming back?"

"He says that every time and every time he comes back."

Gabe stopped his sorting and looked over at Jacob.

"We do a lot of fixing things. We fix things that go beyond the contents of coffee cans and spare parts." Gabe pointed off in the direction the man had taken down the runway.

"Let's go take care of our boy there, looks like he gets a tank of gas and a new tire. I'll handle that and you can get him something to eat."

Jacob walked the duster to the diner where they sat at the counter and talked about flying over bologna sandwiches while Gabe worked.

It felt good to have someone to talk to, even if it was

a stranger who was short on words.

"Yeah, been flying round in circles I guess. I been flying all night I think, been trying to get down to Florida... Heard there's work down that way."

"Where ya from...?" Jacob asked.

"All over..."

"Well you know you're pretty far from Florida."

The man rubbed the back of his neck and then his face with open hands, a smoldering butt sticking out from between his fingers his rough hands caked with the dust and chemical residue.

"Yeah I'll tell ya, you all ought to consider getting somebody to move that radio antenna. I just bout clipped it on the way in."

He crushed the cigarette in the plate, took a bite from the sandwich and washed it down with a mouthful of coffee.

"Yeah I know, almost did the same thing myself. Listen, did you see any towns on your way in? I mean, did you see anything that looked like a runway?"

The duster sat there, his head on one palm thinking. "Nope, can't say that I can recall, though that don't mean much. I suppose there's a field around here somewhere... Always someplace to land, that is if you look long enough and you don't run out of gas first." The man smiled coyly at Jacob as if he new the answer to a mystery.

The engine of the tractor suddenly kicked over and fell into a rough idle.

"Sounds like your boss is finished with my ride, what's the damage?" He yawned, stretched, slipped off the stool and stood digging in his pocket for a roll of cash.

Jacob hesitated, surprised that Gabe had finished the work so soon. He did not want the man to leave. He wanted the man to stay and talk, to give him some assurance that this was real, that there were other places, other runways out there beyond the field and that he could find them.

"Listen, what say you stay for a while? I mean we don't get many folks out this way. You stay over, I could look your plane over and maybe you and I we could do some flying together?"

The duster walked toward the door and lit another cigarette. "Wish I could son but, you know how it is. I've got work to do and well the weather round here is too temperamental for my liking. No I've got to push on and find that job down in Florida."

"Don't go…" Jacob said, his words belying his anxiety.

"Got to son, now what do I owe the old man?"

"I think you're even with the old man. Look, I know this sounds crazy but, I'm lost too. I was in this accident see and I've been trying to find a way out of here. If you could maybe give me a lift, say to an airport or the next town along the way, I've got cash, I'd pay you for the trouble." He was surprised with these words; he felt a sudden fear for the old duster and his situation. He wanted to keep the stranger with him. He wanted them to be together to find someplace, some way out.

"Well I can't say that I'm not grateful, but I only got a single seat in that old airplane and I gotta tell you it ain't likely I'll be down this way again any time soon."

"Look it doesn't have to be anyplace out of your way, just the next town, the next airport. I just have to know there is a way out of here, someplace else somewhere. I've got to get back…"

Jacob's words grew more desperate.

"Look brother, you seem like a good kid, so I'm gonna

let you in on a little secret. I've been flyin around for what seems like an eternity and well, this is the first strip I've seen." The man scratched the back of his neck and looked down at his feet as he spoke, almost embarrassed by the secret.

"Truth be told, I can't say that there is anyplace else. Sounds nutty but, try as I might, I just ain't seen no place else. My advice to you is that you stay put here. Stay here and don't ever leave the ground son. You'll be better off by a long shot…"

The man turned and walked without a further word of explanation to the waiting plane with Jacob standing in stunned silence behind him. It was idling slowly, its engine coughing blue puffs of exhaust.

"You might want to check that compression!" Gabe yelled over the engine noise.

The old duster nodded and climbed up onto the wing and plopped down in a heap into the cockpit, hunching down to avoid the prop wash.

"Thanks for the advice, I'll do that soon as I get to Florida!"

He looked over at Jacob, "So long son, remember what I said."

Jacob looked at Gabe as the man departed, drifting over the runway then making a low pass and a quick snap roll farewell as he disappeared over the horizon, the sound of the plane's engine fading off into the distance.

"He'll never make it to Florida in that wreck." Jacob said.

"He's not going to Florida…"

"What do you mean Pop?"

"There's a lot that can happen between here and Florida son."

"Like what?"

"Men get tired son. They get tired and even though they do, they try to push on. They try to do things they can't do anymore. It's a dangerous thing when men realize at the last moment that they are too old and tired to do the things they want to anymore."

"I guess I'm supposed to know what that means?" Jacob asked.

"Nope, I suppose not…" the old man said as the aircraft disappeared.

"Like I said we fix things here." Gabe said with a sense of finality as he turned and shuffled past Jacob, letting the screen door to the diner slam behind him.

The radio came on almost as if on queue. The radio preacher took up his harangue and the sound of gospel music filled the room. Jacob listened as the hum of the radio, the words and the music mingled with the sounds of distant aircraft engines.

He felt a brush against his pant leg. Hop sat there at his feet, panting and staring up at him expectantly.

"Your old man's nuts boy…"

Hop yawned and hobbled off to find his favorite spot on the diner floor.

Chapter 7

The sky was an ink black sea filled with stars and wisps of cloud that hung in the air at altitude. They drifted like angel hair in a lonely abyss that stretched from the horizon up to the heavens.

Below, towns appeared as glowing splatters of luminescence, shining through the veil of misting ghosts. No more than fragile strands, broken by the long open darkness between them they looked like spider webs that sparkled in quiet disregard to a passing aircraft.

Jacob looked down at the lights below and his thoughts drifted as the twin engines pulsed and throbbed with a muffled beat that resonated through the airframe, and the props bit at the heavy air. His mind drifted and turned to the Mustang in the hangar and the face of the old duster he had encountered days earlier. It seemed to him a familiar face, a face that he should know, but could not remember. Like many things it seemed too unbelievable to have been real. He wondered if the whole incident had really happened. And yet, there he was, the reality of the moment was upon him again. He knew that his destination would be the same and that he would land at the field, see the hangar again, and see the old man there waiting for him. He wondered if maybe the duster had somehow conspired with the old man and was playing some crazy prank on him.

There's no way that old duster could fly that Mustang out of there. Why would he even care? He was on his way to Florida, to a job, probably a thousand miles away from here, he thought. Again the face of the duster returned to his mind and he searched his memory in an effort to remember who the man was.

The vibration of the airframe tugged at him as if trying to lull him to sleep. An icy finger of cloud drifted over one wing and the slight bump of turbulence brought him back to the moment. He reached over and turned the air vent open slightly to introduce cold air from the outside into the warmth of the cockpit in an effort to ward off sleep. He looked at his watch again out of habit, the hands still frozen at the time of his crash landing, then one of two fuel gauges on the panel in front of him. Deftly he switched on the fuel pump, and switched from the left to the right fuel tank in an effort to maintain an even drain between them and balance the fuel load.

He wondered about the towns and the people there below, sleeping quietly in the night. He wondered if they knew about the field, if they knew about the lonely road and the tower. He thought for a moment that he would look for another field, an airport, a beacon of alternating amber and green, and the two lines of lights, green to amber to red bordering an asphalt runway. He had looked for them before, considered them before, there were none to be seen. It was as if there were no other safe places in the world save the field, Gabe's field, a lonely island in a sea of cold inky blackness and the spaces, the open dark spaces down below.

They could be safe? He thought. They could be flat, level places where he could land, then find a farm house, a road, a passing car that could take him to a town. He had considered this a number of times, thought about the possibility of getting out of it, of leaving Gabe and going on his way. He thought about it but could not, dared not try to come down to them. It would not be safe to do this. It would not be safe to go down so low in the darkness. He thought about this again and again, that it would not be safe. In his thinking he could remember something, a vague shadow in his memory, of going down in the darkness. He could not do this. He could not go down to the dark places between the lighted spaces. He must fly on to the field.

He had lost track of time. Had it been days…weeks? He could not remember. Gabe had managed to fill his mind with questions. They drove him on in the night, made him fly on, and pulled him into a routine that defied any logical answers. He had grown used to the process and to the empty space between the memories that made him fear the dark spaces below. He sat in the cockpit now flying one of many old wrecks that they had recovered.

In practically every case the corroding remains would make it from its resting place to its final destination under the same routine. Jacob and Gabe would ride out to some deserted location together in the dark of night. Gabe would drive the truck in quiet silence turning from one back road to another then to a crumbling drive or gravel lane to an open clearing, a flat spot of grass that had been converted to a makeshift airstrip. With predictable consistency, Gabe would waddle over to a waiting derelict and after a few moments of poking around under the cowling, moving the control surfaces and so on, declare it "airworthy". He would then give Jacob a motion to climb in and ferry it back to the field while he drove the truck home. Within minutes Gabe would be on his way back to the field and Jacob would be left alone with the aircraft and all of its decaying metal, leaky hoses and frayed fabric smelling of dank mildew and motor oil.

There was always the smell of decay, he thought, It permeated everything in the cockpit.

He had learned over the course of these trips that he should expect to encounter several near catastrophic system failures during the flight home. In every case, the engine, electronics or airframe had been stretched well beyond the end of its useful life and the aircraft had been left to die alone and abandoned. Jacob was regularly surprised at Gabe's ability to ferret out these relics.

He could not explain it, but he felt fear with every relic and the fact that no one else was ever there when they arrived to collect them. He never saw the owner, never heard a conversation regarding the aircraft. Gabe would simply tell Jacob that he had a ferry that they needed to fly, and off they would go.

In a similar way, he had no idea where the aircraft ended up after he had managed to land it on their runway. Gabe would ask nothing about the flight, the problems or any encounter that Jacob might have had on the way. He would simply be there, standing on the tarmac, in the early hours right before dawn holding a large electric lantern and waiving him on, directing the aircraft to a position outside of the hanger at the end of the field.

"I'll take it from here son." he would say as the plane's engine coughed to silence and any loose bolts or fasteners dropped off onto the ground in a last fitful protest.

He would connect a hand truck to either the nose or tail wheel then wait for Jacob to move off to the main building before he would darken his lamp, slide open the hanger and slowly pull the corpse into the darkness. He knew from the size of the building and the number of planes that had gone through its doors that they could not all be stored in it. He speculated that maybe Gabe was stealing them, chopping them down and stripping the useful parts to add to the seemingly endless supply of junk that he stored in boxes and coffee cans strewn about every available corner or shelf in the diner and the other buildings. It seemed conceivable that he could store even larger wings and pieces of fuselage in the hangar however he imagined that if Gabe had been practicing this habit for some time that he would have clearly run out of room long ago.

He could not understand why, in the midst of this open, seemingly endless expanse, that an almost continuous supply of hapless derelicts lay rotting in fields and barnyards or why Gabe would risk stealing such junk. Gabe did not seem capable of any wrongdoing. Oddly, it had not occurred to him until now, that this ritual had probably been going on for a while. It was as if they were performing some service, like a mortician coming to pick up the remains.

He thought of the place where they had found this latest project sitting in hapless disarray on the edge of an abandoned field in the middle of nowhere.

Gabe had been silent during their drive and only responded to Jacob with grunts and feint replies.

"Hey son, get the bolt cutters out of the truck." Gabe said as he made his way to an old hangar that stood in silent decay in the middle of an empty field.

"You sure you have this right? Don't you have a key?" Jacob asked.

Gabe ignored his comment, "Just get the cutters and come on."

With a single snap the padlock gave way. They entered and found the plane sitting there quietly as if it had been waiting patiently for them. The tires were flat and the engine stiff and reluctant to turn over even after they loaded gallons of fresh fuel and worked clean oil into the crankcase of each engine.

At first Jacob was uncertain that they would get them started, but Gabe, opened the cowling on both engines in succession and worked in patient silence as various parts badly rusted and corroded were either cleaned or switched for others that he had brought along with him. Finally after several hours he closed the cowls and stepped out in front of the windscreen and pointed to each engine in turn with one hand while spinning his other to indicate that he wanted the engines started.

With coughing protests they both finally came to life. Gabe turned his back to him and waved as he climbed into the truck and headed for home leaving Jacob alone in the cockpit of the grumbling machine.

The aircraft managed to struggle into the air and after an hour of bone rattling flight he began probing the darkness in search of the tower.

He looked again at his watch and cursed its frozen hands and broken crystal staring back at him, reminding him that no time had passed; he was uncertain that any time had passed, and questioned his time there. How long had it been? He did not know. He knew intuitively that soon he would be within range and tuned the AM receiver in an effort to pick up the signal that had now grown familiar. He knew that it was out there and on his present heading he would pick up the signal soon then get down, have a drink and get some rest.

The air was cold and thick with the ethereal, drifting static of a thousand voices that congealed into a cacophony of sounds flooding the radio waves and filling the space inside the cockpit. Like ghosts the voices moaned and sighed as they pressed against the frozen atmosphere, then skipped across the heavens like lost phantoms, condemned to an eternal journey without rest.

He tuned the radio and picked up the sudden rush of gospel music. The needle swung around and then stopped pointing 45 degrees to the right of his current heading. He knew that he was not far from the field. Not far, only within an hour or so, he thought.

He gazed out of the cockpit through the windscreen and for a moment thought he caught a glimpse of another aircraft approaching him from off of his left wingtip. It seemed far away from him, and he was surprised at himself for not having seen it sooner. He had caught a glimpse of it as it turned toward him in the moonlight.

Strange, he thought. Looks like he has been paralleling me for some time? Why is he turning toward me?

Cautiously, he put his feet back on the rudder pedals and held the yoke in both hands.

He'd seen everything from runaway trim to broken control cables, loose seats and a propeller pitch on one plane that spun out of control and over-revved the engine nearly shaking it loose from its mounts. Given even the slightest excuse anything could happen and he wanted to be ready to jump on the controls when the autopilot was disengaged and wanted to make sure that he would be able to maneuver away from the approaching traffic and give the other plane plenty of room.

He bit his lip and gingerly nudged the yoke to disengage the autopilot. Without warning the yoke snapped back in his hands and refused to be moved.

Oh this is great, he thought as he worked the control wheel harder back and forth in an effort to move it. Again, the controls snapped back to their positions. Frustrated, he reached for the autopilot master switch and disengaged it expecting the airplane to relinquish control. It refused and continued on its course and altitude as if caught by some invisible force. Then he noticed that the controls were not frozen but were responding to inputs as if from an unseen hand, the plane turning to a new heading, responding to gusts and chop keeping the aircraft on course. He felt a sudden twinge of anxiety with the realization that the aircraft was no longer under his control.

"Shit!" he said to himself, "He's closing on me!" The plane continued toward him, its dark shape like a black cross in the darkness, approaching ever faster with each passing second. Its engine screamed wildly as it passed overhead within feet of the fuselage.

"You crazy son-of-a bitch…! What are you trying to do, kill us?"

Then without warning the communication radios suddenly came to life and blared with static. An unseen hand began to manipulate the dials and volume control flipping the radios through the selectors landing on snippets of voices who called out tail numbers, call signs, headings and vectors, static and hums that filled his ears and drowned out the steady noise of the engines. Then it stopped on a frequency.

"Beech 15414, Chicago Center squawk 1223... What's your current position? We have you off course." The radio called out the voice calm, businesslike, suggesting, as if trying to remind without alarming the pilot of his wayward course.

Jacob reached for his mike button in an effort to reply when he was stopped short by the frantic call of a small child's reply.

"Hello! Is anybody there?! My Mommy and Daddy are sleeping and I want to go home!"

"Ah 414 this is Chicago Center was that you?"

"Hello? My Daddy won't wake up, I'm scared and I want to go home now!"

"Whoever is calling Chicago Center, this is an air traffic control frequency, and we need you to switch your radio off or tune..."

"I need help!" The voice interrupted.

"Ah..." Silence then, "Person calling Chicago...Are you in an aircraft?"

"My Daddy let's me talk on the radio sometimes." The small voice replied, cold and afraid, then several long moments of silence.

Jacob looked frantically about the cabin and keyed the microphone in an effort to break in.

"Ah...Attention...All aircraft on this frequency, please change frequency to 124.25. We have an in-flight emergency." The voice from the air traffic controller called out, interrupting him with a calm, controlled, deliberate voice.

Jacob looked out into the darkness for the aircraft that had just passed over him. He could see the aircraft off of his right wingtip no more than a half mile away, it was turning toward him again, this time closing on him from much closer.

"What in the hell is he trying to do? He's going to kill us!" In a near panic he fought with the controls in an effort to free himself from the grip of the autopilot and the suicidal pilot trying to collide with him.

He could hear several responses as other planes in the area acknowledged. He clicked his push to talk button in an effort to reply but was unable to break-in.

Several moments passed, and then suddenly the plane screamed passed him again, this time only feet from his nose. He could feel the wings buffet in its wake as it passed and the voice on the radio changed from a cold impersonal drone to the voice of a young woman.

Jacob listened and imagined the confusion in the control center.

Good, don't scare the kid anymore. Get somebody on the radio that can get some answers. They must know that there is a lunatic up here trying to ram me! Jacob thought.

"Little boy, what's your name dear?"

The voice responded, "Can you wake up my Mommy?"

Jacob could feel the fear well up inside him with the words, his heart raced and pounded in his temples. He sat in silent panic, his mind locked on the problem of what was being said and the reality of his situation.

"How old are you dear? Is your Mommy in the front seat?"

"Mommy and Daddy are sleeping but I can't get

them to wake up. My head hurts and I don't know what to do."

"Dear, look at Mommy what do you see?"

"Mommy is cold, very cold. Daddy's eyes are open but he won't look at me! Please wake up Daddy, please!"

"God help me!" Jacob said to himself, "Give me control of this heap before its too late…!"

Again the dark specter made his turn off in the distance, the plane charging toward him at full speed.

He came to the realization now, the voice was emanating from the cockpit. He looked around, over the seat behind him in an effort to find its source. He could see the image of the boy, the boy from the road, sitting quietly staring through him as if he were not there.

"Dear?" the woman asked.

Silence and static as the pause continued.

"Honey, please talk to me…You must listen to me now and do as I say. Can you do that for me dear?"

"Yes…Yes Ma'am I think so." Jacob could hear the voices, but the boy made no effort to reply, no movement, a silent ghostly form sitting quietly as the events unfolded before him.

"Good. Now a big boy like you, who knows how to talk on the radio, can count to ten, right?"

"Yes…"

"Good, when I tell you, I want you to push on the talk button and count to ten for me loud and clear then let go of it. Can you do that?"

"Yes."

"Great. Ready? Go ahead now, count for me, then stop and let go of the button."

They are trying to get a fix on our position. Jesus, here he comes again! Jacob's mind raced as once again the plane passed, ever closer shaking the airframe as it passed.

The little boy counted to ten, then stopped, then was told by the woman to count again. This went on for several minutes, the woman's calm voice would ask, the little boy would respond, the black ghost plane circling and lunging like an angry hornet, until finally the woman stopped.

"Wait a minute dear."

Where the hell could we be? Jacob thought as he felt the panic well up inside of him and imagined the little boy, frightened and alone in a runaway aircraft rushing through the night sky. He looked out the window and suddenly could see the shining glimmer of moonlight on the water, waves and white caps washing up over large ice blocks floating in the depths below.

There was silence again, several heavy moments of silence. The boy sat behind him, quietly, dispassionately as the woman spoke.

"Honey…?"

"Yes ma'am?"

"Does Daddy keep life preservers onboard?"

"What…? Life per-serves…?"

"No Honey, does Daddy have those yellow things you wear to the swimming pool?"

"No ma'am, I don't think so."

The woman's voice began to grow impatient with fear.

"Honey, can you look for me? Look in the pockets behind the front seats, but dear don't touch anything else O.K.?"

There was another moment of silence and static.

"Answer me dear. Do not touch anything else alright?"

"Yes ma'am."

Suddenly Jacob made a connection between Chicago Center and the water below them, "He's over the Lake! Oh my god, he is over the…!"

He yelled out loud but was interrupted by the boy's voice and the whine of the aircraft making another pass this time directly beneath them.

"Ma'am, I looked and looked but I don't see any."

Jacob could hear the woman's voice, choked with fear and anxiety as she struggled to maintain her composure.

"Sweetheart…? Can you read the dials? Did Daddy ever show you how to read the dials dear?"

"Sometimes… Sometimes we play a game and he points to things and I tell him what they are!" The boy replied, his voice a mix of fear and innocence, wanting to believe that the woman's voice alone would make things alright.

"Oh that is wonderful, I'll bet you're really good at that game aren't you?"

"Yes ma'am."

"We'll dear, tell me can you find the two fuel gauges there in front of you? They should be between Daddy and Mommy, there in the middle."

"Oh that's an easy one. I can see them both."

"Can you tell me what do they say?"

"They both show close to the 'E'."

Jacob looked rapidly down at the panel, the gauges suddenly drifted down to empty and a panic welled in his stomach as he realized that he was trapped.

There was a pause, "Are you sure?"

"Oh yes ma'am I know for sure."

Another long pause and the low humming of static on the radio as panic stricken minds on the other end of the transmission tried to take control of the situation and work a solution.

Jacob's mind raced and imagined the pain of the people in the control center. He could see them huddled about the radio, some on phones to the coast guard, others talking in hurried tones, still others thinking thankfully of their homes and families, children sleeping peacefully in their beds.

The radio came to life again.

"Now my dear, I want you to listen to me carefully now. We know where you are and we have sent some men in boats to come and get you and your Mommy and Daddy."

"Will they be here soon? I'm really tired."

"Yes dear they will be there soon. The airplane is going to come down in a little while and then they will be there to take all of you home very soon. Now I need to have you do something for me. I want you to move to one of the back seats and buckle in real tight. But just like before I don't want you to touch anything O.K?"

"Can Hoppy sit with me?"

"Who is Hoppy dear?"

"Hoppy is my dog. Mommy let's me keep him and my blanket with me when I go to bed."

"Yes dear, hold Hoppy real tight too O.K.?"

"I can't reach to talk to you if I go back there."

"That's alright dear. I'll be right here with you."

"Mommy sometimes tells me a story or sings me a song when I'm really scared. She stays up with me until I go to sleep."

"Would you like for me to tell you a story?"

"Yes ma'am. Do you have any little boys at home?"

There is silence and a pause and the woman's voice returned.

"No dear, I don't have anyone at home."

"I'm sorry...I know...let's pretend then. I'll be your little boy."

"Yes. Let's pretend. Now are you ready?"

"Yes ma'am."

"OK. Go on now, buckle up tight! I'll wait a minute then start a story."

"Don't go OK?"

"Dear, I won't. I'll be right here, now go."

The woman talked to the little boy in the doomed plane, her voice struggling to maintain a measure of composure.

She spoke for several minutes as Jacob struggled to free the controls. He pushed hard on the yoke and worked the pedals in a fitful, useless effort to regain control, while the remaining fuel onboard burned off and the aircraft slipped into one engine. He tried to respond to it.

Kick the dead engine! He thought as he banged his feet against the rudder pedals in vain.

Then, in the corner of his eye he saw him, the image of a man, a small bespectacled, little man who had been too impatient to wait, in too much of a hurry to check things, to make sure things had been in order.

He sat there in the passenger seat next to him, dripping wet, little straggles of moisture on his bare head, his shirt and tie dripping wet, clinging to him, his eyes all but two wide black macabre spots through the fog of his misted eyeglasses. He sat there his hands on the controls staring, frozen in position, shaking his head in disbelief and fear.

"Let go Damnit!" Jacob screamed at him as the airplane refused to release itself from the grip of the little man.

"God Damnit you little shit! Let go of the controls, you're going to kill us!" He reached over and pounded furiously on the little man's grasp of the yoke but could not get him to respond, could not get his hands freed from the controls.

The little man looked at him, his face bloated with fear and drenched wet with the icy water of the lake. His mouth opened suddenly in a wide gape of final resolution and choking, he forced out water and blood foaming in panicked retching; a drowning man's last breath, not of air but of water.

The aircraft snapped over on the dead engine as the black plane made a final pass that rocked the aircraft over and caused it to spin as the second engine strangled itself and died. Helplessly they spun downward, the little boy's cries mixed with his own epithets and the whine of the wind against the airframe screamed as they plummeted toward the lake.

The woman whose soothing voice trailed off into the distance knew that they were going down. She knew but could not hear the cries as she held down the mike and tried to comfort the little boy.

The aircraft picked up momentum as the frigid black water rushed toward them. Jacob braced for the impact pushing against the yoke as the spinning aircraft fell out of control. He was certain that the end would come within seconds.

Then without warning, the whining and the rotations stopped as suddenly as they had begun. Both engines returned to life and the plane recovered to a level attitude less than a hundred feet from the lake's surface.

A man's voice interrupted on the frequency that had now been re-opened to traffic.

"United 21 Heavy turn 230 maintain 3000."

"United 21 Heavy Rodger.., Chicago... Did 414 make it down alright?"

"21 Heavy, Chicago, Ah…no information on 414, we will advise on the ground."

Jacob didn't need to know the details; he knew what the outcome had been.

Suddenly, the plane rolled slightly left and the yoke freed itself from the autopilot. He was in control again and turned back to line up the ADF needle with the radio tower.

The voices were gone, the boy's image gone from the seat behind him, the little man his pitiful face and panic stricken stare, the black phantom aircraft all gone. It was as if the incident had never happened, as if he had dozed in a moment and dreamt the entire thing. He could smell the dank mildew of the seats and the carpet, the molding smell of soaked fabric pulled from an icy black grave at the bottom of a lake.

His clothes were drenched with sweat; his skin was cold and his stomach churned with nausea. He was sickened and disgusted with his own fear and with the helplessness that pulled at him as he fought to regain his composure and forced back welling tears and the heartsick sadness of the little boy and his end. He felt overwhelmed with fear and a desire to get the aircraft on the ground, to get out of it, to get down and away from airplanes.

Within another few minutes he was back on course, far from lakes or cities or aberrations. He managed to fly on in the darkness, to avoid the tower and bring down the old aircraft. He rolled to a stop at the tarmac turned off the master switch and sat alone for several moments, his hands shaking. Gabe came out of the hangar and approached. He was visibly tired.

"You can get someone else to fly the next one Pop." Jacob said as he collected his charts and climbed out of the wreck. He wanted to explain the incident and the haunted aircraft when Gabe interrupted.

"I know all about it son." He reached out to take the logbooks.

"What do you mean you know all about it? You weren't there."

"Like I said, I'm not your boy. You need to get someone else. I've had enough."

Gabe walked over to him and put an arm around his shoulder, "What say we have a drink?"

Gabe left the plane on the tarmac and they made their way to the warmth of the diner where he produced a bottle of scotch and two glasses, poured and handed one to Jacob who sat on the couch cradling his head in his hands.

"Here…" Jacob looked up and took the glass, inspecting the contents.

He emptied the glass with shaking hands and with a large swallow held it up.

"Refill..." Jacob demanded, his voice shaking and exhausted.

"No problem." Gabe replied calmly and poured again. They sat for a moment.

Jacob wiped his eyes and ran his hand through his hair then tried to light a cigarette. His hands were shaking to the point that he could not hold the match to the tip. Gabe calmly took the matchbook and held out a lit end for him.

"That coffin out there damn near killed me!" he said as he blew the smoke out with a deep sigh.

"That son of a bitch tried to ram us and that little shit would not let go! I could have helped them but he would not let go. And that kid, that poor kid."

"Yeah, I know." Gabe looked down and swirled his glass lightly on the counter top.

"How could you possibly know who the kid or the family was, why the hell that guy wanted to kill us or why that pile of rivets and rust decided to fly itself?" Jacob said, his voice filled with frustration and with a shaking hand, offered up his glass for Gabe to refill it again.

"Oh and that was a great joke by the way, that little shit that was in here a few weeks ago, all of that 'He'll be back' crap! Thanks but I'll wait and find out what my real name is, get my things, my plane and go!" He said as he raised the glass to his lips for another drink. He was frightened, angry and frustrated that somehow he was linked to this place. He thought about the words and recounted the incidents and airplanes in an effort to make the connection.

"I saw a kid on the road, the first night I was here. He was asking for his mother. I thought it was a car accident or something. I was so pissed at the time I forgot about it until now."

Gabe listened then turned toward the window and motioned with his glass.

"Don't know what you'd call it, this place." Gabe's voice softened with the words, his eyes, tired and distant.

"It's always been this way, as long as I've been here. Suppose it's as good a place as any though. The tower is the beacon. It draws them in. They come like moths to a candle flame."

Jacob ignored his comments and sat engulfed in his own anxiety.

"Why the hell are you collecting all this junk? I mean

that deathtrap I flew in here? What are you going to do with them? And that guy, that plane, that guy tried to ram me I tell you!"

"I'm going to fix em." Gabe responded solemnly.

"Chief, I would classify that aircraft as salvage scrap, that by some miracle I was able to get off the ground for a few hours. The only thing worth doing with that junk is to part it out and maybe make a few bucks. And as for that pilot out there, unless you're a shrink or a good pilot with a full load of machine gun rounds, you're not gonna fix him anytime soon!" Jacob took another quick swallow and a drag from his cigarette.

"What is it you got going on here Pop, some kind of a racket? You cutting these old hulks and selling them?"

Gabe ignored him as he spoke, and poured another measure into Jacob's glass.

"Yeah… Fixing each one... We'll need all of them soon."

"Hey did you hear what I said? I wouldn't climb back into that deathtrap if my life depended on it! Let alone go up there with that lunatic flying around! Somebody needs to stop him before he kills someone!"

Hop ambled over to where Jacob was sitting and sat in front of him and yawned. Instinctively, Jacob reached down and scratched him behind the ears.

"Hear that boy? Your old man wants to sell those old kites out there in that hangar. And you, you're in this too aren't you?" The old dog looked at him askance as if he'd expected Jacob to have known this all along.

"Who said anything about selling them? I said we would need them. As for our friend up there, that's your concern."

"What the hell are you talking about?"

The old man looked through Jacob with the wisdom of an eternity of experience, "You'll know when the time comes."

"What are we going to need them for?" Jacob asked.

Gabe paused for a moment bracing for Jacob's response. "To fly to heaven of course..." The old man said this in a way that was so matter of fact, as though he had been asked what direction the wind blows from on a clear day.

Jacob stood up and threw his hands into the air in resignation, the weight of the liquor thickening his tongue.

"That's it! You're right! I don't know why all this should surprise me, I mean dead folks, ghosts, that crazy pilot and that spooky radio preacher!" Jacob's eyes widened and he motioned with his arms and hands to make a point with his sarcasm. "Now we are going to have a big ole revival right here in the middle of nowhere! Sure! That makes all the sense in the world Pop! Lord knows we get a steady stream of folks out this way, why we'll have such a crowd on our hands we'll have to call in the state highway patrol! No! Wait! Ain't no highway patrol in heaven right Dad?"

Gabe would not respond to him but only look at him patiently, then down at his glass on the counter.

"Well! That's just wonderful! I guess it doesn't matter then? I'll just climb into that pile of scrap out there and screw it into the ground! What a show! We'll have that nut up there come on down, land right here and we'll help him get some religion! That'll fix it!" He took a drink and got up.

"I'm going to bed and hopefully, I'll wake up and this whole thing will have been one bad dream!"

Jacob grabbed the neck of the whiskey bottle pulling

it off of the counter with a splash, pulled off his jacket and slapped it into a chair then staggered toward the bedroom doorway.

Gabe walked over to the window and looked out at the night sky and the tired aircraft sitting quietly on the tarmac.

"I'm sorry son, but it ain't a dream."

Chapter 8

"You have a student who desires to learn the science of aviation at the hands of a skilled and experienced pilot!" Gabe said as he pulled the sheets down in an effort to wake Jacob.

"Look, I don't know what you're talking about? I'm not an instructor." It was early and Jacob was barely awake, his head heavy from the bottle of whiskey he had finished the night before.

Gabe ignored him and continued, "Hurry my boy; we do not want to keep her waiting!"

"Don't you get it Pop? I'm not playing this game anymore. You can find someone else to fly those old crates for you!" Jacob protested as he rubbed his temples and pulled his hand through his matted hair.

"Oh come on now, you're a tough nut. Get up. You don't want to miss this." Gabe grabbed a pair of trousers and threw them at him. "Besides, she's been asking for you."

"She..?" Jacob asked.

"Yeah, let's not keep her waiting."

He could not think of who she might be but, he knew that he had to find out and stumbled into his trousers, slipped on his boots and was finishing with his shirt buttons and his jacket when he walked out the front door after Gabe.

"I'm no instructor and with that guy flying around..."

Gabe turned back to him and whispered. "That's alright son he ain't around and besides she's not much of a student." Gabe said as he turned his back to him and approached the form of a thin, small woman.

She was young, in her early thirties. Her face white, almost pale with sharp porcelain features and eyes dark with curiosity. She stood gleaming in well-kept beauty, her age hard to discern at a distance, her arms casually folded in front of her. She was dressed in a flight suit from the early, popular days of flying, when men took daring chances in kites of canvas and wood and flew over open oceans without any chance of survival should they loose an engine or fall into bad weather. It was a tailored affair, trimmed in beaver fur with matching high-laced boots and a leather flight helmet and goggles. A small wild shock of blonde hair poked out from under the front of her leather helmet and curled up over the edge shining in the early morning sun. She moved a hand and waved about in gesticulations and illustrations as she talked about flying and tweaked at Gabe's collar. She was standing in front of an immaculately maintained Duisenberg town car complete with an equally well maintained, uniformed airman who stood beside her dispassionately, his mechanic's togs clean and neat.

She looked over Gabe's shoulder and saw Jacob standing in front of them.

"Oh there you are!" she stepped passed Gabe and held out a gloved hand. Gabe turned and in formal introduction turned his open hand to her.

"Jacob, I'd like to introduce, the Lady, Angelica Fonseca… Angelica, here's the young man I've been telling you about, Jacob…"

"Charmed…and what a handsome fellow…I do say Jacob, you do fly well I presume?" She looked directly at him and then flashed her eyes down to his waistband and slowly back to his eyes again.

Jacob was unsure at the reference, and then came to a sudden realization as she turned her glance back to Gabe.

"Jacob, be a dear and pre-flight the aircraft…I'll be along directly." She said coyly, her gloved hand held under her nose in an effort to hide her giggle.

He moved off in red-faced embarrassment, pulling up the zipper on his trousers as he walked away swearing under his breath.

"He's got to be kidding…" he said to himself as he tramped around behind the hanger in search of her aircraft.

Suddenly, he stopped in his steps and looked with open mouthed, awe at the waiting Tiger Moth that sat in quiet majesty in front of him. The aircraft was a trainer used by RAF pilots prior to transitioning to Hurricanes and Spitfires and later a few remaining ones were used as circus performers after the war. It looked so new and well maintained that he thought it to be a reproduction.

He walked up to it and gingerly touched the doped canvas skin. It was there in front of him, clearly real. He walked around it, checked tires, fuel, oil, rigging, control surfaces, handling them to validate what his eyes were telling him. It smelled like an organic, living thing, not like the metal aircraft he had been close to recently. The wood, leather, natural rubber and caster oil smelled of fine furniture, the wooden propeller a thing of beauty, artfully crafted and fixed neatly into position with a circle of hex bolts that faced upward as the aircraft sat back on its tail skid. The rudder and ailerons moved quietly in response to the slight morning breeze. It reminded him of the Stearman and how much he missed seeing it.

He noticed a small wooden stool; sitting next to the front cockpit position and within a moment could hear the shuffling of feet and muted conversation behind him.

"Well then, Jacob, I assume that all is in order?" she said as she deftly stepped by him, and with the help of her driver, stepped first onto the stool and then into the front cockpit.

"Ah…yes, it looks to me to be ready to go…" Gabe stepped up behind him and put a quick hand on his shoulder in an effort to reassure him. He handed him a leather helmet and goggles, "Now look boy, take it easy and don't rush anything. That old girl has a lot of time on her." he whispered.

"And which old girl would that be Dad?" Jacob replied as he snatched the helmet away from him, climbed into the rear seat and slid the helmet and goggles down onto his head.

Ignoring him, Gabe moved up to the front cockpit.

"Have a good lesson." He called to the woman smiling as he spoke.

"Oh Colonel McCabe, I am certain that we will have a splendid time." The words gushed forth from her in droll, class-consciousness and sophistication.

The mechanic took his station at the propeller and had both hands on it now, looking up at the front seat.

"Contact, Miss."

"Contact Mr. Stewart…!" she called out to him in reply.

With that the mechanic pulled the prop through and immediately it began rotating in response as the engine coughed and came to life.

Jacob looked back and could see the relative wind of the propeller blowing the grass as he pushed the rudder pedals and began taxing the plane to a position on the airstrip. He could see the head of his student poking up slightly in the front seat cockpit. She reached up with a hand and held up a set of spindly earphones connected to a fabric-covered cable. He looked over and could see his, hanging on a hook next to him and quickly put them on.

"Captain, if you would, please. Use the microphone and confirm that you can hear me."

Jacob opened the microphone, "I have you Mrs. Fonseca."

"It is Miss, darling and please, I must insist that you call me Angelica when we are flying together! One simply should not tolerate such formality in one's sport, don't you agree? I mean so stilted and uncomfortable."

Jacob continued to move the plane into position.

"Look Miss..."

"Oh my goodness boy, that won't do at all! You shall call me Angelica and I, I shall call you Jacob or Captain…"

"Alright then, Angelica, are you ready to take-off?" Jacob asked as he quickly finished his run up and turned the aircraft into the wind.

"Yes Captain, let us proceed!"

He advanced the throttle and the aircraft began to roll slowly forward. It quickly picked up speed and began to flex as the airflow increased over its wings. A single slight bounce of the wheels and the Tiger Moth was off the ground and climbing away from the airfield below.

It was a fast little beast of an airplane, its sleek nose and small airframe presented the light, nimble flutter of an aircraft well suited to its name. He pulled the stick back slightly and the biplane bore its way through the morning sky. He was caught off guard by it at first, used to the heavy handed control inputs that were needed to keep Gabe's relics in the air.

"Well then, Captain, what do you think of her so far?" She asked cheerfully.

Jacob could hear her relaxed nonchalance through the headphones. He was too busy to reply at first, too heavy on the rudder pedals struggling to keep the antique climbing straight and true against the bite of the propeller and the torque of the engine rolling the stick in his lap, the ailerons and the wings wagging with his every movement.

"Gently, gently my boy, you must treat her like you would your best girl." the woman's voice called to him over the headphones.

"I have the airplane." he replied in a low condescending tone as he struggled with the rudder pedals and the ailerons and fought to gain control.

"So far so good…what would you like to work on today?" he panted, expecting her to have some desire to work on basic flight maneuvers, take offs, landings and other skills rudimentary to flight training.

"I say Captain, have you ever heard of an Immelmann?"

He thought for a moment, unsure that he had heard her correctly.

"I'm sorry Miss, what did you say?"

"Angelica Dear, I said an Immelmann!"

Sure he knew what she was talking about. It came to him in an instant; he had done this stunt many times in the Stearman, he recalled the movements of his hands and feet and the many times he coaxed the airplane over into a near perfect pirouette. In flight school he had practiced it and old as it was, it had stood the test of time as a deadly dog-fighting maneuver.

Flight school…? When and where…? He tried to think, to remember when suddenly his train of thought was interrupted by a sudden thermal that brought the plane down into an unseen pocket of air on the other side. He clutched the throttle and advanced it to pick up altitude.

"I'm not sure that this old bird is up to it, Ma'am."

"And which old bird would that be, Captain?" she retorted with an omnipotent satisfaction.

Jacob repositioned his feet on the rudder pedals, "Ok then. Hold on." He throttled up, pulled the aircraft up from a shallow dive to near vertical, then rolled the aircraft over stiffly and completed the maneuver much to his satisfaction.

"How was that?" The cold breeze beat at his face and was beginning to make it grow numb and hard to form words.

"Thrilling…! Simply thrilling Captain! Would you mind terribly if I gave it a whirl?"

"Would you like to follow me on the controls first?" He asked, uncertain that she could handle the aircraft and unsure that with his hangover he could handle a spin this early in the morning.

"No. No, I say, I think I followed you closely enough, let me give it a try." She replied as she snatched control of the tiny airplane.

Immediately, Jacob was pinned back in his seat as she shoved the throttle forward and broke into a near perfect example of the maneuver.

"Now my boy, show me a split-S." She said.

"Tighten your harness lady!" He yelled at her, dumbfounded by her apparent ability and irritated with her nonchalance.

He dipped the nose to pick up speed then quickly rolled inverted and allowed the aircraft to dive and reverse course leveling off at the bottom of a downward loop.

"Superb Captain…!" She called to him, her tone more businesslike, more curious.

"Show me a series of loops and vector rolls please!"

"What do you want me to do?" Jacob replied both surprised and curious.

"A series of loops and vector rolls please. Let us pretend that you are being pursued and you wish to loose your pursuer then get into position behind him. Show me how you would do that." Her tone had changed more businesslike, more aggressive.

"It's your nickel! Hold on!" He forgot about his head and his stomach and quickly snapped the aircraft over into a spin, letting it turn in on its self then stalling one wing sending the tail spinning the plane whirling like a spinner falling from an old maple tree.

A thousand feet per rotation… He thought as the plane tumbled downward. Again, a rule that had emerged from his memory came forth, a quiet reminder from the log of many reminders, many things a pilot keeps stored away in the recesses of his mind.

He broke out of the spin, stopping the rotation and then transitioned from the stall at 500 feet, added full power and climbed at a shallow arc; snap rolling over several times as he gained altitude. The engine roared like an angry hornet, its sound a buzzing Doppler echo as the airframe and engine mounts pulled against the torque of the spinning propeller.

He gained altitude, and then half way through a snap roll, stopped and held the wings perpendicular to the ground, pulled the stick sharply, turned hard and then stalled in the turn and fell through it to a steep dive that gave him the momentum with full power to climb to the apex of a loop, he then transitioned to straight and level at the top, the plane twisting, the fuselage binding and creaking under him as it strained against the forces of gravity and the drag of the air around them.

He felt one with it now, the living thing that it had become, himself alive with it, the two of them together as one thing, one moment in their own small space of an endless sky.

"Wonderfully done Captain…!" her voice called out to him in encouragement. "I believe that you would win a flying ribbon anywhere with that series…However, we are not flying for sport. We are flying for more than ribbons here my boy, much more." her words now stern and laced with forewarning.

She suddenly took control of the aircraft again and repeated his maneuvers. In every instance finishing them tighter and with greater authority, her hand moving the stick in subtle ways that he could feel as he followed along his own hand lightly touching the stick his feet light on the rudder pedals. At the end, she would titter with laughter and ask him periodically if he were alright. He sat there, in glum resolution all the while being pushed and pulled against his harness, watching the stick and rudder pedals move in front of him as she danced the vintage airplane in and out of the clouds. The moments passed and after an hour of punishment, he decided that it was time to break off their lesson and return to the field. His head was still throbbing with the whiskey from the night before, his stomach was empty and churning from all of the rough handling and he felt that they had both had enough. He keyed his microphone.

"Miss…"

"Angelica, I simply refuse to answer you unless you address me properly Captain."

"Angelica…!"

"Yes Captain."

"I'd suggest that we head back now, I'm sure they are starting to worry about us."

"The Colonel and I are old friends Jacob. He and I have an understanding. He allows me to fly my aircraft as long as it pleases me and I've agreed never to learn to drive an automobile."

Jacob considered this for a moment and thought about them as friends. Gabe was right, he thought. He imagined what a real danger she would be behind the wheel.

"Oh very well, Captain." She released the controls, "You may take us home in a moment, but before we do, I'd ask that you find a smooth spot…say down there." she motioned to him and pointed. "Down there my boy, please set us down, I'd like to have a moment with you if you aren't in too much of a hurry?"

Jacob looked down at an open meadow that was ringed by tall trees on all sides. He thought it odd that she would think him too impatient and with somewhere to go. I've got nowhere to go, he thought.

"I don't know, it looks a little tight to me, you sure you want to land there?" He called out to her.

"Quite sure." Her words were reassuring as if she had

been there before and knew that a landing was possible.

"Alright then, I'll put her down." He retarded the throttle and lined the nose with the edge of the meadow, gliding down and touching the rough ground, bouncing several times to a stop. He killed the engine and sat there slipping the helmet from his aching head as the propeller came to a stop. He climbed out then held out his hand as she made her way out of the cockpit in front of him. She pulled the helmet from her head and let the breeze flow over the curls of her hair, the long wafts of hair blowing as the gust came and went.

"Walk with me." she said and she took his hand.

He felt strange walking with her, holding her hand. Her flesh was cool and soft and its touch was like magic that spun up feelings in him. He felt as if he knew her, as if she were a part of him from some distant past. She did not look at him as they walked through the tall meadow flowers but rather stared out over the field, and to a line of distant trees.

"I so love trees." She said, as they stopped at a large oak tree.

It sat near the edge of the meadow and she sat down in the shade of it, coaxing him down with her. She held his hand as they sat there together. She looked down at their hands, clasped together as she spoke then out over the field, and at the aircraft sitting quietly in the distance. She breathed a long sigh as if there were many memories and much that she wanted to recount.

"Do you like them?" she asked.

"What?"

"Trees my boy, do you like them?" she repeated.

"Well, I suppose so, I never really thought about it much."

"Yes, well, I suppose it's easy to do that." She said.

"What?"

"Take things for granted. Things like trees and flowers and other things."

"Yes, I suppose." He replied.

He looked at her sitting there with him. It was as if a great peace had suddenly taken hold of him. She was like a calm breeze, a wind that moved like a steady stream directly down a runway. She was like the kind of wind that a pilot liked to have when he was sitting there at the end of a runway, ready to take off, the kind of wind that blew steadily without gusts or cross winds to mar his advance as the airplane picked up speed. It was there to lift him steady and true off the ground, wings level, a firm pressure that he could feel in his hand through the stick and in the pedals. He felt a great comfort in it.

"I feel as if I know you." He said.

"I am glad Captain. I'm glad that you feel that way."

"Should I?" He asked, his heart opening to her with the question, his emotions beginning to take hold of him.

"Yes, I suppose you should. That is to say, I believe that if you do, then you are the right one for what there is to be done."

"What do you mean? What is there that needs to be done?"

"Do you think that you have seen me before Captain?" She asked not answering him but asking another question, as if probing him or trying to help him with his thoughts.

"I don't know... I have seen a lot of women and been a lot of places." He replied.

"Yes, I would say that you have Captain, you have seen a lot of things." She looked down at their hands clasped together and squeezed his slightly as she spoke.

"I'd imagine that you have seen me many times before and that you would remember."

"When would I have seen you?"

"Why I would say many times. I have been with you with the clouds up there. When you have been alone, flying when the sky opens and the air is thick and heavy. I am there with you when its early morning and when in the evening the sun is low and the air is calm. I am there with you." She said this as if she were thinking of something else, thinking of another place and time, as if remembering her time with him up there.

"I'm confused, I don't remember seeing you."

"You have Captain. It's just that you have always been too busy to look, too busy until now at least." She looked over at him smiling; her eyes bright like the morning sun on the horizon.

"I know that it has been difficult for you." She said.

"Yeah I suppose. I mean this place." He said matter of fact and in agreement with her.

"No, not this place, I mean the other things, they have been difficult." She replied knowingly.

"What other things?"

"The time on the ground Captain, the years there, they have been difficult. I know how hard that has been for you. It's hard for a pilot to be on the ground, its not the place for a pilot."

He knew that she was right. He did not know about the years, he did not know how long he had been on the ground or what she was talking about precisely, but he could feel that he had suffered for some time and that there had been a long time, waiting on the ground. He could imagine the sound of aircraft engines off in the distance and a man who had looked up into the heavens in response to their sound as they drifted off into the distance.

"It is very hard for pilots, when the time comes for them to stop flying. They take it very hard. Its not right for them to be on the ground."

He thought about what she said. She was right, he thought, I don't want to be on the ground. I am not supposed to be there.

"If I told you how important it is that you are here and that you will be able to fly again, would that make things better?" she asked.

He thought about the question, wondered at it, wondered at the many things that had happened and if his being there was a purposeful thing and not simply an accident. If it would matter to him or make things easier. He did not know.

"I can't say. I don't know what I am supposed to do? I don't know why I am here." he responded.

He could feel his emotions welling up from inside him, a weight like a great load on him slip away and the touch of her hand in his, melt his resistance.

"Can you help me?" he asked.

"You do not need my help Captain. You have all that is required to find the answer all that is needed."

"Then tell me, what is it I am supposed to do? Why am I here?"

She leaned back against the trunk of the tree and let the breeze blow against her. It seemed that she savored the feeling of the summer sun and the breeze. That the things of life, the smells and the sight of living things were like a relaxing bath that she wanted to be immersed in.

"It is a wonderful thing."

"What?"

"Life…It is a wonderful thing Jacob. So few realize how wonderful it is. I dare say I have missed it…Missed it more than I thought that I would."

"I don't understand? We are here and this is like any other day."

"No…It is not…Each day is like a fresh breath, a great gift of possibility that is beyond measure."

"You sound like Gabe or that preacher."

"Really." she replied, as if embarrassed by an inadvertent compliment, "You flatter me my boy. I can never preach. I can only do what I do."

"And what is it that you do?"

"Fly of course." She answered.

"What else? I mean you do other things, things other than flying?"

"What else is there my boy? For us there is nothing else. Flying, it is what we are." She said.

"Then tell me, what am I doing here?"

"There are terrible things in this world. There are horrible longings that tear away at the light of day. The freedom of life is the great paradox Captain. There are choices that are laid out like a great banquet. We choose the things we desire as much out of taste as from hunger. We confuse the two. In the end, we find ourselves filled but not satisfied. Do you understand?"

Jacob looked at her face, her gaze looking back at him; her eyes welled with tears, pleading with him to understand. He thought about the words. His mind reeled with the many things, the choices that came to him but seemed not a part of him. It was as if he was thinking of someone else, of another man's life. There had been missteps but they seemed not his own. There had been many hours of idle contemplation, of desires that were not fulfilled, of distractions and pressing matters that swallowed up the hours and turned the days out in ways that served to no one's benefit. He could imagine many of them, the places to be, the things to do, the transactions of working and comfort and safety, all the things that in the end turned about a single column in an obituary page. These were the horrors that men were left to recount in the end.

It occurred to him that men desired an afterlife much as their life had been. He reflected on it for a moment, looked back at the man that existed in his memory. He considered that man, that if it were him, he would not wish for an eternity like that.

"I think I do." he said.

"That's good." she responded, "There is only the great wish for pilots. It is about a desire that you must find for yourself. It is terribly important that you find it Captain. It is the most important thing you will ever do."

She spoke to him with the tone of knowing and having experienced this, "You have an opportunity here, in this place to do this. There is nothing here to distract you or keep you from finding it. You have every opportunity here. We are all here for you. Here to help you find it. However in the end, it is up to you and what you do. No one in the end can do that for you. That, my love is why you are here." She stood up and pulled him up to her, holding him in her arms, embracing him tightly.

He could feel the tingling rise in him and instinctively he put both arms about her and held her close to him. He held her tightly, wishing that he could stay there with her, be close to her to have her with him always. It was not the emotion of love that one would have for a lover, but rather like that of a child, a little lost boy looking for his mother in the darkness.

"It's time for us to go Captain, I'm sure our Gabriel will worry if we delay him further." She loosed her grip on him and began walking toward the aircraft. As they walked to where it was patiently waiting, Jacob noticed that a number of small headstones sat leaning in sagging sod filled plots, a small family cemetery alone in the meadow.

"Odd, I don't remember seeing these when we landed?" Jacob asked, curious, "Do you know anything about them?"

"Old friends and loves my boy." she said in a quiet almost mournful tone. She seemed to him momentarily distracted by the words as if remembering something of them and of her self.

They propped the engine and climbed into the Moth then sped off down the meadow and climbed into the afternoon sky. Jacob turned the airplane back toward the field. They cruised along, straight and level for what seemed only a few moments, all the while he listened as she returned to character and carried on about her acquaintances, European royalty, wealthy industrial barons, parties, and summers in Kennebunkport, on and on. Nothing in the conversation meant anything to him but it seemed to him that none of this mattered to her nor did it matter to him. Indeed, she treated him like an old acquaintance, someone who had just been away from the club on holiday for a time and needed to be caught up on the affairs of court.

He felt that he knew her very well, that she had known him, long ago.

Then it occurred to him that she might be able to help

him find another field, another place to land.

He interrupted, "Listen, you know this place better than I do, is there a town around here somewhere? I mean do you know where we are? What's this place called?"

"Questions, so many questions…! My Darling Captain, why do you want to know such things? Look out over the horizon there, isn't it grand?"

"Yeah, sure it's great but, to tell ya the truth I had this accident and I've forgotten some things."

He felt her pause for a moment, silence in the earphones. He sensed that he had struck a chord with her, that she was thinking, and then regained her composure.

"What are memories Captain, but wisps of cloud? They pass before our mind's eye like so much mist."

With this she stopped her conversation with him.

The aircraft droned on toward its destination and Jacob tuned the old radio to the AM frequency of the Bible broadcast and turned to follow the needle to within a visual sighting of the airfield. He could clearly see the structure of the antenna standing guard in close proximity to the field. The station was playing the scratchy nocturne of his dream. He listened as the music wafted about in his headset, the French lyrics ringing in his ears.

She began to sing to him, her voice a quiet soothing maternal voice, her French intonated with every nuance of provincial accent. In the subtlety of her words he sensed sadness, a wish to be a part of something to which she could no longer be a part.

As they approached the field he turned off the music. He could see Gabe standing in the grass next to the strip looking up at them.

"Captain, would you mind terribly if we had a bit of fun with the Colonel?"

Jacob thought for a moment and with a sudden pang of delight realized what she had in mind.

"I'm in!"

"You go on then, I'll tend to my knitting..." she tittered in an impish response.

Jacob immediately pulled the plane off into a wing over and dove on the figures standing at the edge of the runway. Full throttle at maximum airspeed, he leveled suddenly as if flying a low strafing run over the field. He waggled the wings back and forth and closing on them, could see Gabe's eyes open wide with panic as he ducked low and turned around sharply as they passed closely over head.

"Oh Good Show, Captain...!" she exclaimed as they climbed away from the field.

He made a wide slow turn and after flying outbound for a few moments, positioned the plane up wind and retarded the throttle. The old aircraft transformed itself from dancer to ungainly goose as the wheels touched down and it bounced to a stop a few yards from where Gabe stood. Both of the men approached them as the propeller wound down to a stop.

"Switch off Madam?" The mechanic said as he nervously mopped his brow with a handkerchief.

"Switch off Mr. Stewart." She replied, still giggling with delight.

He replaced the stool and helped her from the cockpit. Jacob now saw her in a completely different light. She pulled the leather cap from her head; her flowing blonde curls danced about her face. She was touching up her lipstick with the aid of a compact mirror when he saw that she had changed. He could see that she had an elegant beauty that had somehow been transformed by the experience of the last several hours. Jacob returned to the notion that this entire episode was but an extension of a long running dream constructed solely for his benefit. She looked at him, her face hopeful that he might recognize her.

She was someone he had known, someone who had been close to him. The notion appeared to him. He remembered a woman there next to him. He was only a small child, the beautiful image of her looking back at him in a dream.

"Well a good lesson I take it?" Gabe asked, in a vain attempt to hide his irritation with the low pass that they had made.

She broke off her gaze, "Marvelous Colonel…! Simply wonderful…!"

Gabe looked up at Jacob with a stern glance, "I assume he passed then?"

"Yes, quite satisfactory. He will do well. Of course the aircraft will be much faster, but I believe that he will be able to transition to it nicely." She gave Jacob a knowing look and passed between the two of them toward the car.

Jacob pulled Gabe aside as she passed.

"Alright, Colonel I need to know what is going on!" he whispered, irritated that he had been made the unknowing party to some evaluation.

"Colonel, if you would please provide the Captain with his manual."

Gabe looked up and waved to her, ignoring Jacob's words, "I'm to take care of it then?"

"That would be fine."

"Next day or so too soon…?" Gabe asked.

"No I would say, let's move with all speed, Colonel."

"Very well..."

Jacob continued to whisper his protest.

"Look Dad, I've gone as far with this as I'm going to and I'm not buying another round until I get some answers!"

The mechanic opened the car door and she slipped into the seat. He closed the door and through the open window she called out to them.

"Oh, and Colonel, please ensure that the Captain is in uniform. I do so much like a uniform. You can manage that Jacob?"

"Will I see you again?" Jacob asked.

"I will be around, though I doubt you will see me again for some time."

"But, I have plenty of time. We could go fly again, tomorrow maybe?"

She looked at him coyly but did not answer. The Duisenberg drove off the gravel lot then onto the roadway and out of sight.

Gabe put his hand on Jacob's shoulder and before he could continue to argue he was stopped.

"How bout some lunch Captain?" The old man asked, grinning with satisfaction.

He walked past Jacob to the Diner, slid behind the counter and grabbed the coffee pot in his fist.

"OK, Colonel what's the story? I mean that Tiger Moth looked brand-new and the car, the driver? What's with this Captain bit?"

Gabe ignored him, poured them both a cup of coffee and tossed two bologna sandwiches on a plate and slid them in front of him. He picked up a triangle of meat and bread bit off a corner, chewing a mouthful as he spoke.

"What a nut. I'll tell you though, that plane, in that

condition? It's worth a small fortune. Hell I've never seen one in such good shape, at least not since I was a kid."

Gabe was sifting through a box that he had sitting on the end of the counter, searching for something. He stopped momentarily at Jacob's words.

"So you remember seeing one then? When was that son?"

Jacob took another bite and thought for a moment. "Yeah, let me see here, I remember seeing one once, an old field somewhere…Yeah one almost like that one?"

"And the pilot, do you remember any of that?"

"Yeah, I think so, wait. Wait a minute!" He stopped chewing and dropped the sandwich on the plate.

"That woman…! I've seen her before! I know I have! But no, that was hell…that was years ago!"

"So where did you see her son?" Gabe asked calmly coaxing his memory along.

"It was at a fair I think? Yeah a county fair… She was, Angelica the...Oh what the hell did she call herself?" Jacob struggled.

Gabe reached into the box that he had been searching through and produced an old air show program, yellowed and dog-eared.

"'Lady Angelica, Heaven's Fallen Angel'. Here take a look." He said and handed the program to Jacob.

"This program I remember it!" Jacob held the pages in his hand and stared at the picture of the woman, young, beautiful as she had just appeared to be when she climbed down from the Tiger Moth only moments before.

"It can't be Pop? I mean I remember I was only a kid…"

"Yeah I know, take a look at the bottom there." Gabe peered over the page and pointed at an ink pen scrawl.

'To my wonderful Jacob, Love always...'

"It was her Pop! I remember her now, she was a big draw, every guy in town wanted to see her, somehow I got in to see her…I can't remember how but I did. She gave me this program…"

"So you don't know how?"

"No, but I remember her. She was like a queen or royalty or something. No wait, that was the act, she made out like she was. Man what a looker, she had a silk flight suit, white silk. She'd come out on the field in that big 'Duesie' and then climb into the Tiger Moth and fly all over the place. I mean it was wild the things she could do."

"You ever see her again?"

"No. Just that once I think? God, I'd forgotten her somehow…I was just a little kid, no more than…"

"Eight or nine…?" Gabe asked quickly.

"Yeah, you're right, just a kid…" he responded.

His heart turned over as he thought of her, the memory of her and of missing the opportunity to say what he now realized when she was there with him. Another memory then made its way to him.

"Wait…Something happened to her. Wait a minute, she crashed. She was killed! She was doing a show when it happened. I remember, they said she was doing…"

"Doing what?"

"An Immelmann, she was doing an Immelmann when a wing spar gave way. That plane, it was a wreck! She's dead Pop! She's dead and I…She was just out there, plain as day!"

"You remember your mother son?" the old man asked as he continued to search the box.

"No, I never met her, it was just me and my old man, though I didn't see him much either. He was always gone.

I had a Granddad who looked after me for a time, I think though that's kind of hazy too to tell you the truth."

Gabe took the program from Jacob's hand as it slipped from his fingers and he pondered, dumbstruck the revelation.

"What is this? How did you get that program? What kind of game are you running here?"

"No game boy..." the old man said as he pulled a small paperback book from the box. He threw it to Jacob.

"Here, you're going to need to study that. You'll need to look over every page. There isn't much time so you'll have to take the crash course I'm afraid."

Jacob looked down at the manual, confused.

"What? What's this all about?"

"It's like I said, we fix things around here." Gabe responded as he lifted the box from the counter then turned and went outside toward the hangar, leaving Jacob to think.

Jacob gazed at the worn cover of the manual, its pages yellow with age. 'Flight Manual, Republic P-51D Mustang'.

Chapter 9

The truck pulled up to one in a line of tired wooden and cinder block buildings. Hardly more than a widening of the road, the town seemed only slightly larger than the airfield. There was a short row of road weary cars and trucks parked out in front. A buzzing neon sign on the front of a brick façade hung over the door, 'The Ole Town Talk, We're Always Open', in pink illumination, the words of the sign flickering in frail defiance.

From the time he arrived, Jacob had seen nothing of other towns, only the airfield and the diner. He was happy that there was another place, somewhere else, an island in a sea of open fields and lonely roads. They climbed out of the truck and Gabe opened the door to the tavern.

They were immediately immersed in their surroundings as a draft of warm, thick air from inside the room wafted over them and the clinking of china and beer bottles inundated Jacob's senses. Gabe raised a hand to wave a deft hello and was greeted by an elderly woman who was busy working to make change at the cash drawer and fill a shot glass on the counter at roughly the same time. She spoke to them as they came through the doorway, in an automatic way as if they had been expected and without looking up.

"Colonel McCabe, What brings you out this way? Who's your friend?" The questions came from her in a hurried, pre-occupied tone as if she had no other words to say and wanted him to know how distant and disinterested she was. She wore a worn pink dress that at one time fit a figure that had long since past. The pink material puckered open at the buttons and the seams stretched and rolled under the strain of her shape. Her hands were red and swollen from dishwater and calloused and worn from hard work. Several fingers were adorned with old engagement rings and wedding bands that dangled carelessly about like odd trinkets from several old marriages or near misses that had long since past into history, all but her left hand ring finger which stood bare in anticipation of the next opportunity. The work had drawn deep furrows around her eyes and drew crevices about her lips. They were grey eyes, blue grey like cigarette smoke, framed deep in a face of aged puffy marshmallow cheeks and too much makeup. Her hair sat in a misshaped heap on her head like a helmet of steel wool, died a blazing orange, the grey roots sprung up from about her scalp, the mass pinned down around the ears with bobby pins exposing a pair of dime store earrings that hung from the sagging lobes of her ears like Christmas ornaments on an old dry pine. She slipped two menus down on the counter without being asked and turned her back to them with a hurried sigh as they sat down at the counter.

The air inside was heavy with the smell of cooking fat, beer and tobacco smoke. A line of booths bordered the walls on one side and under the window front. Tired, well-worn split vinyl stools lined the counter. Like hundreds of run down small town watering holes it sat as a pale reminder of a town that was once active and alive with local commerce but had seen its zenith and was now slowly crumbling away with neglect and decay.

While Jacob was not certain he had been there before, he knew that he had been in many like it. He glanced around the room at the faces, the tired desperate eyes and cold stares over plates and beer bottles as if trying to reconcile what had happened, what they had done and had left undone, regrets that smoldered like cigarette butts in dirty ashtrays. They sat about the room estranged from one another. They drifted about in shadows like victims in a slowly churning whirlpool, resigned to let it wind them down into a cold dark sea of empty existence. It seemed to him that the town like the airfield had long been bypassed. There was no reason to come here, nothing and no one of interest, just a small town slowly decaying like the peeling paint on the walls.

"Rita, dear, this is Jacob." He slapped him gingerly on the shoulder.

The old woman turned and wiped the counter with a towel she had draped over her shoulder, "Another one of your crop duster bums looking for a handout? What's it gonna be boys? I've got meatloaf on the special."

"We will have the biscuits and gravy please and do not spare the gravy."

"You've got it." she said without a change in expression as she returned a liquor bottle to its spot behind the bar and disappeared into the kitchen. As the old woman made her way through the doorway a young girl emerged.

She was in every way the antithesis of her surroundings,

as if gliding on invisible wings, beautiful in a way that almost defied his description. Beyond earthly beauty, olive skinned, eyes shining like black pearls in almond shaped lids, her body a comely shape that fit into a small tight dress and spoke to him with the tone of youth. Her hair was shining black silk that fell to her shoulders in streams of light. It was a light that no one except for Jacob seemed to notice.

"Who's the girl?" Jacob whispered emphatically.

"Shoosh…Don't say nothing to her boy…" Gabe whispered in a knowing response as he watched her make her way toward them and watched Jacob cautiously.

Jacob was surprised with his reaction.

Within moments, the old woman returned with two large plates of food and sat them down on the counter as the young woman worked quietly behind her.

"Here you go." The woman said as she moved down the counter talking to her self.

Jacob looked up at the girl as she turned to remove several bottles from the counter and smiled at her in an effort to get her attention. He thought he saw her pause for a moment, as if she had been reminded of something and had been momentarily distracted. She reached for a coffee pot and he felt her eyes on him as she poured coffee into two cups and pushed them in front of them.

"The Colonel there tries to stay away from me for as long as he can, living out there all alone." the old woman said as the girl poured, "Then he gets his fill of bologna sandwiches and makes the trip in for some real food. But I know that it's not the food that he's here for…" the old woman continued.

The girl looked at Jacob as if she had to be spoken to before she could speak, as if she were holding in some clue that required his asking the right question before she could divulge it there in front of the others.

"So you from around here…? You look like I should know you?" Jacob said this then, embarrassed caught himself suddenly.

"I'll take care of these two you go work the other end of the counter." the old woman said as she stepped in front of her to break up Jacob's attempt to make conversation with the girl.

The girl stood there for a moment longer.

Jacob interrupted, "No, no that's alright, I don't mind. Really…I…well…I flew in the other day…"

Gabe coughed suddenly in response to the words, in an effort to hold down a bite of food. Jacob gave him a quick side glance annoyed by the old man's reaction.

"Like I said, I flew in and well I've been doing some work at the airfield."

The girl looked over at Gabe, suddenly interested and with anticipation as if she expected him to say something in response to this.

"He's right, flew in a few days ago."

Jacob interjected, "Have you ever been up before? You know ever been up in a plane? I mean if you'd ever like to…"

The old woman interrupted him suddenly, "She don't take to pilots." She diverted the girl away to another customer at the end of the counter where other men were sitting drinking beer and quietly smoking.

Jacob looked down at three huge biscuits and fried potatoes all swimming in white sausage speckled gravy. He then looked over at Gabe, who had already finished a third of his portion.

"Go ahead boy." he coughed out between bites, "It's

not good to let your food get cold."

The old man grinned at him then turned to Rita, "Look…Rita, I've been looking for our boy. He disappeared the other day and well I thought maybe you might have seen him in here?"

Jacob listened and ate. The food went down in large lazy bites as he savored the first hot meal he'd had in what seemed to be a very long time. He thought about that as he ate and fought with his memory in an effort to remember what he had eaten, where he had been, who he had talked to, what was said. The memory was fading; he could not make out the faces.

He looked over at several men sitting on bar stools at the counter. They looked tired, worn as if from a long trip, their clothes creased with the wrinkles of sitting in cockpits for long hours, their eyes tired from watching instrument panels and searching the ground below for waypoints.

"Is that Colonel Gabe?" A large, loud man suddenly approached them and put a hand on each of their shoulders as he leaned in between them.

"You know Gabe. I've been trying to get hold of you. Where ya been?"

The voice was unusual with a soft, southern, hypnotic rhythm to it, a voice that was well trained with years of experience, a Virginia drawl that poured out words like poison into the open ear of its sleeping victim.

"You know where I've been." Gabe responded stiffly.

"Yeah I know those shacks and that air strip out yonder. I've wanted to give you a call, ask about the offer." His tone was almost a pleading ballad.

"Phone's been acting up…" Gabe snapped.

"Really now…? Not getting any calls?" The man

smiled knowingly then stepped back and positioned his large frame on the stool between them.

He was of a sort that Jacob felt he had seen before, a man who slipped in around the misfortune of others, who knew how to recognize an opportunity and take advantage of a situation.

"Can't you see we're trying to have a quiet meal here?" Gabe said in response to the man's sudden intrusion.

"Sure, sure I see that." He looked Jacob over, scanning him, sizing him up like an old bear looking over an unsuspecting fish in a stream, trying to figure out which end he was going to eat first. He lit a cigarette cupping it in his swollen bear paws and moved over to the stool next to his.

His suit looked as if he had slept in it. It was a gaudy pinstriped affair of dirty white linen with robin egg blue lines that marked the hills and valleys of his immense frame. He wore a large flat tie, the flowery print bulged out from under the rolls of flesh around his neck, the shirt a dirty soiled white poplin, was stretched and the collar points strained under the paunch of his jowls. His hair was an auburn mass of wiry curls that was in need of a trim. It was thick with pomade, combed over in an effort to make some sense of the matter.

He wore a gold watch on his wrist and in a practiced move pulled a sleeve down with his elbow on the counter to expose it and let it flash in the light over the bar.

"Son… Don't I know you? You look like someone I've seen before. You know the Colonel?"

Taking Gabe's cue Jacob sat eating, trying to ignore him.

"Let me tell you, you have a fine sense of character boy. This here is a good man, a fine and caring soul." He gestured to the girl tipping up his closed fist and extended thumb, suggesting that he wanted a beer.

"Charles William Beauchamp." He extended a heavy hand to Jacob as if he were trying to slip some cash to him under the table.

"Folks call me Lucky, sometimes other things, some just call me Bo." His lips pursed almost like a kiss as he said the name.

Jacob dropped his fork and briefly clasped hands then resumed eating. Without hesitation, the man returned his focus to the conversation, talking through Jacob loud enough for Gabe and several others within earshot to hear.

"You look like a smart kid to me… Let me ask you this, if you had 40 acres of worthless farmland out in the middle of nowhere, and a man came to you and offered you 500 an acre for it, what would you do?"

The man grabbed the brown beer bottle by the neck and tilted it up for a swallow. He grabbed the ashtray and slid it over in front of him, and sat hunched over the counter. Without a beat he continued, not interested in Jacob's answer, but filled with his own purpose.

"I mean, 20,000 dollars is a lot of money son. These days, land around here wouldn't sell for half that. Folks don't like the smell," he sighed, "and well, this here is a town that don't get a lot of attention." He casually sucked in a large drag and blew a mouthful of it up into the air then allowed the rest to drift out of his nostrils as he talked.

Gabe continued to chew and stare into the mirror over the bar.

"Look why don't you leave me and the kid to our meal?" Gabe interrupted.

"I'm not bothering the boy, am I son?" the old Bear replied then quickly picked up where he had left off.

"Yep this is a town that nobody pays much attention to. You ever see anything like this? I mean I been all over this country every small town between here and ever where else. New Orleans, been down to Mexico, up to Canada, traveled over seas, London town, Singapore, Tokyo. But this place, man it really beats all!" He laughed a practiced chuckle and looked around slightly nervous and uneasy as he said these words in an effort to stir up some attention and draw others into the conversation. He leaned into Jacob and whispered. "It's like a mausoleum in here. Nobody talks to nobody…" He chuckled uneasily then glanced about again, shifting his eyes a bit and raising his tone.

"Where you from son…? No wait; don't tell me, you're from out east I bet?"

Jacob swallowed a mouthful still distracted by the young girl moving silently behind the counter.

"Iowa." Gabe interjected this before Jacob could say anything.

"I knew it! A boy from the heartland uncorrupted by the sins of the big city! There's some great country out there, yes sir, open spaces, a man can stretch out and breathe. You know what I mean? Yeah been to 'I-o-way' a number of times, on business mostly…Great place, great place…" His words trailed off in a well-practiced cadence.

"So what kind of business are you in Mr. Beauchamp?" Jacob asked, drawn in by the bear's words.

"Why I'm glad you asked son. I appreciate a young man who takes an interest in the vocations of others and shows a real interest in one's fellow man, in the welfare of this great American engine of commerce. Why I am what you might call an agent my boy."

"As in real estate..?" Jacob asked.

"Real estate, horse flesh, risk, sports folks, all sorts... I'm an agent who represents the interests of other parties you might say." the bear smiled with satisfaction as he took another drag on his cigarette and waited for Jacob to respond.

Jacob continued to sit there as if he weren't sure it was his turn to speak. The old bear got impatient and moved on with the conversation.

"So you and the Colonel partners…?"

"Well I…"

"Yeah, boy the Colonel's a great soul, but let me tell you, he's no business man. With all due respect, he just has no head for business."

He grabbed the ketchup bottle, salt and peppershakers, moved his ashtray and began his presentation, "Did he tell you bout the property? About the deal I've been trying to strike with him and how he could fall into some real money?" He didn't bother to wait for the answer but began positioning the condiments on the counter.

"Here, say these shakers mark the town and those shacks… Now this here bottle represents that radio tower across the road and over here…"

He made a sweeping motion with his hand. "Over here is nothing, I mean a patch a woods here and there, ole farms, houses, barns, nothing… Now, in all this there's what my client calls a topological oddity. Any idea what that might be son?" He interrupted before Jacob could reply, "Didn't think so… So I'll tell you. The Colonel's airstrip and that damn radio tower represent the highest point for miles from any direction!" He poked the ketchup bottle top with his index finger, laughed in satisfaction and tipped up the beer bottle, holding up his hand to pause while he gulped then resumed.

"Now, I happen to represent an interest that wants to acquire that property and is willing to pay top dollar to get it!"

"Well what do they want it for?"

"Oh that's confidential son. I mean privileged information between my client and me. Can't indulge you I'm afraid."

"In other words, he don't know." the old woman interrupted, as she walked past the bar strangling the necks of several beer bottles in each hand.

"Now then, we have this odd piece of land out here in the middle of nowhere, nothing else around for miles and no chance that anything will be, any time soon…" He raised his voice and leaned in the old woman's direction repositioning his girth on the straining bar stool as he said this, then leaned back to Jacob and continued.

"I've been working with the Colonel here for some time now and he is either too slow or too bullheaded to even talk about my offer!" He sat there his arms crossed over his barrel chest looking satisfied he had made his case.

Gabe finished his meal, wiped his mouth with a napkin and tossed it onto the counter.

"Pie…?" the old woman asked as she reached over quickly and picked up their plates. Her question was direct and implied she wanted them to say no, "We have apple, cherry and coconut cream."

"No thanks. How bout you Jacob, pie?"

"No that was plenty."

The bear shifted himself from off of the stool and crunched the cigarette out.

"Gabe, I'm not going to push it, but you and I both know that the time is coming when you and I are gonna need to talk serious. I mean that property ain't worth $1,000."

He killed the contents of the beer bottle with a few more quick swallows slid a five-dollar bill from a huge wad of small bills and placed it on the counter.

"Darlin, you keep the change". He slipped off the stool and headed for the door. The girl looked over at the old woman who snatched up the cash from the counter and pushed it into a pocket of her dress.

"I'll be around to see you." the bear warned.

"Yeah sure…" Gabe responded.

The man turned with a serious look, "By the way, I understand you had a visitor recently that you can't seem to locate. You need any help? I could ask some questions, you know poke around?"

"Don't know what you're talking about Charlie." Gabe replied disinterested.

The old bear smiled as he pulled himself together and smoothed a shock of hair back over the side of his head carefully inspecting it from the mirror behind the bar, "Oh, I think you do Gabe."

He paused, then turned to the door and looked out on the street, "You think about it now. My client has been patient, a lot more patient than he's used to."

"So long son…" The salesman held his look at Gabe for a moment, and then slid out the door and into an old Cadillac parked out in front and then drove away in a cloud of blue exhaust.

"You know he's been nosing around a lot." the old woman said as the girl slipped up to Jacob and gingerly poured refills.

The girl touched Jacob's hand slightly as she held his cup and poured. He wasn't sure that it was intentional or in an effort to say something. He held his grasp on the cup as she poured and did not move his fingers or try to slip away from her touch. She did not move hers either and poured slowly. He could feel an odd energy in her touch, the feeling he had gotten from Angelica before but this time different, a feeling that flowed from her finger to his hand and up his arm. He felt light headed and a swirl of emotions washed over him.

"I thought I told you to go to the other end of the counter girl?" the old woman said as she separated them.

Her touch was broken and as suddenly as it had come, the feeling disappeared.

Then the old woman leaned into both of them from across the counter.

"I got no idea why I keep her around. She's dumb as a post. Ain't said anything since the day she showed up." The old woman looked over at the girl, "She just showed up. I tried to get her to leave, but she kept coming back. I guess I'm too soft, I don't know…"

"You mean she can't hear?" Jacob asked.

"Oh she can hear just fine, she just don't say a word to nobody. Don't even know her name… She comes run-in when I call her so that suits me…" The old woman looked over at Gabe, "By the way, I think your boy is at the end of the bar down there." She shifted a quick glance to the end of the counter. The man looked up at them both then quickly down at his glass in an effort to blend in.

Gabe looked over at him again then leaned forward to whisper to her.

"How long has he been here?"

"Since early this morning... Tried to talk to him but he hasn't said a word."

Gabe made another observation, whispering to Jacob,

"I think that's our boy."

Jacob looked over at the young man, "What do you mean our boy?"

"Thanks Rita." Gabe whispered to her.

"Just get him outta here. I've got enough drunks in here as it is. I don't need another." she replied as she went about wiping down the counter.

Gabe started moving down the counter and began fishing for bills in his pockets.

"Get my ticket." he called over his shoulder as he approached the figure at the end of the counter.

The girl pulled the bill from a pad and silently slipped it into Jacob's hand. He looked at it silently and quickly counted out bills from a wad he had taken from his satchel. He handed her the money, looked at her with a faint nod and slipped the paper into the pocket of his jeans.

Gabe made his way to the end of the counter and turned a glance toward Jacob and motioned for him to stand at the doorway. He then turned to the figure leaning in close to him, casually inspecting him as he spoke.

"Hi friend…" Jacob could hear Gabe say, then muffled whispers as the figure refused to answer; took a long drink and stared down at the bar. The stranger continued to sit quietly, trying to ignore him. He was a young man, probably in his twenties; he was thin and his clothes were wrinkled and fit loose on him like old cast offs that he had picked out of a discarded box of rags. His hands and face were swollen and tired, smudged with several small cuts and fresh dried blood.

There was a short conversation between them, then the figure shouted.

"I don't need your help." Gabe now more confident

sat down next to him and continued to speak to him in quiet whispers as if counseling him. Gabe looked up at the mirror behind the counter.

Again the boy spoke up, "What's it to you? I'm just minding my own business here. Why don't you go on and leave me alone?" Gabe motioned as he spoke, as if re-telling a flight, moving both hands in tandem, one chasing the other through maneuvers as he spoke.

"You still here old man…?" The young man waved his empty glass at the girl signaling for a refill.

Gabe reached over and tugged at the collar of the boy's clothes.

"I don't know what you mean? These are just old work clothes, got em from surplus that's all. I told you I don't know what you're talking about!"

He moved to get up and Gabe put an arm around his shoulder and held him against the counter.

"Wait, wait! Don't worry son, nobody's going to hurt you. We're here to help." He tried to comfort the boy who had stood up from the bar and shifted his eyes around the room in a rising panic, like a cornered animal.

"I don't know what happened I tell ya!"

Gabe now in consolation, "I know boy. Now come on with me, we're going to take you home." As they passed, the boy looked into Jacob's eyes with a cold fearful look of someone who's seen something that they wanted desperately to forget.

"Have you seen any of them? Have you seen him?" The questions slammed into Jacob's mind.

The young man clutched at Jacob's jacket and held him within inches of his face. He peered into the boy's eyes. The man leaned back on the bar resting his elbows on the counter top to steady himself against the onrush of the alcohol. Jacob could feel his breath hot and dry, the smell of liquor wafted up from him. He could feel the chill of fear rise in him, his neck and scalp tingling with the words. He could not speak. The look on his face was evidence enough to the young man.

Jacob stood transfixed by the words. He could see a familiar fire in the man's face. It was familiar like someone that he had known before. The familiar scent of after-shave wafted up from the beads of sweat on the young man's face and with it Jacob suddenly felt that he was looking at his own reflection. He stepped back away from the man, terrified.

Gabe slipped in between them and loosened the man's grip on his collar. The man slipped into unconsciousness and slumped forward into Gabe's arms. Gabe put him into an open chair at a table where the drunken body sat limp. He then repositioned his arm and slipped it around his neck in an effort to lift him out of the chair and carry him.

"Help me get him into the truck."

Half stunned Jacob grabbed the door and then helped him lift the man up and carry him out to the truck. They slipped him into the cab between them, where he immediately leaned in against Jacob his head slipping back against the top of the seat.

Gabe took a close look at him, "He's out cold. We'll take him home."

"Gabe, what the hell is going on, he looks…Who is he?" Jacob asked, fearful of what the answer might be.

Gabe slid behind the wheel. "He's our pilot son."

Chapter 10

The late evening sun cast long shadows and a chill blew through the open window of the truck as it bounced over the tired asphalt toward the airfield. The gospel radio droned on in familiar intervals with a testimonial that sang a sweet lullaby to the young pilot propped between them. It was a field hand's tune. A song sung in the cadence of hard work in open fields under the blazing summer sun; an old Negro spiritual. It stung Jacob with its irony.

"We are climbing, Jacob's ladder, to his kingdom, in the sky…" the words rang out, repeated in harmony and a round of voices, straining with fatigue and labor.

Jacob glanced over at his face, cold like a death mask then stared out over the dash at a dwindling distant mirage that drifted up from the pavement.

It drifted in front of him on the horizon of his consciousness the image as fleeting as the setting sun. He could see it shining in his mind, a sepia photo of the young woman and a dream.

He could remember a man, a man he barely knew. He searched his memory for the earliest recollection, a collection of pictures and comments that formed a collage in his memory. He remembered when he was a kid. He would sit in an old pickup parked at the edge of a small town airstrip, half-listening to the radio, watching planes take off and land. He remembered the aftershave that would waft about the cab in mentholated drifts. A young man, his face lean and gaunt with a look of deep contemplation; he would follow the aircraft as they broke from the runway and struggled to climb. He would follow them as they lifted off, and angled up toward the clouds, biting the air, propellers pulling them skyward. He would sit for many hours, his mind absorbed in each passing plane, a loneliness fed by the empty runway and open prairie grass that shifted in the prop wash as they passed.

He looked over at the man sleeping between them, looked deep into his face. He could make out memories of the face, of the man and stories about the image, some he thought he had read, others he had manufactured, of the man cutting through angry thunderclouds and pouring rain. He could not understand the duality of the image and the myth, nor with the many flights his remaining longing, his painful yearning to fly. It left him wondering if perhaps too many spaces, left between expectation and compromise were not to blame. It was as if his shadow had been brought to life and sat at his side. Like a silent stranger who kept a carefully guarded secret.

There were many shadows and of them, one emerged always, and came forward. It was the shadow he thought, that pursued all pilots, the patient specter that waits in the quiet depths of lonesome introspection. It slips into the thoughts that come after hours of propeller blades turning invisibly in front of a never ending horizon and long lonely miles in air that is thick and still. It counsels, it suggests offering doubt in the face of growing experience, coaxing out fear and anxiety or dull complacency, a heavy half-sleep in a growing log of near misses and over-extended flight plans, a quiet ghost that sows the seeds of uncertainty and indecision and spins its web of miscalculation and indecision in an effort to lead it's victim to a final violent end.

I have seen them. I have seen him, he thought.

There had been a young man who late one night, tired from too many hours of low passes over a field, clipped a telephone wire or something on the ground in a moment's lapse in concentration. He remembered the scene as if he were hovering above it, suspended in space. He could see them, the farmhands and the curious from a nearby town that came to see the wreck as it lay burning, half buried in an open field, a twisted skeleton of wood and canvas.

Finally Jacob gathered his courage and broke the silence. "So who is he?"

Gabe did not answer him immediately but paused for several moments as if he expected him to answer his own question then replied, "Its like I said, he's our pilot."

Jacob shook his head, frustrated with the answer, "What do you mean?"

"The Mustang..." Gabe said, letting the words settle on him.

"Look there's no way, that plane was there for years. This guy's no older than I am."

He glanced over at Jacob then returned his eyes to the road.

"Now look, I'm me and he, well I don't know who he is. I'm right here alive and no way am I buying in to some crazy idea that this guy flew the Mustang into that field!"

There were several moments of silence then Gabe spoke up, "You believe in anything boy?"

"Like what? You mean spooks, the boogey man? Hell, around here I'd say if you don't you're going to be playing a lot of solitaire!" Jacob answered him, his words thick with sarcasm.

"Do you believe in heaven?" Gabe asked solemnly.

Jacob was stunned by the words, the power that they had to bring him still further into another memory. He recalled a large white tent, in a small valley nestled in a clearing of trees at the edge of a small forgotten town. He was small, only a youngster clutching a man's hand. The man tall, thin barely twenty his eyes deep set and tired, his face tanned brown as tobacco. Jacob was startled as the truck hit a deep pot hole in the road.

"I don't know Pop, never really thought about it much."

"Well I expect you will be soon."

"Why? What is this guy to me and what does any of that have to do with it?" Jacob asked.

"Cause sooner or later everyone does…" Gabe said in a matter of fact way as if he were talking about the weather.

"Right Pop…!" Jacob responded, frustrated with the notion.

"And I suppose that town back there, is supposed to be heaven?" he said sarcastically.

Gabe didn't answer for several moments.

Jacob nervously spoke up again, "That town." he said in an effort to calm his anxiety in a tone as if he were talking about some half-witted farm hand.

"What about it…?"

"Well you got to admit that it's about as glum as it gets.

And that gal behind the counter, what's her name ah…"

"Rita…?"

"No the other one, the girl with no name, I saw that girl…I mean I think I did at least. What's wrong with her, she can't speak?"

"Don't know. My guess is she could if she had something to say and someone came along who would listen. We all have something to say boy, jus different ways of making ourselves heard is all."

Gabe continued to drive on for several moments. Then he asked, "You ever been really scared? I mean so downright rubber legged that you can't even run away?" Gabe paused as if he expected Jacob to respond.

"That's what its like for some folks. Some live their whole lives, just scared. They got no choice in the matter. They try to hide it, do things to fool themselves into believing that they got things the way they want them. They just keep on turning over the same field, avoiding the things they're afraid of, circling around and around."

Jacob noticed a change in Gabe's tone.

"Those folks in town son, they're all scared."

"Scared of what?"

"Scared of the same thing you're scared of son."

"And what would that be Pop?"

"You know what I'm talking about, that thing that hangs out there and waits for you. You're scared. Like a kid who almost drowns in a lake and when he grows up won't ever cross a bridge." Gabe responded seriously.

Jacob thought about the words. Deep in the recesses of his heart there was a whisper, a suggestion that stirred in him. He knew what it was to be afraid. There had been times when in his own impatience he had struck out impulsively and had found himself trapped. The specter had reached for him several times and he had narrowly avoided the ground. He could remember the sense of helplessness and anger, his struggling with the controls, his mind racing with panic and indecision. It was a sickening thing to be cornered in such a way, without options, caught in a tight spiral in heavy clouds, unable to see the ground but knowing that it was rushing up to meet you.

"So what is she doing here?"

"Waiting…" Gabe said with a grim determination in his voice, as if he had been struggling with a great problem that refused to be solved.

"Waiting? Waiting for what?"

"Not what, who…"

"Well, who then…?"

"I'm not sure yet." Gabe responded with deep contemplation looking over at Jacob as if he had been sizing him up and had expected his questions.

"What about that salesman guy? I suppose he's from heaven too?" Jacob asked changing the subject.

"Charlie? He's harmless. It's like he said, he has a customer."

"You mean that whole story and that 'topological oddity' bullshit? What would anyone want with that old broken down airfield?"

"It's not the airfield, it's the tower."

"O.K., so what's with the tower? Where is this preacher I keep hearing on the radio?" Jacob asked.

"Lost..." Gabe made this statement in the way that one would speak of some great loss or deep regret.

Jacob responded to the whole exchange sitting up in the seat overcome with a mounting frustration with a situation that had grown to full blown insanity, his voice filled with sarcasm.

"Well sir, this is one fine community! I mean, everybody's lost! The girl doesn't know where she is, our pilot friend here, you got guys flyin in who don't know where they are and I sure as hell don't know where I am!"

He sat back and pulled his hands through his hair, and continued, "So, when did all this start Pop? Did ya all just decide one day that this here is where it was gonna be and hung out the old heaven sign for anyone who might decide to come down for a visit?"

"This ain't heaven son and it ain't my idea. It's always been here. I been here to watch over things, watch and take care of the folks that stop here. Folks like you. There's nothing else son. That tower gives folks the signal. It gets picked up if a guy gets lost and can't find his way down. They use it to find the place. Most the country around here is as flat as a frying pan and they come to know how far they can descend through the clouds and not hit the ground in the process. They all come back. Seems fitting I suppose, a guide for a wayward soul. You listen to the words coming from their mouths once they get down but you know that sooner or later they'll be back. You can hear em, the planes circling on top of the low overcast probing it from the clear sky up on top, lining up their approach with the tower. Eventually they all get up the nerve and decide to commit and drop below the clouds. I sometimes sit outside and watch for them. They come down out of the clouds the fog misting over their wings as they break out searching for the runway. You can see em come in waggling their wings, throttling up and down in a panic and then the look they have when they finally make it down and manage to get out of the cockpit. They all have it, that look. They walk as though they did it all on their own."

"But why here? I mean why the hell do they come here in the first place?"

"Same as you, flying around, lost. Some ain't come down yet. They keep circling for a while, and then they give up and move on. But sooner or later they all come back."

Gabe looked out over the dashboard in reflection, deep in his own thoughts. He paused for a moment and then asked as if he were speaking his thoughts out loud, "You ever wish for anything boy?"

"You're kidding?"

"No, I mean it now, most folks have em. What's yours?"

Jacob thought about the question. He thought about a great wish that he had buried deep in his heart. A deep longing to be away from the earth, to be suspended in the sky above all the mundane routine. The sky was open unpretentious unconditional, a precious thing so bright and shining that he could not bear to look at it for too long at a time. Jacob had held it in, pushed it away. There were things that made it possible for him to keep it away, to daydream in doldrums and to exist day to day with the dream, the great wish tucked into the recesses of his mind.

"Wishes…? Wishes are for kids Pop. I've learned that if I want something, the best way to get it is to get it, not to wish for it."

"And why is that?" Gabe asked.

"You can spend a whole lot of time wishing. People can make all kinds of promises, they can swear on a stack of bibles but in the end, you can't rely on anybody."

"That makes for a pretty tough go, doesn't it?" Gabe asked with a stern look.

"Life is all you've got Pop and let me tell ya, its not near as tough as praying and wishing and then having people turn around and shit on you."

Gabe did not reply but kept driving.

"I'm just saying, you rely on people, but in the end, it's every man for him self."

"Like that Charlie guy. He's got it right."

Gabe looked over at him, a somber, defeated look on his face.

"Charlie's dead son." Gabe said, then paused letting the words settle on Jacob.

"He spent a lifetime running after something. His big ambition was to make the big play. Cut the big deal. He traded everything for it, his family, and friends. Now he's just circling. He wants to come down just like the rest of them but he can't bring himself to do it. He tried once, failed and decided he would never be able to make it so he put a bullet in his head." Gabe said this, his voice trailing with sadness.

"What do you mean? He was right there sitting at that counter? He was as alive as you and me?" Gabe's expression remained serious with the words and Jacob grew anxious with his silent rebuttal.

"So who the hell are you Gabe?"

"Me? I'm just an old man. Guess at one time I was a lot like you, wanted to leave, go fly off, and keep to my own business. Guess I decided it weren't right. Guess I found something better."

Jacob did not respond, but sat quietly thinking about all of it.

"It's OK, son." Gabe said in a consoling tone.

Jacob stared down at the floor of the cab, "The whole thing is just crazy. I mean, I've never seen this place before. He can't be anybody that I know because I don't know anybody!"

Gabe didn't answer but looked over at him as if he were aware of something that he should already know. "You know the girl don't you?"

He realized that he did know her and that she was there. She was not supposed to be but she was. He had known that there were elements there from his past that Gabe, the Mustang, the town, the girl they were all pieces to a puzzle that he was to assemble. It was all circling about him. He was no longer apart from what was happening; he was at the center of it. It became clear that there was something, some plan that had put him there and a purpose that he must realize something more than his desire to get away, to run.

The radio hummed as it passed by one in what seemed to be an eternal stretch of power poles lining the road. The ever-present chorus of evangelical tunes and down home homilies scratched in protest at the interference. They didn't speak again for the rest of the drive but sat in silence until the truck rolled onto the gravel of the drive.

"Well were back." Gabe announced as they got out and pulled the young man from the cab.

"Tell you what, son. You go in now. I'll take care of him."

He turned for the door then turned with an after thought, "You ought not to tell him anything yet. He don't know you son. He don't know who you are. Don't give this any more thought OK? You turn in now, and get some sleep. We'll talk some more when you've had some rest."

Jacob walked into the diner and back to the room that he had occupied since his arrival. He threw his bag on the bed.

What would I have to say to him, he thought, even if he knew me, knew who I was; I don't know what I would say?

The evening sun had drifted below the horizon and a sullen moon illuminated the darkness through the windows of the diner. He was pleased to be able to sleep and escape the questions. He pulled off his boots and clothes and slid under the sheets. He looked around the room with a renewed interest, as if he were looking at it for the first time. It was neat and orderly. Pictures lined the walls. Pictures like the ones in the adjoining room. Small trinkets and knick-knacks from world's fairs, tourist traps, air race banners and trophies all stood neatly grouped and draped about the room. Small paper and balsa wood model planes hung from the ceiling. A small box with a glass lid sat under the lamp on the nightstand. Jacob looked over at it as he reached for the lamp. He could see that it held items neatly displayed; a Distinguished Flying Cross, Iron Cross, Legion of Merit, and several medals with which he was not familiar. They sat there in the little wooden box in mute testimony to the heroic acts of men who he guessed were old now or probably dead and long forgotten.

A quiet breeze grazed his forehead as the ceiling fan overhead moved in slow rotations. He looked up at the fan, watched the blades and without effort, drifted back to the slow rolling chop of a midsummer ride in the back seat of a wood and canvas kite as the heavy hands of sleep moved over him and drew him into its embrace. He reached over to the jeans he had left at the foot of the bed, pulled out the dinner bill that the girl had given him and read the note scribbled hurriedly across the bottom of it.

TOWER.

The words seemed urgent, pleading, her eyes frightened when she handed him the slip.

“I have to figure this out.” He whispered to himself as his eyes grew heavy with sleep.

There would be time to figure out the pilot and the girl. Time tomorrow...

Chapter 11

Jacob drifted down into a deep pool of sleep, his mind filled with images of a place far away and of aircraft that raced across the sky like dark predators, their backs gleaming, darting about like angry hornets. There were so many of them, so many planes and voices, altered by the static scratch of radio transmissions.

In his dream it was as if he were there, in each cockpit. He could feel the controls smell the air and sense the weightlessness and the invisible force of gravity pulling and pushing him as the heavy aircraft seared deep furrows through an endless sea of turbulent air.

There were Mustangs, their tails painted in orange standing out against a bright blue of the high altitude sky. He could see great lumbering giants of drab olive green, each in succession as he drove through the swarm of aircraft flying in tight circuits about them in an endless race, high over the tops of their gun turrets. He could feel the sudden bumps of thermal turbulence and prop wash as he banked in steep turns to slip past other aircraft fighting for position.

The Mustangs, silver streaks throwing bright flashes

of light from their wings as they banked in steep turns, lethal killing machines great fighters built to fly through deep brooding skies, images that came in sudden spasms flashing through the landscape of his mind.

An aircraft screamed past, first one then a second then a small clutch of others chasing the first all firing as they went by, muzzle blasts flashing from their wings. A short respite of several moments of straight and level then again another pass closer to the giants that stood as forbidding obstacles as he cornered round fighting the centripetal force of tight turns and the rough air churned from a thousand engines. His mind wandered and the flurry of images and thoughts mingled with fear.

Suddenly in the middle of a turn he could see it, the tower standing directly in his path. He struggled to avoid it to slip past in the split second opening between the steel beams and an unseen aircraft that was pressing him from behind. He banked hard narrowly avoiding it as he passed.

Then the dark ghost slipped up on him. It came into view, its wing becoming visible in the corner of his peripheral vision. It was coming for him, fighting for position, pushing its airframe and engine to the edge in an effort to get into position behind him. He struggled to see the face in the opposing cockpit. He felt the fear rise in him, fear that it would be on him, take him, and bring him down. He felt that he must not let the aircraft into a position directly behind him.

Then again in the middle of another quick turn he looked down the wing and was taken into another image. He was suddenly in the clouds, flying blind through a white curtain of mist. His eyes jumped instinctively to the panel in front of him, his sense of reality was now measured in the scan that he maintained of the instruments, their hands jumping in nervous protests, arguing with his senses as to the attitude, airspeed and direction of flight. He was climbing; straight and true like a silver dagger. The outside visibility was zero, the canopy a white opaque sheen of mist and cloud.

I must trust them, he thought.

His mind returned to a place that it had been to many times before, the second nature of all pilots, the lesson burned into their minds. It was the religion of the pilot, the faith that all pilots practiced, the notion that without the horizon there was only the panel, only the instruments. The glowing needles were all that he had, all that there was to link the ethereal with the reality of the earth below.

He was consumed with a mixture of both fear and of faith, enraptured in a moment of speed and limitless freedom from the abandoned earth below. He cared little about the other aircraft, of pilots and the giants flying in lockstep formation. There was no time for thought or analysis of the situation, no dull pounding of chop, no thought of a pursuing aircraft. There was only the purity of the shining silver ghost, gleaming in the sun as he rolled and bobbed in the morning sky. He drifted in endless tight turns and climbed to the limit of the protesting propeller blades clutching at the thin air in an effort to break free from gravity's pull. He nosed over again and leveled the wings.

What did he want? The question slipped into his mind once more. He pondered it as the aircraft leveled and then trimmed, droned along in level flight.

It was to be there, in the sky, off of the ground, to be up here, he thought. He wished that time could hang motionless and that he could remain there above the clouds forever. There could be no redemption on the ground but only waypoints, markers to intersections pointing to the invisible highways in the sky. He knew like all pilots knew, that God wanted no part of the earth, but rather had chosen to drift on the ethereal, eternal sea of space. Earth was meant for others; for those who feared the unknown reaches that lay above the clouds, beyond the blanket of atmosphere, the silent spheres coursing through the heavens and the edge of the dark abyss that called to them from above.

The horizon beckoned and his heart opened ever wider to the notion, and the great wish seemed less like a dream and more like a revelation. It was the great impossible wish of immortality that travels beyond the pain and suffering of men to find something beyond their grasp. The elusive single answer, the rune that deciphers the why's and how's and renders the truth from all doubt, the love from all ego, the shining metal from all impurity. The hours became moments that pushed the sun to the other side of the horizon as he flew on and the cloud layer below him formed an alabaster, rose-marble floor for the sun.

He slipped on one wing, closed the throttle and the aircraft seemed to hang there, motionless as the engine slowed. He could see the gleam of the sun on the wing and imagined the image of his aircraft from a distance. He thought that they could probably see his shining reflection for miles. He shone like a star, hanging there high on the horizon. He wished that he could be there shining forever.

Then the dark image returned to him, the pilot chasing him through the clouds. It seemed to him not human but rather a thing. He thought of the trappings of it, the symbols and reminders of what it once had been. It seemed that he could feel the pain of the thing, desperate and alone.

He retarded the throttle further. The clouds wafted over the canopy encasing him in mist as he drifted downward and then broke out below the floor of the cloud layer. The world below rose up in his windscreen again and a bleak landscape lay out before him through the canopy. He could make out an ocean below, blue green waves and white chopping foam boiled and lapped against a lonely shoreline. He lowered a wing and rotated round it in a tight high-banked turn.

He could hear nothing, no sound but could see the vibrating nose and the ghost of a whirling propeller in front of him. He looked down at the panel again, at the stick between his legs, then down the wing in an effort to make sense of his situation. He looked out of the canopy down at the open expanse of sea below, then up at the ceiling of thin clouds above.

Nothing…

He looked out over the nose, pushed the stick forward and could make out more of the shoreline, cliffs chalk white and beyond, a grey brown expanse of fields and grass, flowing in ashen waves beyond the cliffs. There were no buildings visible, no other aircraft on the horizon. As he approached the shore he could see it, the black lines of the tower again standing in an open field below, a lone structure it stood on the precipice of the cliff. He could hear the static emanating from it as it called out to him through the radio. It sang to him, vibrating the headphones with the songs of lonely men, singing to him, calling him to come with them.

Then suddenly, the engine shook violently and the rudder kicked back and forth under his feet. Without warning, the aircraft began to roll and pitch forward. He pulled back hard on the stick and almost immediately the engine roared in protest and the nose pitched up. He could feel himself lose weight in his seat and the airplane slip backward in a stall that brought the nose down sharply. Immediately the entire windscreen was filled with the view of the churning waves. Instinctively he brought the power down and pulled on the stick to get the nose up and lower his airspeed. Sluggishly the elevator responded and the whining of the propeller blades subsided as the aircraft's nose came up to level attitude. Though it was flying, the plane was barely under control. Jacob fought the panic and the drifting haze of confusion that danced through his mind. The nose bobbed and the stick continued to shake as he frantically struggled toward the coastline.

Then without warning, at almost the moment of cognition, he was caught in a stream of tiny contrails and tracer bullets. He could feel them hit the fuselage, enter the cockpit and penetrate his body. He could see them pass through him and into the instrument panel in front of him. He could feel no pain, only the dull pounding of the slugs as they passed through him and the sickening anxiety and helplessness of the situation as they slammed into the instruments, breaking the glass faces of dials, sending electrical sparks and sucking compressive sounds through the cockpit.

The dark specter passed over and in front of him, filling the windscreen with its presence. He could see the dark mottled gray on black camouflage, the square, paned canopy, and hear the sharp whine as it swooped down and passed in front of him from behind. Though he caught only a glimpse of the pilot, he could make out features, like a lifeless doll sitting there in the cockpit, surreal against the seascape before him. The image loomed forward and filled the windscreen for several moments, weaving and bobbing, taunting him, an easy target for his guns, if he could hold the nose in position and maintain control of the dying machine.

Then, in a sudden change of fortune, the black form in front of him suddenly rolled over, underneath him then climbed up to a position along side. The lifeless face of the pilot turned toward Jacob. He could see the face, a young man, maybe in his twenties, maybe younger, smiling at him, the face of a boy, young, proud, enjoying his sport with him. He could see his uniform, fit tight at the neck with a silken ascot and iron cross, fitted neatly over it.

The boy raised a hand to his leather helmet in salute, his goggle covered doll eyes gleaming his mouth in a tight smile. Then suddenly the black and gray Fouke-Wolfe 190 broke off and rolled away out of sight.

Without warning there came an explosion that shook the air around him. The concussion rolled his left wing up and over, and he was again diving to the sea. No control, no altitude, airspeed climbing and the shrieking wind blowing through the holes in the cockpit. Totally out of control, panic stricken, he struggled with the stick and rudder pedals, the sea racing up to meet him, his bloodied hands slipping on the controls, fighting to avoid the inevitable collision with the sea below. Then as quickly as it had come, the image disappeared.

Jacob sat up quickly, his mouth raised in a silent scream. He was awake, back in the room in the diner. It was silent except for the slow ticking of the ceiling fan overhead. He lay there in a cold sweat. He fought the fear welling up in him in the darkness of the room and his mind struggled as the distance between his dreams and his consciousness collapsed in on its self.

Am I dead? No…

He could feel the sheets around him and smell the damp mildew and dust in the room. He was afraid, overcome with the desire to get up, go into the next room, to seek out the old man to talk to him, to ask him if he knew the specter, to make sure that he was in fact alive and that the thing had been only a dream.

He wanted to move. He felt compelled to do it but in his fear felt unable to. His ears strained to hear a sound, any stirring that might indicate either the presence of the old man or the thing waiting there in the darkness.

It seemed as though it was with him now, that it had entered the room and was there with him, looking at him from a darkened corner. He moved carefully, quietly shifting his eyes about the room in the darkness, silently scanning the black shadows for an image.

A sound came to him, a quiet rhythmic tapping on the linoleum floor. The panic welled up inside of him as the sound stopped, and then quietly approached the soft tapping broken by several moments of silence. He lay still, braced for the moment when the thing would be upon him, reach for him in the darkness and take him.

If I can only reach the lamp, turn on the light before it gets too close, he thought, as he calculated his next movement, how to time it, how to get to the lamp before the thing could reach him.

Suddenly a leaping scratch against the floor and he lunged for the lamp and struggled to turn on the switch.

The form was on him now, in the bed with him. The light came on as he moved from the switch in an effort to fend off the intruder. Then the wet tongue, the familiar lapping whines.

"Hop…! Jesus…" he caught his breath, "What the hell? You scared the living shit out of me!"

The crippled mutt sat back on his haunches licking Jacob's face then looked at him tilting his head in a perplexed one-eyed stare. He felt embarrassed by his childish emotion over a dream and a reaction to such an obvious explanation.

The old dog lay down next to him and yawned wide as it settled in the sheets. It lay there looking at him with a soft self-assured gaze as if it had known that the dream would come and that a part of it was not a dream but something real that would require his attention.

Jacob fell back on the pillow and the dog slowly crept up and settled closer beside him turning his gaze to the window. Jacob looked at the window and then at the dog for a moment. It occurred to him that it might have heard or seen something there, something that he could not have sensed. He reached over to turn off the light and in the darkness that fell again on the room, the wind rose with a gust that shook the windowpane. Hop stirred for a moment, looked up again and then settled.

The gust receded and was replaced by the sound of a single aircraft engine that droned rhythmically off in the distance. It was far away, so far that one could not tell if it were approaching or moving away. It was throttled down and the crackling of the exhaust revealed the pilot's intention to lose altitude in an effort to land.

He's too far away to be landing on their runway, he thought. It seemed strange to him that a pilot would choose to land in an open field when their runway was there.

The whine of the engine was reduced to a slow drone that receded further until only a muffled rumbling could be heard. Jacob thought again about the dream and struggled with the images and how real they had seemed.

He's down now, he thought as he imagined the aircraft sitting quietly, far from the road, the town or their field, a pilot hiding from the approach of the dawn and the light that lipped the edge of the horizon. He shivered with cold as he thought of the thing, the pilot.

Chapter 12

Jacob laid sprawled on the bed as the dim light of the morning cast a pall over the room. There was a grim reality to it, the atmosphere was tired and worn with depression.

His mind moved between sleep and a drowsy, muddled awakening, thinking of the dream and the night before. He thought of his plane, the Stearman and of the Mustang, both undoubtedly lying in heaps of torn metal and rusting parts in the hanger, probably little more than the mass of junk that they had been some time ago. He thought about the men in the tavern, like somber ghosts, the pilot in his dream and of the girl. He could see her face, the picture in the wreckage. The woman in the dream, it was her face, he thought.

He was sure that the idea that the pilot had flown the Mustang into the meadow was as improbable as the notion that it even existed or the idea that Gabe would somehow be able to put its remains back together on his own.

He felt a sudden tug at the sheets and the weight of Hop on the mattress then with several awkward thumps the warmth of the animal's body curled close to his head and a hot breath next to his face. He opened an eye and met Hop's face only inches from his own the dog's single eye staring with curiosity into his.

"Damnit dog…!" he whispered, pushing the dog back as he sat up and reached over to grab a cigarette from a pack on the stand.

Suddenly, his thoughts were interrupted by the sound of a faint muffled discussion coming from the adjoining room. He sat there straining to listen to the conversation. He quietly moved closer to the door in an effort to hear them.

Gabe and the pilot were talking. It sounded as though the subject of their conversation was something familiar to them both. He could make out Gabe's tone consoling and calm, the pilot's hurried, insistent and direct. The exchange of their words bounced back and forth between them and escalated in intensity as they talked. He could tell from Gabe's voice that they had been talking for some time, possibly since the early morning hours. He moved as quietly as he could in an effort to avoid being discovered.

He can't be the pilot… He thought. It stirred in him, the white tent, a congregation; he remembered the image of these things though he did not know why. His curiosity turned to concern as he thought of the drunken pilot and Gabe, the old man. He thought too about the salesman, Charlie. Gabe's words echoed in his mind, Charlie's dead son… The thought of it chilled him.

He turned to get up from the bed when the voices stopped suddenly and the front door of the diner slammed a final exclamation point to the conversation. Hop jumped off of the bed and walked to the door. Jacob put out the cigarette and quickly slid off the bed and cracked the door open as the dog squeezed his way past.

"You okay Pop?" Jacob asked as he feigned a yawn and looked out into the adjoining room.

The old man was standing behind the counter, washing coffee cups. He looked tired, very tired as if he had been up all night.

"You look like hell." Jacob said as he pulled together the last button on his shirt and reached across the counter for a coffee cup.

"If you want breakfast you're late." Gabe replied.

"No, coffee will do just fine. Where's your boy?"

The old man turned dispassionately and filled his cup from the pot on the grill.

"He's outside trying to sober up."

"Everything O.K. …?"

Gabe did not respond but turned and resumed washing dishes.

Jacob sipped and looked over the counter as Gabe worked.

"Thought maybe there was some trouble?"

"No. No trouble…"

There were several moments of awkward silence, "I suppose now that you have your pilot, you'll want this back?" Jacob said, sliding the Mustang's flight manual onto the counter.

"Don't give it to me, take it out to him. Ask him if he wants it back." Gabe answered as he wiped down the counter with a towel.

"I don't understand? I thought you said he was our pilot?"

Gabe stopped his work and looked over at Jacob, "I've got something to tell you son…"

"What is it?"

"That man out there, he's someone you know." Gabe said this to Jacob, his voice trailing off almost fearful, afraid of what effect the revelation might have on him. Jacob sat there at the counter for a moment, unable to move. It was like he had been told that he had only days to live or that the only love of his life had died. It was a truth that he had suspected, that in the images of his dreams had made itself known to him but in his own denial, his own desire to cling to another reality, he did not want to accept. He got up from the counter, walked to the window and looked outside.

"Mind if I go introduce myself?"

"Now don't go and tell him you know him boy…I mean he knows who you are…" the old man said.

"That doesn't make sense. I want him to know, I want him to know. He needs to know that in spite of him that I made out alright."

"And just what did you do with your life son? What did you make of it in spite of him?"

"I made it as a pilot; I made it as a fighter pilot Pop." Jacob replied sternly. The words came out by themselves. He had not thought of them, it was as if something deep inside of him was speaking, something that had to be let out.

"I've had time to think about things Pop. I've been able to remember some things and I know that I was somewhere else before the Stearman and that storm. I'm not sure where yet but I know I am a good flyer."

"How do you think you got to be a pilot?" Gabe asked resuming his work behind the counter.

"Work, Pop. That's how, lots of work and lots of nerve."

"That nerve, where do you think you got that from?" Gabe asked.

Jacob looked outside at the man struggling with a

fire hose, trying to get water flowing from it, his hair a jumbled mass his face white, with the effects of too much alcohol.

"Not from him…" he said.

"No, you're wrong boy, that's exactly where you got it from. You got the good and the bad from him boy, the things that make you who you are. You been trying to run from it son, you been trying but you can't."

Gabe looked down at the counter, "I guess all men try to do that one way or another. They try to be something else all together. It's like there's something they resent about where and who they're from, even the ones who tell everyone how much they love their folks."

"I'll be outside if you need me OK?" Jacob called out ignoring Gabe's words as he opened the door.

"Don't tell him boy…" Gabe called back in acknowledgement as Jacob walked toward the door and made his way outside.

He walked around for a moment, pulled a fresh cigarette from a pack in his shirt and lit one holding it with his coffee cup.

He found the pilot by the service bay with the water hose and a bucket. The man had the water running and was holding the flow over his head, bent over the bucket letting the water rush over his scalp in an effort to wake up. He suddenly lifted his head and shook it like a dog would, trying to shake the water from his matted hair.

"Oh man that hurts," he said rubbing his neck, "I'll take one of those if you've got an extra?" The pilot groaned the words his voice dry and sore like a toothache.

Jacob pulled another cigarette from the pack and handed it to him and flipped open his Zippo, lighting the end. The pilot took a deep drag on the smoke then coughed a horse cough and wiped a crust of dried sputum from his mouth.

"Gotta find someplace to dump this bucket..." he sighed.

"Take it over to the weeds there." Jacob responded.

"Listen sport, would you mind? I don't have my land legs yet."

The pilot pulled the bucket up by the wire handle and held it in front of him. Startled, Jacob took it and dumped the contents in a patch of weeds then took the hose that the pilot left on the ground and began rinsing it down while the stranger leaned weakly against one wall of the hangar.

"So, what do they call you?" the pilot asked, taking the smoke from his mouth then replacing it as if there was a special place for it between his lips.

"People around here call me Jacob."

The pilot smirked, "That's your name or is that just what people call you?"

"I suppose it's my name." Jacob replied.

"You suppose? Sounds to me like you're in worse shape then I am sport?"

The pilot wiped cold beads of sweat from his forehead with his sleeve.

"Doubt that..." Jacob said as he washed down the last remnants of the pilot's stomach contents from the bucket.

Jacob looked up at the man leaning against the wall. He could see his bare forearm, muscular and dark like a cigar. It looked like the kind of lean muscle that had come from a lot of hard work, a forearm that had been exposed to a lot of hours of sun. The man was lean all over, his clothes wrinkled as if slept in, his boots were beaten up and the soles and heels were worn from hours of shifting rudder pedals, his hands rough and bruised like a prize fighter's. His hair was like Jacob's, black and course, long on top and shaved close on the sides, strands of it framing a dark suntanned face and deep set smoke grey, steel bearing eyes.

"So, how'd you get here?" Jacob asked.

"I got here by luck." the pilot replied.

"What do you mean?"

"I mean I took one too many rounds to the oil cooler is what."

Jacob thought quickly about the Mustang and the holes that Gabe had found in the wing and fuselage.

"You mean the Mustang?" he asked.

"Yeah…You got any idea where it is?"

"It's in the hangar there." Jacob replied glancing over to the hangar door as he turned off the hose.

"That old man brought it in then?"

"I brought it in. Took me the better part of a day…"

"Yeah?" the pilot said, looking at Jacob and smiling slightly.

"Well you know then that I banged it up pretty good. So…You been inside there yet…?" the pilot asked cautiously and nodded in the direction of the hangar door.

"Nope…The old man doesn't let anyone in there." Jacob responded.

"Well, just as well." The pilot said as he propped himself up onto both feet and started toward the hangar door.

"I wouldn't go in there if I were you." Jacob warned.

"Don't worry boy, I'm not going in there." the pilot replied as he stumbled and then caught himself after a step.

"Whoa, better let that settle a little." he said as he

stumbled back from the door. Jacob grabbed his arm as the pilot lurched forward.

"You better come over and sit down." He took the man a few steps over to the picnic table under the apple tree and sat him down, "I'll bring you some coffee."

"Don't bother with the coffee sport; better make it a tall glass of ice water. Don't know that I could hold down any coffee just yet."

Jacob dumped out his cup and filled it with water from the remaining dribbles from the hose then handed it to the pilot.

"Here, drink this." he said. The pilot drank the water down and motioned for some more. Jacob refilled the cup.

"Where you from…?"

"Up there." the pilot replied, motioning skyward with the cup."

"Before that…?" Jacob asked.

"I don't know…flying around, can't say as I remember much before that. I've been here for as long as I can remember." The pilot said this, his face distant, his thoughts pre-occupied. He looked over at Jacob suddenly realizing that he was being watched.

"So sport, where you from?"

"Gabe says Iowa, but I suppose I'm from up there as well. I was flying an old Steerman, got lost and ended up here. I can't say for sure, but it seems to me to be the only place that makes sense. I've had a few things come to me, some other places, but I think mostly up there…"

"You say you've had some things come to you? You remember much?" the pilot asked as he continued to nurse his hangover.

Jacob thought for a moment about Gabe's request to

say nothing, "No not a lot. Not anything that I can put a finger on really."

He then changed the subject, "Gabe tells me you're the pilot he's been looking for?"

"I don't know about that sport, there's lots a pilots around here."

"Yeah seen a few but, not too many that could fly that Mustang." He replied. "Look, I saw something when I was bringing that plane in; there were some holes in it."

"Him…" the pilot replied, as he rubbed the stubble on his chin, his face grim with familiarity, as if he were recalling an incident.

"You said something last night. Who were you talking about, when you said *him*? Who would be out here shooting at planes?" Jacob asked.

"How long have you been here sport?" the pilot asked, in response to his question.

"I'm not sure, seems like months but its hard to say."

The man took a quick drag on the cigarette, "So you say you've been here that long and you haven't seen him yet?" the pilot asked, sizing Jacob up with the question.

"Seen who?" Jacob replied.

The pilot didn't answer but asked another question, "What do you think…about ghosts I mean?"

"Hell I don't believe in ghosts. As far as I know I'm nuts, maybe or having a bad dream, lying in a ditch somewhere sleeping one off, I don't know. Maybe you're just a figment of my imagination."

The pilot pulled another deep drag on his cigarette and said with an exhale, "Well, let me tell you sport, you best start believing in them, right now."

"And why would that be?"

"Because sooner or later you're gonna have one on

your tail and you'll need to believe that what you are seeing is real and not some dream…" The pilot's words were stern, bitter as if he were recalling something from the past.

"What are you talking about?"

"You'll see…Sooner or later everyone sees a ghost. They may not think that's what they're looking at when they see it, but it's a ghost just the same."

"Hell, you're not making any sense." Jacob replied, and then thought that possibly he had seen something.

"You'll know what I'm talking about soon enough. You've probably already seen him and don't know..." he said, looking knowingly into Jacob's eyes, rubbing his face with one hand.

"So how would a guy know if he had seen this ghost, you're talking about?"

"Can't say that I can tell you exactly what your ghost will look like but I can tell you something about what I saw...That is if you're interested?"

Jacob didn't reply but sat down at the table curious.

The pilot looked over at Jacob his eyes distant as if recounting a dozen deep regrets as he went through the story.

"There is a thing that's out there. He's always out there trying to take you…"

He interrupted himself with another drag from the cigarette and then paused for what seemed several moments. Jacob felt that the pilot was trying to piece together the story, as if the details of the incident needed careful attention and that it was important that the story be right. Finally after several moments, he spoke again.

"There was once this guy, flying through the soup" he began letting the words come forward on their own, not hurrying the story but rather letting it tell itself. "When… when suddenly the clouds began to glow under him, like lightning and thunder..." He pulled the smoke from another drag into his lungs and exhaled with the words.

"The guy was lost, afraid, he had no idea where he was, and then in an instant he saw something. It was the thing, like a dark shadow... He wasn't ready for it. He didn't expect it to come so soon. The man thought he would live forever that he had killed so many shadows that he didn't have to worry about them anymore. I guess you could say that he got careless…"

He sipped some water from the cup and swirled the contents around thinking, trying to recall more details of it, of the story that he had buried deep inside of himself, something it seemed, he did not want to recount, but was compelled to. Suddenly he collected himself and dove into it again.

"He broke into a wing over and tried to follow him, but he was too slow. Then the thing came in, his machine guns tore through one of the bombers. He could see it roll over and spiral down. It spiraled several times as he dove down after it. He looked for parachutes. There were none, no survivors, only the flaming carcass falling."

The pilot paused again for several moments, and then said in a final ending phrase, "It was him…"

"Him…?" Jacob asked.

"Yeah, him. He's there always; he knows right when to come for you. He'll roll over and down he'll come, right out of the sun. He'll be on your tail before you can turn. He'll open up and catch you when you least expect him."

The pilot flipped the butt of the cigarette into the cup, "Anyway, a few rounds caught my engine, a few more into the left wing tank. I thought I'd had it. I dropped down and started looking for a place to land. That's when I found this place."

"So how'd you end up here?" Jacob asked skeptically.

"Don't know but, I'll tell you it didn't matter at the time where I was, just as long as I could get down in one piece."

"Well I didn't have anybody shooting at me… I…" Jacob thought for a moment, that plane, that dark shadow…?

"I did see something a while back, yeah; several times I saw something, some crazy fool…" Jacob said.

The pilot paused, as if waiting for Jacob's reaction, "It's him sport."

"So what am I supposed to do, I mean what can a guy do if its always there?"

"Ain't much you can do really? All you can do is keep flying, stay up there and keep fighting him off as long as you can. It's not that you can change things, the ending I mean. When he comes, finally, and you're too tired to fight him, well…" The pilot sighed.

"Anybody ever beat him, I mean shoot him down?"

"Not that I know of… I'd say a pilot wouldn't have much of a chance alone. But I suppose if a man has good eyes, if a man can see far enough out on the horizon and see him coming, turn soon enough or get up above him then fight him off when he comes, and also if he had someone there or rather something, I guess. I mean, something more than a man or something of a man's creation, then I suppose he'd have a chance." The pilot swirled the cigarette butt around in the cup.

"Hey sport, want to see what's behind that door?" the pilot asked, suddenly changing the subject.

Jacob could feel a fear suddenly well inside him. It was like the fear that a kid gets when he looks up at a carnival ride, a sparsely rooted rollercoaster thrown together in a farmer's field, an inviting maze of color and metal beams that give one the illusion of flying, a dangerous contraption that barely supports itself on the ground, cars spinning and the frame shifting with every turn.

"No..." He replied, suddenly fearful at the prospect of seeing something that he did not want to see, as if the ghost was there behind the door.

The pilot got up slowly and began to walk toward the hangar door.

"Come on boy, you ready to be knocked off your feet?" the pilot said as he reached for it. He stood there as if taunting Jacob, daring him to defy the old man and see things for himself.

"Gabe said not to go in there." Jacob warned, self-consciously, aware that his fear was showing through his words.

The pilot looked at him knowingly, grinned and then grabbed the door in an effort to pull it open.

"Hey I thought you said you weren't going in there?" Jacob asked, looking over his shoulder for the old man.

"One other thing I've learned about this place sport," the pilot responded impishly, "nobody around here plays by the rules."

The pilot pulled on the door that was locked tight, "Well," he responded his eyes peeled with a determined look, "looks like we'll have to break that lock…"

He walked over to a pile of junk and produced a length of steel rod that he slipped into a crack of the doorframe and began to pry it open when Jacob spoke up.

"Pa…" Jacob said suddenly, his voice uncertain, the

word slipping from his mouth.

It caught the pilot by surprise. It was as if he had known something, that they had both been keeping this thing like a silent, gentleman's agreement between them and had kept it at a distance out of some courtesy, some mutual desire to keep their speaking path clear of encumbrances. He had wanted there to be some distance between them but the word had closed a gap between them suddenly and without warning. He stopped his work and stood there, his back to Jacob, waiting for something that would correct the situation. As if there were some word or action that would make things as they had been only a moment before. He heaved a great sigh.

"My son is dead boy…" The pilot replied.

"No…No I'm not dead, Pa. I'm right here with you. I'm here and you're here too. I know that it makes no sense. That you should not be here, that I should be somewhere else too but, it's true, you are here and so am I."

"No boy, it's not true. It's a dream boy, a dream that you have fashioned for yourself. Don't listen to the old man boy. He's wrong about this. There's no such thing as 'great wishes'. I thought that there might have been once but, I can tell you there's no such thing. There's only the sky and the thing…That's all there is…"

"Why do you say I am dead? I know that can't be, I'm here, I'm alive just like you?"

"That's just it boy, I'm dead too. We're all ghosts. You wouldn't be here if it weren't so."

"Look, let's go in there then. You're right, I'm ready to go in there and see it, whatever it is. Let's break the lock and open the door then!" Jacob said, his voice pleading. He wanted to fix things too. He wanted to make the misstep of his words right and make things like they had been before. He realized that it was not the hangar that he was afraid of, it was the man who stood there next to him and the words that the man had said.

He suddenly realized how painful the realization was. That everyone there was in pain. Everyone there wanted to ignore their visions, ignore their own personal condemnation.

"You were right before boy," the pilot said with a sudden distant tone, "we best not go in there…"

The pilot dropped the rod and turned, walking off in the direction of the runway.

"Wait! Where are you going?" Jacob called out to him as he turned to follow.

The pilot stopped for a moment, his back still turned to Jacob, "Back to town, sport… You stay here now; you stay with the old man. He'll take care of you son, I'm only gonna be gone for a while…Just going into town for a few drinks, I'll be back for you later…"

The words came out as if the pilot were recounting something from the past, as if he were talking to a small child, someone he had lost a long time ago.

"Come back!" Jacob called out to him.

"Go on now boy, you just stay there. I've got some flying to do, some fields down south need to get done, and I have to go away for a while, but you be a good boy, you stay with the old man and I…I'll come back for you in a few weeks after the season is done." The pilot walked on, his voice drifting like a sad song over an open cornfield in the dead of winter, his words an unsuccessful attempt to calm a young boy's crying.

Jacob looked for him, watched for him as his image drifted off into the distance. He felt his heart grow heavy and a deep sob rise up in his chest. He listened for his voice but heard nothing, and then a distant engine as a propeller turned idling revolutions as it waited.

He knew that his father's ghost was out there waiting and that there was nothing that he could do to fix it…

Chapter 13

Jacob returned to the diner to find Gabe, to talk to him about the man, the pilot, his father. He walked in expecting to see the old man there, still working behind the counter, but he was nowhere to be found. Like the man, Gabe had left, suddenly without warning. Jacob wondered if his words, his disclosure to the pilot had done something to the old man as well.

The hours slowly turned over as Jacob waited for him. He could hear sounds of toil echoing from the hangar. Odd, moaning sounds like an animal trapped in a cage and sharp reports from a hammer on metal. It was as if something was trapped in there, something that had been caged and made angry. He wondered if Gabe had somehow slipped passed him during his talk with the pilot, and had decided to work in there apart from him. That he had said something that had made the old man distant. He could hear the sounds of machinery and hand tools, metal being formed into shapes light enough to fly, to cut through the clouds but heavy, heavier than air.

With all that he knew about flying, about the aerodynamics of the aircraft he had spent so many hours in, it seemed to him still a miracle that these things could fly. They were heavy, very heavy things, too heavy to fly and yet, the metal, the wood and canvas could be shaped, made into things, that by human hands could reach the sky, climb up into the clouds and the heavens. It did not seem possible that they could do so, but they did. He thought of the planes in the hangar, the times he had stopped and listened to the sounds of aircraft overhead, flying, circling off in the distance, beyond his vision. He thought of the weight of them hanging there in the great expanse of open sky and of the earth sitting quiet and still below them. The earth seemed still and distant, the countryside a never ending patchwork of fields and farmhouses, pockmarked here and there by towns and then cities, that sat like great open sores of concrete and steel on the landscape. The people too seemed small and insignificant in a universe too big and with too many questions to ever be understood.

"It's right not to believe in anything." he said to himself as he worked and continued thinking about the dark thing and his father…thinking about what he had said. He recalled the images from his dreams, the sound of the lonely aircraft from off in the distance, the many aircraft engines, similar in sound that he had heard but never saw hidden in the clouds. The specter began to take shape in his mind. I have seen him, he thought. He thought about the girl again, the girl in his dream.

He went outside and found the hose and holding it over the asphalt, washed down the spots of oil and aviation fuel that stained the tarmac. The water mixed slowly with the oil and brought it to the surface. He could see the rainbow puddles of oil and water whirling about on the pavement as he let the water flow over it. He could see her face in the sheen; make out her features, in another place, another time. She helped me once, a long time ago he recalled but could not remember how or what it was that she had done. It seemed like something that had never happened but with thinking about it again and with each remembering, a little more of it returned to him and for the first time he felt that it could have been. There was a part of it that he wanted to keep remembering, a part of it that made him feel whole. It was a longing, a love for something that made him feel that way. However there were other parts of it that he could not, did not want to remember. He could not put the entire picture together in his mind, but he was certain that while there were parts of it that were good there were others that were not, that in remembering them, he would reveal things that he did not want to know.

He looked over at the hangar as he shut off the hose and rolled it into a loose bundle of loops on the ground. It occurred to him that maybe Gabe was holding something in there, a wounded animal that needed to be put down, put out of its misery. He dropped the last loop of hose to the ground and pulled the faded flight manual from his pocket and sat down at the picnic table under the apple tree. He thumbed through it and looked at the notes that had been made on the pages, notes to remind him to open the oil reservoir to contact the batteries and to prime the engine and so on. He looked at the script in his own hand, worn and faded as the pages themselves, written by his hand but done so it seemed, a long time ago. The book had become familiar to him, its diagrams and information not as much absorbed but rather recalled from his memory as if the details of the Mustang had been buried within him and the book was there only to remind him of these things.

I know that airplane. I know it like I know my own boots, he thought. The book had become like a possession, a thing that belonged to him.

"I could fly it…I could fly it if it were in one piece." he said, "But its not, it's a heap of old junk in there. There's no way it will ever be anything but an old hulk, a memory of what it had been. "

He put the book in his pocket. "I need to see the girl, she will have the answers." he said to himself as he started for the diner.

The room was empty, a single coffee cup on the counter and the remains of a smoldering cigarette in an ashtray. The cigarette, a fleeting reminder of the pilot, his father a man who like in life had only brushed against him in passing, a man who had been there at some time but was now gone.

The radio was silent. He thought it odd. He reached up above the counter and turned the knobs. There was nothing, no plaintive sermons, no gospel music, only the silent static hum of warm tubes inside a wooden box.

Jacob retreated to the bedroom, took off his overalls and opened the closet to find some clean clothes. He found an old flight suit, clean, neatly hanging there, and captain's bars on the collar. He thought about the woman pilot, Angelica and her words about being in uniform. He smiled and shook his head as he put on the uniform and reached under the bed in an effort to find some clean boots.

Then he felt it, a leather strap lying next to a bootlace on the floor under the bed frame. He pulled on it as he dragged out the boots and the strap came out, a worn leather holster clinging to it, a holster cradling a black

45 caliber semi-automatic pistol. He pulled the boots on and tied the laces as he hopped from one foot then the next. He looked down at the holster. He was struck by the impulse to take it and strap it on, that the gun was his and that he should take it. He pulled an arm through the sling of the strap and buckled it on. It went on instinctively, its buckle and the strap worn in a way that made it conform to the shape of his shoulder and chest, as if he had worn it many times and that it had been a part of him for a long time.

He made his way to the counter and poured a cup of coffee. He walked over to the door, and looked out through the screen at the abandoned lot and the tarmac. The morning was low and cold, no sunshine no breeze only the gray overcast sky that met the open prairie in a pencil thin line. He found the keys to the truck and made his way across the gravel toward it.

He listened intently as he walked; not wanting to let Gabe know that he was leaving. No sounds from inside, nothing but the sound of hop panting behind him.

"Ok boy, why so quiet?"

The dog stared back at him with a bored, experienced look then let out a rough bark and stepped in front of him and looked back at Jacob as he put his front paw on the running board of the vehicle.

"So you think I should ignore the old guy and take a little ride?" Jacob said, "Well, suppose I should probably check things out. What do you think boy?" The dog only whined in reply, and continued to stand there impassively.

He thought of the note again, of the girl. He thought of the words, the pleading of her eyes. She too wanted him to go, to find her.

He slid behind the wheel and closed the door. Hop was sitting there next to him, panting with anticipation looking over the dash as if he had been sitting there for some time and knew where they were going.

"How the hell did you get in here?" Jacob asked as he slammed the door, "You aren't going."

The dog whined slightly and laid his head on Jacob's knee and looked up determined to stay.

"Oh, alright… The hell with it, just don't cause me any trouble." The dog responded with a quick yelp and sat up with anticipation waiting for him to start the engine.

He threw his cigarette out the window, gunned the engine and pulled the truck out onto the road. He was not sure what he would find there at the edge of the asphalt. There where the tower stood in quiet solitude. He was not even sure that she would be there. It seemed to him that she was not one suited to the dreary overcast. That she would not materialize unless the sky was clear and the sun shining. There was something about her nature that made him think her fearful of the dark. He recalled her form, beautiful, deep and warm. What would he say to her? He did not know. He only knew that he must go there, to the tower, find her and try to understand.

It didn't take long to make his way to the end of the field, then down the road to the crumbling cinder block building and the rusting steel skeleton of the tower. He shut off the engine and sat on the shoulder quietly smoking. He looked around, thought about getting out, then decided for some reason it would be best to remain there and wait. He stared down the length of the road to a point where it met the line of the horizon.

It seems so empty, nothing out there, he thought. He's out there flying. Ghosts, he thought, you've been acting like a little kid, there's no reason to be afraid...Just an old dirt road and rusting old tower out in the middle of nowhere.

He felt that he needed to wake up. That if he could, he would wake up somewhere and that wherever he had been would return to him and he would laugh to himself and then go on to wherever he was going. He thought again about his aircraft, thought of it repaired, sitting there in the hangar waiting for him, and the Mustang, its gleaming features shining there as well. Both of them were waiting to take him in a different direction. Which one of them would it be? Which direction would I go if I had to choose? Hell, where would I go? Either way I don't know where I would go...

He thought that maybe it didn't matter, that either way the plane would take him. Like flying that broken down old Beech, the plane would take him where it wanted him to go and that he would have no decision in the matter.

Hop had been sleeping, his head on Jacob's knee, his breathing quiet and slow. He stirred slightly and with a yawn sat up suddenly and looked up over the dash as if he had heard something.

"What is it?" Jacob asked startled from a doze in the warmth of the cab. He peered out to the horizon in an effort to see what the dog was looking for.

The morning sun had begun to shine down on the dark asphalt warming it and causing the air to rise up in silvery waves from the pavement. As if materializing from a mirage, a form appeared to him, drifting toward him from out of the distance, moving like a cloud billowing upward from a rising thermal. It moved with slow almost imperceptible progress toward him.

Moments passed as it approached him. He looked out toward it, his eyes watering from the bright reflection of the sun that had broken out from the overcast; its rays reflecting upward from the surface of the road, smearing the windshield with glare. He thought for a moment to turn the ignition and to drive toward it, to meet whatever it was that was approaching him before it could get him into a compromised position; it was second nature to him, to consider his position in relation to others. He began to start the engine when he felt a presence within him that calmed his anxiety and urge him to do nothing, to wait for it.

Then he could make out the image, her shape in the soft illumination. She stood there shining; her beauty almost beyond his capacity to bear it. She was dressed simply, her dress common white linen that spoke of an Iowa farm on a bright summer day. Her hair shown like shining black obsidian pulled back away from her face in a tail at the back of her head that flowed in a cascade down the middle of her back, in flowing strands.

He could hear the sounds of the nocturne playing, feel the warm breeze, see her face and through the beauty to a silent pain that clung to her features. He opened the door and climbed out cautiously as the remaining distance between them closed.

He did not know what to say to her. He wanted to comfort her somehow, to tell her that in spite of her fear that he could make things alright.

"Who are you?" he asked.

She looked at him. A tear welled in her eye. It formed in a small pool at the corner of her eye then, like a crystal stream, rolled in solitary silence down the ivory rose of her cheek. Her eyes stared back at him and urged him to look into them. It was as if she could see over the miles and time that had been lost over the years, as if she knew a secret buried in him that he did not know. His mind reeled to another moment, a dream within a dream. Suddenly her face changed. They were both somewhere else.

It was morning once again. He was far from the aircraft, lying there on the ground. There were odd unfamiliar sounds, mocking, distant sounds of monkeys arguing in great frenzies of hoots and shrieks.

Suddenly he felt a sharp stick poke him in the ribcage. He flinched and instinctively reached for his holster to retrieve the pistol. He looked up and saw a small child with an elderly man who looked to be at least ninety years old. The old man had relieved him of his weapon but was not pointing the gun at him. He could see that the boy had found a flight helmet and was wearing it on his head. He was dancing around him, playing; the helmet bobbing back and forth as he hopped about pretending.

Jacob could feel himself numb again, numb from morphine and a fall through the trees. He struggled to crawl, to move away from them when the old man put his fingers to his lips and said quietly, “No V.C., No, No V.C.”

He then motioned to a large water buffalo that stood quietly in the shallow creek a few yards away, chewing its cud. He continued to motion to him with his stick and then helped him to his feet. He could feel their hands on him; the old man and the boy as they helped him up onto the animal; he could feel its hide course and warm as he slid over its enormous girth. They covered him with several large grass mats and secured these under the animal’s belly. He could feel the animal moving under him as they then began a slow prodding hike winding along the creek bed and down over the mountains to an area cleared in the jungle. Then after some time, he could see the clearing, a handful of huts stood with quiet ribbons of smoke streaming from openings in their rooftops. He could only make out a few figures through the mats that covered him; women, children, old men, and wounded men lying on mats. They were barely clothed. The naked children were running and playing or helping with the work.

He passed close by a small child clinging to the leg of his mother. The child looked up at him and made eye contact through the matting. He was maybe 8 or 9 years old, his face, neck and hands horrendously scarred and his scalp exposed and mottled with scarring on one side. It looked to him that the boy had been very badly burned.

He felt himself sicken with the sight of him and wondered if this child had been a casualty of a napalm attack, and if possibly he had been responsible. Then it became clear that this child was not the only one. That there were dozens of children and adults whose flesh had been burned or who were missing one or more limbs.

The animal stopped at a hut and several children came streaming out, chattering all the while and looking at the helmet that the boy had found and was now holding up away from their reaching hands. Two young women then came out of the hut and after getting some quick instructions from the old man, quickly untied the mats and helped him down, into the shelter and out of the sun.

The hut was thick with the smells of cooking and sweat. The hot steaming jungle air made everything damp and dank. He lay down on the floor on several mats and looked up at his captors. They seemed to be little more than a band of poor farmers, not the enemy that he had imagined, the sinister, fanatics that lay hidden in ambush deep beneath the jungle canopy. He looked at the girls who moved about the single room. One of the girls he noticed was older than the others. She moved quietly about, giving directions to them. A small bowl of water was brought over and they began cleaning his wounded leg and face. He felt the sickness returning to his stomach. He could hear them talking softly and feel the treading of their feet as they moved about. The woman called the young child over and plucked the helmet from his head. She looked at the helmet, inspecting it and the name spelled in block letters on the back collar of it, JACOB.

"Jay-cob..." he heard her say.

Then with the recollection of the scene and her face and her calling out his name, his mind wound forward. He suddenly could imagine them together, days in the quiet peace of the village, of children playing and time slowing to a crawl. He could see the many days he spent with her, healing in the sun, her voice, the quiet singing, her hands rough from labor caring for him, softening his heart, calming his fear like a monsoon shower. The water of time wore down the edges on him.

The pilot's mind sharpened by the speed and abrupt changes that come from flying jets in rough air and death in seconds was hard to unwind in such a way. The mind is a complex thing, a tightly coiled mass of synapse and blood into which are burned many images, many things, real and unreal, wishes, hopes, dreams and in tight, dark corners fears and regrets that struggle to push themselves forward. His training, his experience, what he knew, the process of evasion and escape, the desire to return, they pushed at him too, told him that he must go, must keep distance between himself and these people. They could be collaborating with the enemy; they could be on either side. There was no way to know…

He became worn down by her though, the hardness gone, the pain gone, the guilt that comes from impersonal killing thousands of feet above the ground, all of it worn down, polished with a patina that warmed him like the olive of her skin.

She was lying with him in the night, a thin worn mat in a jungle hut. She is oblivious to the world and of the great giant's that burned white contrails miles above them in solemn formations. She was interested only in his face and the moment. They laid there, quiet, their bodies intertwined. They held each other not with feverish passion but in desperate longing to comfort, to sooth to bind wounds that they both had suffered.

Her features are clear, her body, and every aspect clear in his mind. Her sweetness overwhelming, flawless, every curve and contour, her scent all responding to him, urging him quietly and softly. With every move, she struggled with successive, quiet pleading for him to love her, to take her while the giants loomed above them their engines silently burning casting vapor and aviation fuel in narrow streams as they went. They move together on the bare mat, her warm breath panting with the rhythm.

The giants passed above them, brooding under the weight of iron bombs destined to obliterate yet another set of coordinates in a network of jungle paths and underground passage ways. To seek out and destroy an unseen enemy, a ghost that haunted the jungle. Like a herd of running hooves, pounding footsteps rumbling high over them and shaking the earth off in the distance with manmade thunder as they dropped their payloads.

He looked down at her, his senses overcome with the pleading of her abdomen, her eyes in tear stained disbelief peering into his soul. Another distant rumble like the thunder of an approaching storm and she could no longer contain her self and cried out a lone silent cry. Then, she held his face up from her, her hands strong, rough with work, but small. She smiled warmly, a single droplet from the corner of her cheek, a solitary tear shining in the moonlight, cracks of light that slipped through openings in the canopy of trees and illuminated her face. He brushed back her hair and wiped the tear, the single shining diamond from her cheek. It sparkled like a small sliver of glass, a star shining in the night sky.

He felt loss as the image drifted away and the pain of longing and remorse came over him. He struggled to remember her name through the cloud of distant memories but he could not. It was as if she were a personification of all of the loves, the warm compassionate possibilities that he had once had.

His mind reeled forward. He was again lying on the floor and could make out her sound. She was arguing loudly with a young man. She was standing in the doorway of the hut and the man was out of sight. Whatever it was that they were discussing, clearly they were both determined to have their way.

Finally, she said something and their tone got quieter and less menacing. In another moment, the young man entered the hut with the girl. His black 'pajamas', clung to him from the humidity and Jacob could feel the fear jump inside at the sight of him. In his fear he wanted to escape, in spite of the woman and her love, he wanted to move, to get up and to run.

But, too much time had passed; he had stayed there

too long. Something between them, something now growing inside of her had made it impossible for him to leave. He could feel the pain again in his leg. There too time had worked its way. A slow insidious infection, a demon had worked its way into his flesh, had eaten its way into the bone of his leg, had poisoned his blood.

He had been healing and for a time it had seemed that the wounded leg would be as it once had been. She had placed a bandage soaked in medicinal herbs on it, cleaned it, sang as she worked and smiled down at him. She sang with the music of the French melody.

But he had stayed too long and the shadow of infection would not lift, it would not go away. In spite of all she could do, it would not go away. He lay there again, helpless, wracked with fever.

He could see the AK-47.

Immediately his mind raced with a thousand possible scenarios. His memory was flooded with the film footage he had seen, of airmen shot down and captured, paraded through the streets of Hanoi, beaten and tormented by angry mobs. He thought of his wounds, that they would withhold treatment, that he would be tortured and left in a solitary concrete cell, alone, forgotten, given up for dead.

The young man in the black pajamas then stood over him and in the dimly lit room, stared down at him. His face smoldered with burning contempt. He barked out unintelligible words of abuse and rage. He poked at his ribs with the barrel of his weapon and motioned for him to get up off of the floor.

"Mao! Mao!" the young man ordered.

Unable to understand, he motioned to his leg in an attempt to bring the wound to the young man's attention but he continued to press his demand that he get up. He looked up again and saw the girl standing behind the young man. She placed her hand on the man's shoulder and moving close to him, spoke in quiet, seductive tones. She pressed herself against him. He turned to her and she pointed to a small bowl of rice, some drink and the mats that she had laid out for them. Taking his hand she managed to calm him and led him over to the mat. She knelt and offered the food to him. He squatted down in front of her, the rifle leaning on his shoulder with the butt against the floor of the hut and began eating the rice and drinking in succession, several long swallows from the cup. He continued to stare suspiciously at Jacob as he ate and drank. The girl then, came to him with a water bowl and a damp cloth and began to wipe his face and neck and to sing quietly in a near whisper a seductive lyric. In time, the young man relaxed his hold on the rifle and turned to her. He looked to be somewhat intoxicated, partially as a result of the drink and also, as a result of the girl's enchantment. He looked up at her with a sultry gaze and in a moment the two were lying together on the floor of the hut.

There in front of him, she allowed the young man to open her clothes. He was distracted and oblivious to Jacob and to the figure moving in the shadows behind him. As the young man lay on top of her and buried his head next to hers, the girl looked up at the shadow and then with mute silence, made eye contact with Jacob. Still in the shadows, the figure suddenly moved forward and through the low light of the cooking fire, Jacob caught a glimpse of his face looking calmly down on the two on the floor.

In the next instant, the figure reached forward with an outstretched hand and holding the 45 caliber automatic that had earlier been in Jacob's holster, fired point blank into the back of the young man's head.

The concussion of the blast sent a piercing sound that rang in Jacob's ears; dust blew up in a cloud from the floor, a deafening concussion that startled animals outside and sent them scurrying about in the darkness.

The boy's head lurched forward in response to the shot and a warm spray of blood and tissue splattered the girl who laid there pinned underneath him. Jacob felt certain that the old man would kill them both, kill the girl as well. She immediately cast the boy's limp body over on its back her own chest heaving as she breathed heavily and quickly climbed to her feet. She looked down at Jacob for a moment her eyes welled with tears and with fear at what he might think of her and what she had allowed the young soldier to do. Then quickly she began cleaning her face and body.

Now in the full light of the fire, the old man, held the pistol at his side. He reached over and handed it to Jacob in a nonchalant way and grabbed the body of the young man by the heels slung his rifle over his shoulder and slipped out of sight and into the darkness as if he were removing a pile of rubbish.

"My God…I remember it. I was there, I ejected and you, you and that old man you helped me." Jacob stepped toward her, moved closer to her as she looked up at him.

He was there at the tower in the truck; she was there now, looking at him. Jacob reached over to her and took her hand in his, felt an overwhelming desire to kiss her, hold her like a precious part of him, lost, desperately searched for and now found. He did not want to let her go.

She put up her other hand and held him at arms

length, her face compassionate but her eyes warning him as if to say, "You must not do this. You must see what I have to show you."

She then reached behind her dress and gently coaxed forward a child who had been hiding behind her. A small child whose face looked like his mother's, beautiful, innocent, but the eyes, the eyes were of his father. The little boy looked up at him, as he stood there in front of her one hand clinging to the folds of her dress smiling at Jacob. Hop ambled down from the seat down the running board and then onto the ground and jumped up to the boy. The boy put his hand on the dog's head playfully and smiled up at Jacob as if to ask if the dog were his.

Jacob was struck with a sudden sense of fear.

"Is he…I mean is he…?" Jacob tried to ask her but the words would not come. She simply looked up at him, peered into his eyes, his soul. She gazed into him looking for him to answer the question and to recall the rest of the story. She touched his hand, touched it again like she had before at the tavern and with her touch he began to see the rest of it, the rest of what had happened.

He felt himself roused in the darkness. The faint hint of a small fire caught his eyes as it licked at a small cooking pot. There bent over him was the old man who motioned and tried to get his attention. Early morning sunlight was beginning to make its way through the open hut and voices could again be heard outside. The old man whispered to him in hurried tones and helped him to his feet. The girl hurried over to him and she motioned for him to go with her. They stepped through an opening and made their way to an area a number of paces into the jungle where she had him slip into a shallow pit. Then, she quickly covered it with a mat that had been formed on a bamboo frame that was used to hold a few shallow wicker containers of rice.

Carefully he peered through the slits in the mat and tried to discern what was taking place. He could hear loud shouts and see a young VC regular, apparently an officer, shoving and prodding the old man all the time yelling into his bowed head with a rapid staccato of questions. The officer was angry and his words came forward in rapid succession, the foreign sounds unintelligible, not like words at all but like the sound of a tin can bouncing down a flight of stairs, a jumbled mass of emotion and frustration.

The old man spoke too softly to be heard but within minutes the girl appeared with Jacob's helmet and tags in an attempt to convince the officer that the body of a downed pilot had been recovered. She pointed to an area down wind from the huts and the officer quickly commanded several of his men to go with a boy to examine the body. Then taking the helmet and the tags, he ordered them into the hut and followed them in, examining the tags and the helmet.

It seemed that they were in the hut for quite a time when the men returned dragging the now putrefied body behind them. Time in the jungle heat had taken its toll on the remains and the odor of death and decay was strong even from his hiding place in the pit.

They called for the officer, who took one look at the body and apparently ordered them to return it downwind of the hut. He was reasonably certain that the ruse had worked and could hear them talking in more congenial tones.

Then, without warning, the officer's voice rose to an angry tone. It was clear he had discovered something that did not look right to him. Jacob could hear shuffling in the hut and the sounds of the cooking pot being kicked across the bare floor. The startled creatures all around him accented the commotion, singing in protest and flittering about. Soon the group emerged and the officer ordered his men to round up villagers and line them up.

A bedraggled clutch of scarred and frightened people emerged from the huts and the surrounding bush. They were ordered to sit in the dirt quietly with bowed heads and did so in mute detachment. The officer moved up and down the line, holding a small object between his thumb and four-finger of one hand and a small black book in the other.

For a few moments he addressed the group, and then began prodding each person in turn, looking at them and repeating his words. He was clearly trying to get an answer to something.

What the hell did he find? He could think of nothing small, or of consequence that he had left in the hut that would have betrayed his presence. He tried to think. His tags and other effects had been left with the body when they took his uniform. He looked down at his pistol. He had it in his hand, a fresh round in the chamber. As a notion came to him he was startled by a shot that rang out from the clearing just a few yards away. He looked up and through the cracks in the mat could see the slumped body of the boy. The protesting birds shot out and dove in and out of the trees and brush in a panicked frenzy.

He could see that the officer was now holding a pistol in his hand and was in turn holding each person at gunpoint. Then systematically holding the small object in front of them, pointing at the book that he had thrown in the dirt in front of them then, showing them the pistol and in reaction to their silence, shooting them one by one in the head. Cries from the crowd and wailing children were being silenced one by one as he sat there, hiding in the pit. He knew that the officer was no longer convinced that the body was that of a downed pilot. He had the body stripped and even though it was disfigured and bloated from the jungle heat he could see through the hoax. With the third shot, the officer turned his gun on the old man and was preparing to execute him when he could take it no longer.

"This shit has got to stop!" he whispered to himself as the urge to rise up from the pit and surrender welled up in him. He commanded his limbs to move to stand up from the pit and to surrender.

Covered with mud and filth he would do this, he would surrender and stop the shooting. He would be pulled from the pit, where he hid in anger and fear. He would come forward and be pulled from his hiding place.

He tried to move, to leave the pit, but in his weakness, in the infection that was consuming his leg he could not gather himself up to get out. He tried to cry out, tried to bring attention to himself, but could only lay there, crouched in the filth of the pit while they killed them.

The officer fired again and the old man lurched forward, blood from his temple flowed in gushing spasms as his heart pumped the remaining life from him.

Then Jacob caught a glint of light reflecting from the object in the officer's hand. He could see for the first time, the object that he was holding. The empty shell casing from the 45 automatic rested in his palm. The officer pushed it into the woman's face and muttered in contempt. He brought the pistol to bear on the side of her face; a face like a child, a child who without childhood, had aged well into the years that had been taken from her.

The officer clubbed her to the ground. In a daze, she was then made to sit in the village clearing and witness the continued beating and executions. Each person shot or stabbed in a wild frenzy of brutality and vengeance. The men then looted any usable items and burned the village to the ground.

It was as though this exhibition of violent inhumanity had been staged for his benefit and he sat there in the pit, overcome with fear and pain.

I want to live. I can't let them take me, kill me! I've got to get back to the ship! I want to be far from this place. This was not what I had intended, not what I expected it to be. I can't die; no I don't want to die! If only I hadn't taken that last pass over the target!

A great swell of guilt washed over him. He sobbed as the officer raised the pistol to the girl's head one last time. His only thought now was of the VC officer and his pistol and a small village and people whose names he did not know and whose lives he did not understand. He worked himself up onto his knees. He would not let himself be taken he could not let that happen. He was not prepared when the final shot rang out.

It was a hazy overcast sky, the kind of steamy gray that was part of the regular morning downpour that comes to the jungle. He looked up at it, his chest heaving with fear as he sat squatting in the pit, in an attempt to remain still, his blood saturated with adrenaline feeding his brain and his vision, which in the next several moments dimmed to darkness.

The young girl took his arm as if she knew that he had now come to this revelation. He looked at her.

She had been there with them, taking care of them there at the café. She was there too, waiting.

"I am sorry. I love you. I was afraid. I was a coward. I should have climbed up from that pit and let them take me! I'm sorry do you hear? I didn't want this to happen! I didn't want them to kill you!" he pleaded, begging for her to forgive him, to forgive his moment of weakness, his decision to trade her life for his.

He felt himself slip down to the ground, down to his knees, his hands together pleading, praying for her forgiveness. He sobbed, his shoulders heaving uncontrollably as the revelation of what he had been, what he had done and not done washed over him. He could feel the great weight of it on him, clinging to him pushing him down, crushing him to dust.

Before he could say another word the two of them were gone, drifting to the road leaving him alone under the rusting steel tower. He stood there for what seemed an eternity, unsure what to say or do.

"Don't leave me here alone! I need you; I want to go with you!"

There was only silence.

Chapter 14

The morning light had barely crept over the horizon. He had been there for a long time. He wasn't sure how long, but he knew it had been a long time. He did not know why he was so frightened, did not know what he would find but he was afraid of it. The realization of his connection to this place, the people he had seen, the ghosts that haunted him, all trying to tell him why he was there tormented him.

He thought of the man, his father, the pilot that he did not know, a face that he wanted to recall in full but could not...A man who had once been there for him, somewhere in a distant past. The old man, he had been there too… Somewhere off in the distance, like the road, a road that kept going on forever. A lonely cold strip of asphalt, like the airstrip, it met the horizon and then went on without end.

He laid his hand on the pistol tucked in its holster, gripped it, then let loose his grasp, reassured that it was there, that he had it with him should he need it. He did not know why it made him feel better but somehow it did. He walked slowly to the truck. Hop met him there, already up and about he stood there waiting for him. The dog whined quietly as Jacob opened the door.

"Quiet!" Jacob whispered, "I'm going to go find out what's in that hangar and I don't need you to stir up any trouble."

The dog responded by licking his jowls and bowing his head slightly in contrition in the way that dogs do when they know that they are addressing one another and do not wish to challenge another's order in the pack. He followed as Jacob made his way to the vehicle and together they drove to the hangar. He had managed to hide a pair of heavy cable cutters from the collection of tools he had used on the Mustang. He had kept them hidden under an old oil cloth that lay in the truck bed. He had thought about them now and again, thought about when the right time would come for him to use them, when there might be an opening. He would retrieve them to cut the chain on the hangar door.

He thought for a moment about what Gabe had said to him, about staying out of the hangar. He felt that he needed to know, that the time was now.

He drove to the hangar stopped and quietly pushed the door to the cab closed and then gathered the cutters up and made his way to the hangar door. He nearly stumbled over the dog as it darted past him in response as he reached for it. Hot coffee sloshed around in a cup he had filled from an old thermos that the old man kept in the front seat. It spilled onto his boots as he dodged the animal.

"Watch out dog! Keep an eye out for the old man." he whispered nervously as he put the tool to the chain in an effort to cut it in two.

Just as he was preparing to cut the chain a voice called

out to him from behind, "Hello funny dog." the boy said as he reached down to meet the animal who bounded toward him. Jacob recognized the boy; it was the child he had seen on the road, the child in the old beech that had nearly killed him.

"How did you get here sport?" Jacob asked.

"I don't know." The boy answered coyly as a child would if playing a guessing game, unaware that he was but a shadow.

"Did you come to see the flying lady?" the boy asked.

"The flying lady…?"

"Yes. You know, The Lady Who Flies up in the sky…" he said impatiently as he patted the dog on the head.

"You mean the lady who flies the old airplane?" he responded.

The boy tittered, "No silly, the lady who flies!" he responded as he hopped around the dog playfully.

Jacob grew irritated with the little boy. He had other worries now and wanted desperately to get inside the hangar.

"Look kid, I don't have time to play today, maybe you should come back when Gabe is around."

"You'll see." The little boy responded giggling with anticipation, ignoring Jacob's words, "It's a surprise."

The little boy walked over to the hangar, "You have to open it," the boy said puffing as he hung on the door of the hangar, "it's too hard for me…" Jacob grabbed the handle and with the cutters snapped through the chain lock then opened it with a shove.

The room was a dark cavernous space, much larger then he had imagined from the outside. A musty draft escaped through the opening and blew wafts of engine oil mixed with metal flecks and sawdust out through the door.

It was like a tomb, like a place that had been sealed long ago, its contents never again intended to be seen in the sunlight. There were shapes that sat quietly in the darkness, deep in the recesses and corners. Some were shrouded in canvas or old oil cloths; others were leaning on jacks or propped up with cinder blocks, their frames sagging.

He fumbled about for a moment in the darkness, reaching around the doorframe in an effort to find a light switch.

"No don't turn on the light!" the boy's voice called out to him.

"I can't see…"

"Don't turn on the light, you'll scare him away!" the boy replied, desperately.

"Scare who away?"

"Here, I'll hold your hand and you can stay with me." The little boy said this, his icy fingers slipping into Jacob's hand.

On one wall there hung pictures of aircraft. Many pictures dusty and tired hanging in worn frames, their photos dingy and dust covered with age.

The boy led him up to a single picture that stood there among them and proudly pointed to a single photograph.

"Look at this one." he said.

Jacob approached the picture and reaching up took it down from the nail on the wall. He brushed the cobwebs and dust away and then stared at the image in the faint light that crept in through the open doorway. It was the pilot. He was standing there with another figure, a small boy. The pilot's hand was resting on the boy his fingers threaded through the mop of hair on the youngster's head.

They were both there in front of an aircraft. It was the Mustang, its shining skin bright in the sunlight washed out in the grey of the black and white photograph. They stood there, under its upturned nose.

"It's me…" he said quietly.

"Surprise…!" the boy yelped with satisfaction. Hop sat and looked up at him, barked and panted in reply.

"Now look at this one!" the boy coaxed Jacob to another picture next to it.

He returned his gaze to the wall to another picture, covered in dust, and could see himself again, dressed in the clothes of a naval aviator a flight suit, he is standing on the ladder next to the aircraft the Phantom of his memory.

"It's mine…My aircraft! Where did you get this picture?" he asked.

"Surprise…!" the boy giggled again, playfully mocking Jacob's questions.

Jacob crouched down in front of the boy taking him by the shoulders, "Where did you get these?"

"I don't know." The boy said defiantly and pulled away and clutched the dog's neck swaying playfully back and forth.

He could see himself in the picture; the story of a last pass, a fateful decision to circle a second time not out of duty but out of frustration and anger and of a crew, whose fate had been in his hands, then a moment, the tiny contrails, withering fire from an unseen enemy.

That was what he was talking about… He wanted to know if I had seen him.

It was the thing, the personification of all men's doubts and indecisions, the result of a cascade of failures that piled up too quickly to resolve before the ground came up to meet you. It was too many passes over a target already rendered dead and benign by so much destruction.

He thought momentarily about the café, the faces of the men at the bar and in the booths sulking and a realization came to him. He remembered them, sitting in their flight suits and heavy boots waiting, waiting.

They're here too…They're here waiting…

The young woman, 'The Lady Who Flies', his great love, and the 'great wish', to be up there, to right his single moment of wrong, the wrong that had brought him here, the single moment of indecision.

Gabe was right when he said that they were there to 'fix things'…to fix the one thing. They were all there. He looked at the wall and at the pictures hanging there. He could see familiar faces, of pilots who had been circling and had come down to the tower, to find their respite then return to the sky to find their way.

The pilot…He had sinned too, Jacob thought, we both let it take us… He was sickened by it, the burden of his debt too much to bear written into a book of acts that he had been helpless to stop. The girl and his love, love that had not been strong enough for him to overcome his fear, not strong enough for him to climb from the pit and stop the killing, not strong enough to save her or the son that he never knew. It suddenly occurred to him that a great deal of time had passed since he had been there in the jungle, that a lifetime had slipped by and that he was much older now. That a lifetime had gone by and that the weight of what he had done had been with him for a long time.

"I told you, up in the sky…!" the boy said suddenly, as if reminding Jacob of something he was supposed to do.

"What…? What do you mean?" He responded.

"The lady who flies is up in the sky always."

"She has to come down sometime." Jacob responded, not knowing exactly what the boy was talking about but certain that all things that go up into the sky must come down at some point.

"She never comes down…" the boy said.

"The bad man wants to take her away." the boy whispered, looking around cautiously.

"What bad man…?"

"He wants to take her away…" the boy responded.

He wasn't sure who the boy was talking about but his words evoked a notion that the thing was at the center of it. He felt that he had seen the thing and his work many times. The plane that slammed into the earth as a pilot fought to regain control, the angry men who gave no quarter but shot him down as he struggled to free himself from the pilot's seat. He felt that Gabe had seen it too and the pilot and the others as well, the fear and panic of faces staring out from the windows of doomed bombers as they fell and spiraled down to their end, the impersonal, white smoke trailing rockets that screamed toward him like comets from the earth below, the tracers that flung themselves upward to tear away at a fuselage, countless flights and dark clouds, moments of forgetfulness and items overlooked on checklists, pilots coaxed to fly into dark clouds or beyond their capability, stupid pride, and the countless generations before, before flight and guns. He had been working for a long time, ever since a man first lifted the jawbone of an ass over his head in anger he had been working.

"When do you see the bad man?" Jacob asked in a determined tone his voice wavering with the prospect of his being there with them, hidden from view.

The boy spoke up, "He comes down... he lands and comes. He comes down and whistles for us to come to him."

"Do you ever call him have him come to you?"

"No, he doesn't come for anybody. He does what he wants." the boy said fearfully, "Except when the music is playing...He can't come here when the music is playing. He has to stay away."

"Gabe knows about this?"

"Yes." the boy responded.

"The people in town, they know about it too?"

"I guess so. They stay away."

"Are there more people out there waiting?"

"Yes, lots..."

"How many...?"

"I don't know, lots, you can see them on the road, mostly at night."

"On the road...?"

"Yes, out there!" the boy said and pointed outside.

"They have no place else to go." The boy shivered slightly as he knelt down next to the dog and stroked its flank with his hands.

Jacob felt his own pain and empathy for the souls on the road wandering thinking about what they could have done, about what they did that they should not have done. It's like that for them now, he thought. They've got nothing else, only the road.

Suddenly the boy stood up and looked about as if he had heard something there in the darkness. "Time to go now dog..." the boy said as he backed away toward the door.

"Wait, wait you can stay here if you like, I want to talk to you some more."

"No, I have to go now…" the boy replied then giggled nervously and began singing quietly, "You can't come…You can't come." again, like before in a sing-song playful response.

Jacob stopped abruptly as if suddenly the sound that had made the boy fearful had come to his attention. Instinctively he reached for the pistol cradled against his ribs and turned as the boy disappeared.

"Nein…! Nein! Schießen Sie nicht!" a voice called out sharply.

Jacob stopped, startled and looked about following the sound of the stranger's voice, looking for its source.

"Open the door my friend…" the voice called.

Jacob could feel the tension rise up in him something inside him telling him that he should return to the diner and ignore the voice coming from the dark corner of the hangar. The dog began to growl a low threatening warning to Jacob as he stepped forward toward the sound of the stranger's voice.

Chapter 15

"Ah das hund." the stranger called out in a soothing tone, "The dog, leave the dog there please!"

"Hop...Stay here." Jacob ordered as he continued forward. The dog sat back on his haunches but continued to growl nervously.

"The dog, he does not like me I think...?" the stranger warned, "He is a good dog, he and I are old enemies I'm afraid."

The windows had been boarded over with odd sections of plywood. He could make out a section of corrugated steel that had been cut with a torch into a makeshift door, fastened with hinges. A small square hole had been cut into it the opening large enough for a man to slip his head and a shoulder through. The door blocked the entrance to a small room. It was like a small makeshift cell that housed a single occupant.

"Wo ist der Oberst?" The voice asked.

"What? Who is it? Who's there...?" Jacob called out in the darkness.

"Ah. Sprechen Sie Englisch?" The voice responded. "Das ist gut! Hello friend." The voice replied in stiff English.

Jacob approached the door and looked over at the occupant of the cell.

"Who are you? What are you doing here?" he asked as he inspected the doorframe and peered back at the small face looking back at him through the hole in the door.

"My friend." the voice called back with a sigh of relief. "My friend you have come. Finally someone has come, would you be so kind friend as to lift the lock and open the door?"

Jacob could just see his face in the darkness of the cell, a young man he appeared clean and well groomed.

"Looks like you've gotten yourself in a real spot here friend? Who are you and how'd you end up in here?" Jacob could barely make out the form in the darkness.

"We are friends, old friends I think?" the voice replied.

"I can't say that I remember you." Jacob replied suspiciously.

"I am an old friend of the Colonel's. Surely he has spoken to you about me?" the voice replied.

"No, he didn't. How come you're locked up in there?"

The young face pressed closer and strained a glance past Jacob to the hangar door.

"Are you alone my friend?" he asked nervously his eyes peering from side to side.

"Yeah, I'm alone."

"Ein unkluger Fehler... I ist ängstlich, dass ich unfaller die Tür..! Oh erbärmlich, Englisch verschlossen hat… Yes?" the young man explained then caught himself realizing that he had slipped back into German, "I am afraid that I accidentally shut my self in here."

"Why are you in there? Where are you from?" Jacob asked him, unsure of the young man's explanation.

"Well you see my friend, I had a problem with my aircraft, the, the, ah…Die Kraftstoffpumpe hat versagt, Oh the fuel pump, it was not working properly and I had to land."

"And where is your aircraft?" Jacob asked as he glanced over his shoulder.

The boy quickly shifted his eyes to the pistol while Jacob's head was turned and calculated his next response.

"Mein Kämpfer, mein Faulke Wolfe 190…" the young man whispered to himself thinking about what he would say in English. "Yes my aircraft is over there I think?" He pointed to a rusting heap sitting sadly in one corner of the hangar.

"Doubt that friend, looks to me that that one has been a wreck for quite a while; older than you and me put together I'd say."

The boy pressed against the opening, straining his eyes.

"Yes, yes you are correct. I don't think it is mine. Would it be possible for you to assist me with this door? I have been in here for some time and well it would be quite an embarrassment for me if the Colonel should find me in this situation." The young man smiled at Jacob, a nervous smile as if hiding something from him.

"So how long have you been in there, anyway?"

"Oh…a long time I am afraid. I have been waiting for someone to come and let me out, now you are here with the key. So, you can let me out and we can go together to find my aircraft. That would be good, yes?"

Jacob thought about the answer. He knew that Gabe had been in and out of the hangar dozens of times and never mentioned a prisoner locked inside. He thought too about the dark aircraft he had seen, the aircraft that he had heard before off in the distance, never landing at the field but remained alone away from their runway.

"Look friend, I'd like to help you out, but I don't have any key."

"No…No…my friend, it is not a key, it is…" the young man continued to look about, showing impatience as he spoke under his breath, "Dieser Idiot! Ich werde weiter Spiele spielen! Wie werde ich dies zu ihm sagen?" he whispered to himself as he struggled to find the right words to convince Jacob to open the door.

Then, just as the young man began to speak, Jacob felt it. Not a sound but a feeling, a low bass vibration that shook the walls and floor of the hangar with a low drumming rhythm. He could feel it rise up through him rumbling like a tremor that passed through his body that grew but then faded.

A bird that had been sitting on a low beam overhead skittered away and made a low screech hiding further on a higher frame. Hop whimpered and shifted nervously from behind him at the hangar entrance.

Jacob looked down at the coffee in the cup and could see the liquid in it oscillate as the vibration came forth again this time growing into a sound that shook the foundation of the hangar with a heavy mechanical drone that made the metal skin shudder.

"Verdammen Sie! Ich muss von hier aussteigen! Es kommt!" the young man blurted out as he poked his fingers through the hole in the door beckoning Jacob to let him out. "My friend, you must let me out of here! You must let me out! I must get out of here!" the young man called to him desperately.

Jacob looked down at the door. It had no lock or latch. The door handle was a simple piece of angle iron welded to the steel. There were two additional pieces of iron bent in L shaped retainers welded over the door, they hung on the door and cradled a thin wooden cross that braced it against the frame holding it fast. The cross was simple, just two pieces of wood bound together. It looked like a makeshift grave marker, thrown together in haste, a simple marker that one would drive into the ground with the end of a shovel to mark some unknown person now dead and gone, their name never to be known or spoken of again.

The rumbling came again, this time louder.

"What the hell was that…? Look, I don't know what you're talking about here? You could pull this door open with no trouble. This piece of wood just needs to be lifted up like this."

Jacob reached down to lift the wooden rod from the retainers. It felt heavy, too heavy to lift, as if it had been welded to the door. He pushed hard against it. The wooden cross held the door fast to the frame and resisted his weight. "Man, that's tight!" he said to himself as the door continued to resist his attempts to break the barrier off.

"Maybe a bullet," he said as he reached for the pistol.

"Nein! Nein! Schießen Sie nicht!" the young man yelled.

"No! My friend, please no shooting! This will not work! You will wake the Colonel!"

"What do you want me to do?"

"You must lift it off…" the young man said frantically.

"What the hell are you saying?"

"You must lift the wooden barrier off. Do you know this?" the boy spoke quickly in broken English trying to give Jacob the clue.

"It's too heavy for me…Maybe if you reached through the window?" Jacob asked.

"Nien! I cannot touch it. You must lift it yourself! Yes! You must do this my friend! Quickly now, there isn't much time!" the young man pleaded.

"What the hell for…?" Jacob asked, irritated.

"Please! Please! There is no time to explain it, please just do this!" the stranger begged.

Jacob thought about it, the young man's pleading tone and the odd sound emanating from outside. "What the hell are you doing here? You tell me then we talk about chapter and verse!"

"I am your friend. I am the Colonel's friend. You must let me out of here. It was…it was a mistake you see, to leave me in here."

"Thought you said you locked yourself in?" Jacob asked suspiciously.

"Yah, this is true…" the boy replied, nervously.

"How'd you get this in place on your own?"

As Jacob asked the question, the sound came again. The rumbling shook the ground harder, and caused the foundation of the hangar to shiver. A cascade of dust drifted down and settled at Jacob's feet.

"My friend, it is coming, you must let me out!"

"What is it?"

"It is my prize! A great, thing…You must let me out, to protect you from it…To protect the Colonel… Please!"

Jacob did not know what he should do. The sound raised fear in him. A fear he could not explain. There was something about it that seemed familiar. He felt more fear about what the sound could mean then what it could do.

"Why don't you do this yourself?" he asked.

"I, I cannot…" the stranger replied.

"And why is that friend? If that's all it takes to get you out of here you could have been out a long time ago. What say you tell me the truth?"

"Listen, my friend, I must warn you," the young officer said as he motioned for Jacob to come closer, his eyes darting about, his breathing laboring under the panic that Jacob could see building in his eyes.

"Your Colonel, he has lost his senses. I landed here a long time ago, like you I think? I landed here and your Gabriel, he locked me in here. He is mad you see. He wants my prize for himself!"

The young officer reached through the window suddenly grabbing Jacob by the collar and pulling him closer, "Don't you see my friend, you must let me out. Soon you will be locked in here too and it will be too late!"

In the sickening anxiety, in the fear he began to recall words that the pilot had said, that he was doing something that he should not, but he could not stop himself, he felt that he must do it in order to understand. That he was releasing something that must be set free. Something that must be let loose in order to bring it out into the light of day, to fight it and put it down and not to simply let it remain, locked away, hidden from view. In desperation and confusion he began to lift the wooden brace.

He suddenly could remember a hospital room a white, stark room, the quiet nocturne playing, a dark jungle, in a small dark hut, somewhere, someone had watched over him as he slept in his sweating flight suit writhing slowly with dull pain and morphine. He recalled the nuns, the black on white habits as they prayed over him as he lay in a hospital bed, their olive skinned and almond eyed faces, solemn in the half light as he laid there sick with infection and fever.

He could see in his mind's eye their faces looking down on him as he laid there.

"Yes! Yes my friend!" the voice of the stranger spoke up as the wooden barrier began to slip from its moorings. The young man yelled as he slammed on the door, "Please my friend…!"

Jacob looked down as the wood that held the door suddenly gave way, breaking in two at the center and dropping to the ground. The door swung open.

He was not at all what Jacob had expected. He was but a boy, almost a child probably no more than eighteen. He was slight of build, maybe 130 pounds; thin with a complexion that was pale, his features soft and effeminate. He was no more than 5 feet tall. Jacob wondered how he could reach the rudder pedals let alone handle an aircraft. Suddenly the boy's demeanor changed, he was now quiet, stoic a young officer under control. The boy opened the collar of his flight suit and brushed his hand through a shock of blonde almost white hair that stood in a stiff mass like a brush on top of his head. It was closely cropped at the sides, tight to his scalp and exposed tiny almost fragile ears. He was no longer the young man pleading with him to be set free but a young aristocrat who stood there defiantly and walked from the cell with a swagger as he slipped on a peaked hat, its bill shining with polished black celluloid, the corded band and grey flannel piping neatly brushed for inspection. He wore a grey uniform, a German Luftwaffe officer's uniform. It was impeccable and fit him with neat, perfectly tailored precision. He wore a string of decorations over the pocket of his coat; the neck tightly buttoned at the top and the iron cross prominently displayed itself at the base of the collar, a decoration like those he remembered in his room in the diner. He remained motionless, quiet and erect in his pose, his arms crossed confidently across his chest. It was as if he had just emerged from an officer's quarters, not the dingy bowels of the cell he had been imprisoned in just moments before. He said nothing but walked forward in a determined stride, a defiant prince who had been imprisoned and was now released, coming forward to claim his rightful title. Jacob let him slip past then spoke to him.

"Ok friend I let you out now maybe you could repay the favor and let me know what that noise is?"

The boy ignored his question and walked out toward the doorway of the hangar, marching forward looking out toward the runway, brushing the cobwebs from his uniform with a handkerchief that he produced from within his coat. He peered out in the dim haze as if looking for something.

"It is none of your concern." the boy responded dispassionately calling back to him and raising a hand as if to hush his next question before he had the opportunity to ask it.

He moved out on to the concrete of the tarmac toward an approaching, unseen object, looking up as he walked, searching the sky in anticipation. Jacob could hear his black boots clapping on the concrete and echoing in the morning mist as his shape drifted in and out with the wisps of ground fog.

The young officer looked around inspecting the gloom with satisfaction then glared into space as if thinking to himself, trying to recall something, his eyes like two small blued steel bearings cold and piercing with their defiance.

After a moment the boy appeared to recognize what he was looking for and stood quietly waiting.

"Ah. Was ein Ding der Schönheit. Es ist wahr ein silberner Teufel!" the officer said to himself as he reached out into the empty space and appeared to brush his hand over the invisible metal skin.

What the hell is he doing? Jacob thought.

Again, the sound, this time more familiar, it rumbled like an approaching freight train, shaking the ground under them, a loud mechanical rumbling like great engines laboring to produce power.

"Ah. Mein Engel kommt!" the young Officer whispered to himself.

Jacob thought that he had made a mistake, he remembered Gabe's words to him about the hangar and that he was not to go in there.

Instinctively he held up the pistol, his hand clutching the grip his finger resting on the trigger as he pointed it toward the young officer.

"I don't know what this is about friend but I think it's time you went back to your room!"

"I am sorry but I am already late for a very important engagement." the young man responded as he stood waiting for the unseen visitor.

"Don't do it! Don't go any farther! I'll put a bullet in you…" Jacob warned.

"Vielen Dank Kapitän. Ich möchte bleiben und möchte reden aber ich muss jetzt gehen!" the young officer called out, smiling sadistically as he marched out toward the sound through the gloom.

Jacob pulled the trigger and watched as the round passed through the young officer and spun off into space. The sound of the shot was deafening and reverberated through the corrugated steel ceiling of the hangar. Hop let out a yelp and barked frantically in pain, Jacob's ears rang with pain at the sharp report of the pistol as he fired several more times.

The young boy laughed out loud, then turned round, faced him and smiled. His eyes were sharp and filled with lust, a powerful burning gaze that set Jacob back with fear. The boy walked a few more steps as the sound approached them.

Within moments, there came the whine of a fighter, its engine screaming like an angry buzz saw. It flashed past them and disappeared into the haze. It turned sharply in an effort to line up with the runway. It quickly disappeared again then within a few moments reappeared from the cloud ceiling; its engine throttled back, its flaps down, the landing gear extended. Cautiously he followed the boy to the sound and could see clearly the markings on the wings, fuselage and tail as the plane slowed and passed low in front of them. He could see the mottled grey black camouflage paint and the paned glass of its canopy as it passed.

He could feel the tingle rise in his spine as the aircraft touched down and then taxied slowly to the tarmac in front of the hangar. The rudder deflected suddenly as the plane approach and the aircraft responded by spinning round to face away from him blowing dust and debris kicked up from the prop wash as the aircraft turned. The blowing subsided as the engine shutdown and reeled to a stop.

Instinctively Hop ran for a darkened corner by the hangar slipping behind a wing section that sat propped up against the outside wall. Jacob stood silently and lowered the pistol as the aircraft settled to a stop. It sat silently for several moments as if waiting for an attendant to come forward and wave an all clear. Then the canopy slid open. Jacob could see no one in the cockpit.

The young officer approached the aircraft and deftly swung himself up onto its wing. Two gloved hands grasped the top front of the windscreen then he calmly stepped into the seat and then looked back at Jacob with an arrogant self-assurance.

"Thank you for releasing me Captain. I will see you soon again, I think?" The stranger turned and stepped down inside of the fuselage and buckled himself in.

The sound returned and the young officer moved quickly, closing the canopy. The engine of the grey fighter spun up and started, throttled and moved off toward the runway, toward the rumbling that was echoing in the distance.

Hop moved back further under the wing and lay there whining as Jacob ran to the tarmac and looked after it.

The bellowing roar returned and he looked up and around him not sure where it was coming from. It seemed to be all around him, like a great host of cavalry, approaching at full gallop from all directions. He took several more steps and looked up to the sky, and strained his eyes in an effort to see the source of the sound through the grey marbled overcast.

Unable to see it he returned his attention to the fighter, now taxing to the runway, almost on it. He looked up in reaction to the bellowing rumble and could see emerging from the low cloud the dark form of a huge aircraft. It could barely be seen through the mist, rumbling and waggling as it struggled to remain airborne, its pilot probing for the ground for a place to land. It appeared to be on a heading right over the runway. An eerie, hopeless sight the form struggled like a dying bird and slipped in and out of the clouds, emerging then disappearing as it struggled in the grasp of the next wisp of moisture. It then dropped lower and its form became clear. It was an archaic, drab green giant belching smoke and hanging on its propellers in an effort to remain airborne.

"Jesus what the hell is it?" he yelled over the deafening sound.

Then as it cleared the cloud layer and drifted lower, he could see what it was. He knew its silhouette as well as he knew his own face and yet he was dumbfounded, shocked by its form, out of place, it, was like the Mustang. They were not supposed to be there. He felt compelled to call out to it, call it by name as it broke out.

"B-17 Flying Fortress…" he mouthed the words to himself in reaction as it rumbled toward them.

Black smoke poured out of all but one of its four engines. Three of the engines were running but clearly they were laboring and clanking with the rasping sounds of broken metal that could be heard over the rumbling exhaust.

He stood in a cold paralyzing fear as the size and sound of its approach gripped him with panicked confusion.

The plane was far too heavy to land but was badly damaged with dozens of holes in the fuselage and tail section all streaming oily trails of thick smoke. In its condition there seemed little doubt that it would have to land, it was committed. It hung on to its remaining airspeed as it approached the end of the runway. Then, within moments the form was on them, off course and headed for the diner.

Hop suddenly darted out from his hiding place and ran in the direction of the sound. Jacob ran after him as the dog ran furiously past and onto the runway.

"Hop…! Get back here!" he yelled as he ran after it. He approached the runway, closing on the animal; he could see a grey flash from the corner of his eye.

Within an instant Jacob caught up to the dog and just managed to snatch it away tumbling and rolling past the spinning propeller of the fighter as it passed over them, missing the blades by only inches. He lay there, breathing heavily holding the dog in both hands as it squirmed and yelped in protest and looked about frantically for another place to hide.

The fighter climbed above them and wheeled about in a long lazy arc circling in behind the monstrous bomber.

Jacob looked up at the shadow and caught a glimpse of its nose. The art form stenciled there on the aircraft was the figure of a woman. Though he could only make out a sketchy outline, only the eyes stood out, beckoning, seemingly following him with their gaze as the smoking giant passed by. He could hear the whine of the fighter as it began to close its turn and dive down to pass over them in pursuit of the bomber.

In a single motion, Jacob fell to the ground in an effort to avoid being hit as the dark form screamed past them.

It climbed up to position itself behind the bomber, the sound of their engines mingling a frantic scream and a deafening, bellowing roar. Then, suddenly as he braced for the impact of the crash, the instant when he expected to hear the terrible grinding of metal against pavement and the explosion that he was sure was to come, all was silent.

Jacob rose to his knees and looked out to the end of the runway. Like a phantom the huge ghost that had appeared before them and its pursuer abruptly disappeared without a sound.

"Jesus Christ! Hop! You damn stupid dog, you nearly got us killed!" He tucked the dog under his arm and pulled himself to his feet.

"What the hell are you trying to do?" Jacob yelled as the dog stared out in the direction of the fading engines.

Jacob took the dog and walked to the hangar door.

He felt sick with anxiety and frustration. "You damn idiot!" he said, admonishing himself as he approached the door with the dog in tow, "You really did it. Damnit! I know better. Damn…Damnit!" he yelled as he kicked an old tire and sent it wobbling across the floor of the service bay.

Then the air was filled again with sound, the strains of an old gospel hymn that like the old bomber shook the foundation and the galvanized walls and vibrated and echoed with the bellowing wails of four part harmony and a banjo-bluegrass quartet. Jacob covered his ears with his hands in an effort to shut out the loud painful cacophony of music. He was trying to block the sound, lurching forward, staggering around the hangar floor; his hands over his ears. Jacob looked at the empty room, and shook with panic under the blare of the music. He could see the thin transparent images of young men, fliers their faces contorted into gaunt, hideous images. A pilot, his eyes glazed with shock, his jaw unhinged hung loose from the flesh of his face as he screamed in agony, his hair, blackened and burned with blue black blisters of heat and fire stuck out from his seared hair and scalp. Their uniforms burned away as if under the tremendous heat of a furnace. Some stood shaking as if they had contacted a live power line and were being electrocuted. Then a great flash and concussion as if from a cloud of propane gas that had been ignited. It shook the building and knocked Jacob to the ground. In an instant all of it was gone, only the smell of sulfur and burning flesh remained.

Jacob sat there stunned. He was alone, more alone than he imagined that he had ever been. The weight of it, of letting the thing out was on him; he had been foolish and afraid and had let him out. Hop sat next to him on the floor, licking his face, whining in consolation.

I let him out. I know why Gabe said not to come in here, he thought. Jacob thought of what he would say, how he would explain what he had done. There would be no explanation that would be satisfactory. There would be no excuses. He knew that what he had done was a terrible thing, a thing that had come from his fear his indecision in a moment.

It's out now. It will come for them, he thought.

He sat down on an old wooden box holding his head in his hands, frightened and confused.

The Lady Who Flies, he thought.

Chapter 16

He sat there for a long time. The moments passed and the music from the radio poured over him. He was alone.

He recalled the handful of clues that had been presented to him, the sound of an aircraft engine, distant lonely in the night, the bullet holes in the Mustang's wing, the pictures, the pilot and now the stranger. They were all pieces of the mystery that was playing out for him. He wondered for a moment if he had not been meant to release the German, if it were not just another part of a larger plan for him, something that he was to play out. Something beyond his control.

He thought about the notion that the world had been put into motion a long time ago and that the events that take place, the struggles with fear and anger, desire and love, loyalty and deceit were in fact a part of a winding down of all that had been set spinning in the beginning. He wondered if indeed there were truly any choices that a man can make or if in fact all of them had been made for him. He did not want to believe that. He did not want to believe that there was a world into which a man could not impose himself. He did not want to believe it.

The light of the sun had hidden itself behind a layer of thick grey overcast and slipped almost entirely from the horizon. The wind in the trees began to blow. It blew in steady, rhythmic gusts, as if humming in time with the plaintive gospel strains that rang out from the radio. It caused the rafters to creak and moan as if the spirits from the metal corpses that lay hidden inside the hangar were speaking to him, trying to tell him something. Stray metal sheets, the remains of control surfaces that had once graced airframes, shook and rattled as drafts passed through open gaps in the window frames and from under the hangar door.

It has been that way from the beginning, he thought, they have always talked to me, every one of them, each in its own way, speaking its own way, talking to me through the stick and the pedals, the vibrations in the seat, the hum of the engine, each one speaking, though in different tones, but all speaking.

He thought about the images that had come to him in this place. They were all speaking to him, trying desperately to lead him to the end of the road, to a clearing in the clouds, to a runway, a place to land and to rest. He felt angry about what had happened and that he had been fooled. He felt foolish that he had listened to the boy and that he had panicked. He was sick with remorse at what he had done. He thought of what Gabe had said and what the pilot had told him. He wondered if this was what the pilot had been looking for, the thing that was not to be set free. It was something that Gabe had intended to be held there, not to escape, not to be airborne. I was a fool, he thought. He wanted to go, to leave. He knew that Gabe must have heard the shots and the sounds of the aircraft. He did not know what he would do. It occurred to him that if the Mustang were in there, repaired, ready to fly that he could try to pull it out of the hangar, try to get it off of the ground, try to leave with it.

He thought again about the girl, the jungle and the pit.

He walked over to the door again, looked for a light switch. He reached up and put his hand on the doorframe, weighing his indecision and the impulse to turn on the light, to see what had been hidden from him, to confirm all that he suspected he would find, to see the inside for what it was and to confront the reality of it. He was not certain that it was even in there, though he could imagine it, he could see himself standing there with it, it's nose pointed up to the sky, brushing his fingertips over the freshly painted metal skin. He imagined himself flying it, sitting in the cockpit up in the sky, the instruments singing, the airframe buffeting in heavy turbulence, his hands sweating and his legs cold and unable to move against the protests of the rudder pedals. He imagined how frightened he would be, how the air rushing past him so fast and the controls so sensitive and the engine so great and powerful would be beyond his ability to control it.

It would kill me, he thought. He thought of the fear, the cold impersonal moment, a bounce of turbulence that would make the panic rise up in him. He knew he would panic, struggle with it, fight to get down to earth to be safe. He did not want to fly it. It would be too much…It would kill him.

He thought about its owner, the pilot, his father flying it, trying to protect The Lady Who Flies and all the others. He thought that he must have been quite a man to have mastered such a machine.

He must be quite a man…He would never have been fooled…He would never have been so careless…

He could hardly believe that the drunken stranger he had pulled from the truck was the same man. He was sickened by it, sickened with his own inadequacy and fear, his own lack of ability, his own cowardice. He remembered his father, a man killed while he was but a very young man, a man who carried the burden of miscalculation and mistake on his shoulders. He could see him now, clearly. He could see his eyes, the pilot's eyes.

Men are free to make their own decisions, he thought.

He imagined the man who had carried the moment of self indulgent dozing and inattention that had allowed the German to come in and cut the bomber to pieces. It had happened in an instant, in a single instant, diving through the clouds, guns boring holes in the helpless giant, all of them in screaming and panic as they struggled to free themselves from the centripetal force pushing them with unseen hands against the inside of the dying aircraft. It had been a single helpless moment of cruelty and inaction that he had carried with him. It had held him down, made him old and drawn, tired and impotent. It had been a reminder that stayed with him and came to him every time he climbed into a cockpit.

The lone wire, the unseen obstacle that had taken him had been the last miscalculation. He clipped it as he had missed the flash of the German fighter, in a moment of inattention. Now the man was living in his purgatory, an endless series of flights to chase down the demon that had brought down his comrades.

Men do make their own mistakes, their own compromises and failures. Men are men, not gods nor angels…

Then another thought, his own purgatory, a second pass over the target, a self-indulgent desire to kill to make the area clear of an unseen enemy, to satisfy his lust to burn them to feel satisfaction and power in killing. He thought of his plane, the Stearman, he wanted to take it, to leave, to get away from the ghosts and return to wherever he had been. He reached for the light switch as a hand reached out and grasped his.

"Didn't I tell you not to come in here?" Gabe's voice called out to him in the darkness. He was holding the weapon in his other hand.

"You ought not to play with firearms son." he said as he turned the butt toward Jacob, "Here put this thing away. Won't help you none with him anyway." Jacob took the weapon, the gun that had given him away and placed its cold frame in his hand.

Jacob scrambled for an explanation as he returned the pistol to its holster, "It was the damn dog! He ran out here and I thought you were in trouble."

Gabe looked down at Hop as if asking for an explanation. The dog sat looking up at him perplexed.

"Both of you are too nosey for your own good!" he said as he picked up the remains of the cross a piece in each hand and stood silently as if deep in contemplation.

"He'll be back." Gabe replied. He seemed preoccupied with his thoughts about the situation his tone belying some deep agitation, angry in the way that a father is angry with a miscreant child.

"So you let him talk you into letting him out?" the old man grumbled as he walked to the light switch preoccupied, irritated, thinking of what he would do next.

"He let himself out, I was just talking to him and the door opened. I didn't do anything."

"Don't lie to me son. That bastard was locked up in there and you let him out."

"You're wrong Pop! I told you the guy let himself out!" Jacob protested his voice steeped with anger and frustration, sickened with his own foolishness, defending his lie.

"You let him out boy. You let yourself get tied up with his words. You let him distract you and talk you into giving him the key."

"What key? Look at that door, there's no lock on it. That wood was the only thing holding it closed. If you wanted him locked up you should have put a lock on the door!" Jacob responded as he walked toward the vacant cell.

"Besides what right do you have holding somebody against their will?"

"You don't know what you're talking about boy." Gabe said his words quiet and ominous.

"Well, why don't you tell me what I'm dealing with then? Seems everything around here has to be a secret with you! I'm tired of being the only one left out of the picture here."

"You don't understand. You are the only one in the picture boy!" the old man blurted out the words, then caught himself.

"So tell me, what is that supposed to mean? I went to the tower. I saw the girl. I came here and yeah I broke the lock and came in here because I had an idea that I would get the answers. Instead, it only made things worse!"

Jacob stood there in the darkness, "You don't have it in here do you Pop? You don't have the answers locked up in this hangar do you? You want me to stay here. You want me locked up in there with all your other junk just like that German!"

"You…? No son, I don't want you here."

"Then what the hell am I supposed to do old man?"

"Look son, this is the last place, the last stop! Do you understand? I don't want you to keep coming back here; I want you to go on home."

"What is this place?"

"It's a place for waiting."

"Waiting for what?" Jacob asked.

The old man stood there his hand on the switch, pulling things together in an effort to work off his frustration as he spoke, "Sometimes a guy gets put in a position to do something. Something he doesn't want to do. There are things that happen, a lot of bad things, we don't ask for them but they are there. We have to make choices, don't want to do it but we have to. We have to leave the people and things we love and do things that we don't want to do, things that men shouldn't have to do. We aren't allowed to ask questions, to think about why it is that way, only that we have to do them. People get mixed up in things. They get tied into us, what we do, who we know; others just make stupid mistakes, bad decisions and end up here."

"But what about them…? What about that bomber…? That wreck smoking and him flying off after it?"

"They're like everybody else, trying to find their way. As for him, he's a whole lot of trouble. I caught him in there the other night, had him in there, thought that would be enough to keep him. It wasn't enough…Should have known that it wouldn't be. I should have known that you're being here and him, locked up in there…I should have known better..." Gabe said, as if talking to himself.

"You're not making any sense Dad! There was no lock on the door!"

Gabe did not reply but stood there for a moment deep in thought, weighing his options considering the next move. It was as though a plan that had been thought out and put in motion had suddenly run into an obstacle and had to be changed in some dramatic way.

"Who the hell was that guy?" Jacob asked, exasperated with the situation and the lack of response.

"So, you want to see what's in here boy?" the old man asked his voice tainted with anger and impatience.

Jacob was not certain he wanted to know. He was thinking about what would be there, what he would be asked to see and what he might have to do.

"Yeah…Sure," he responded as if he were being put to a dare, "Let's see."

Gabe said nothing as he reached out in the darkness for the switch. He grabbed it then paused and looked back at Jacob, "You best be ready to take this all the way son. Once you've seen it, there ain't no coming back."

Gabe flipped the switch and the overhead lighting buzzed and flickered in protest then came to life flashing blue, grey illumination over the shapes and flooded the room with the glare of industrial florescent tubes. The light opened the room before him. Hop trotted in confidently.

Jacob leaned against the doorframe, stunned with what he saw. The floor was covered with dust, dirt and cracked concrete, undisturbed by shoes, reflecting in dull tones from the light above. There were workbenches, tools and power machinery covered with dust and age, rusted parts and machines that had not seen a single revolution in years. Slowly he walked past the old man and crept into the room. He stared silently at stacks of aircraft sections, wings and propellers lining the walls, once living, now dead and covered with cobwebs and dirt. There was no sign of activity, no work to recover them. They were as they had been; the rusting hulks of aircraft. Several of the machines he recognized, many he did not. It was as if he had stumbled upon an attic of tired memories, forgotten over many years, the lost inventory of a long dead collector. They faced forward; their oil stained bellies and corroded skins rotting away. Exposed corpses covered in scratches and dents, gaping holes in canvas skins, mice crawling frantically through their bodies in an effort to escape the stark lights that bathed the room with an eerie glow. He stared at them and thought of the sounds that had emanated from the hangar, of an old man working throughout the night, laboring in the darkness.

"What is this…Some kind of joke?" Jacob said to himself.

"It's no joke boy."

He looked further and his eyes settled on a single form that sat alone in a corner of the hangar. It was a single lone aircraft that sat there, away from the rest. It sat there exposed, all but the nose which had a tarp positioned over it, protecting something underneath. He could hear the flutter of wings overhead and watched as a white owl flew down from a rafter high overhead and landed near him. Hop cautiously approached it, his nose sniffing and tail twitching with excitement. The bird totally out of character stood quietly looking at Jacob, undaunted by the dog's interest.

"It doesn't look like the old bird is interested in you boy."

Instinctively he bent down and the bird hopped up on his forearm. He held it up for a closer look.

"So you want to tell me what's going on here professor?" The bird winked and stared past him disinterested and then, leapt from his arm with a single motion glided to the rafters and returned to his perch.

Jacob brushed his hand on his pants and walked slowly toward the machine, touching wings and tires, propeller and cowling.

He reached up and pulled an oily tarp that had been covering the cowling off to expose the nose of the aircraft.

The silver ghost stood completely exposed before them, its shining metallic skin gleaming with confidence, its air intake smiling under the nose with deadly intent. It was the Mustang he had exhumed from the meadow, the aircraft in his dream. It stood in mute silence, its every detail restored.

"My God…" Jacob whispered, "How the hell did you get that wreck back together?"

He strained to make out in the flickering overhead light the graphic design painted on the nose of the aircraft. He could just make out the bright red and black shadowed lettering stenciled in comic script on the side of the cowling.

'JACOB'S LADDER'

The nose blurted out the words on its side, in large bold strokes that arched over a cartoon of a young man who stood hanging onto a radio antenna by one foot and a handhold, and in the other hand clutched a small model airplane, other planes circling like angry wasps about his head.

"I fix things… That's what I do…" the old man replied.

Jacob was overcome with disbelief dumbstruck, unable to put together the reference and the circumstances of the plane and his own past. He was becoming sick, fearful at a realization that he had previously considered but had resisted.

Gabe made his way up on to the wing, his back and aging legs protesting under his weight and peered into the cockpit of the Mustang searching the inside as if looking for something.

"How the hell did you get that plane put together? It was a damn mess!" Jacob asked again as Gabe looked through the interior of the cockpit. Then suddenly he stopped his search and looked down at Jacob, "So you have it I take it?"

"Have what?"

"You know what. It belongs in here. I asked for everything to be brought back and you said you did. Now that you've seen it, I want you to hand it over." Gabe commanded.

He thought for several moments then realized what he was asking for. Sheepishly he produced the photograph from his pocket, "Here, I…well I saw it with the wreck and kept it. I thought it wouldn't matter if I kept it, I don't know why I did."

The old man squatted down on the wing, reached down and snatched the picture from his hand, "Didn't I tell you to get everything boy, to bring everything to me?"

Jacob stood motionless, at first unable to reply then spoke, "So who is she?"

"Who do you think boy?" the old man asked in reply.

"She looks a lot like the picture I saw on the side of the bomber."

"Who do you think she is?" the old man asked again and stood for a moment waiting on the words, waiting on Jacob to think about the question and who the woman might be.

The lady who flies… The boy's words came to him.

"I don't know."

"Like I said, fixing things, that's what we do here." Gabe sighed to himself as he positioned the picture on the panel.

"I thought I had him. I thought I had him here in a place where he couldn't get out. Now he's talked himself out again. Like I said, I didn't want it to be you, I didn't want you here but I had no choice in the matter. I thought you would find your way if we could only hold him for a while, give you time…"

"What the hell are you talking about?"

Gabe looked down at the picture again, and then stood up on the wing.

"He's going to be on them again, soon."

"What does he want with them?"

"Same as he wants with you."

"I think you're a crazy old man! I think you're full of shit. Those guy's, that pilot, their figments of my imagination and you too you're something I've made up in my mind! My guess is this whole thing is something I've made up! I knew the girl once, a long time ago. I was over seas I was flying a mission, I…"

"You let her die?" Gabe asked.

"This is bullshit! I'm not buying it!" Jacob said angrily. "Well, I don't know about you Pop but I'm getting out of here, right now, today!"

Jacob said this as he focused his attention on the aircraft. He was afraid of it, but even more afraid of the thoughts that haunted him, the things he might be asked to do.

"Look kid," the old man spoke, "You can go on and get in the aircraft and try to run if you want to, but you'll be back before you've flown a mile!"

"I won't make the same mistake twice, I'm picking a point and heading for it just as soon as I can get it pulled out of the hanger and collect my stuff!" Jacob thought about the money in the satchel and looked around for it on the hangar floor.

"That money won't help you boy!" the old man called back to him.

He stopped and turned back.

"I know about the money, the whole thing." Gabe said.

"How would you know?"

The old man grabbed him by the shoulders and looked directly into his eyes.

"Look, you have to fight, you have no choice. You can't keep running! That's what I…We have been trying to tell you!"

"Why should I fight this thing, what is that German to me? I wasn't there! I wasn't the one who let him in on the bomber! I didn't kill them!"

Gabe looked at him now, as if to deliver the great secret that he was holding, the thing that he had expected Jacob to know, to uncover on his own.

"You and the German boy, the second pass over the target. You let him out! You let him out then you tried to run… You can't run boy. You can't escape him…You have to confront him, take him on, bring him down. Not just for you but for all of us! "

Jacob could hear the pleading in his voice, the desperation in his words. The old man turned to the hangar door.

"How could I have done that, I didn't even know them before now?" He snapped in an angry response.

"You are special son. You have a very special job to

do. You must do it. I'm sorry but it's the only way." He looked at Jacob, his eyes tired. He pulled the door shut behind him.

Jacob moved without a word and walked stunned and shivering to the diner.

He did not know what he would do. He knew that the German was out there now, that he had let something out that was not meant to be set free. The thing was more than he appeared, more than the ghost of a man obsessed with a long dead trophy from a war that had passed into history. The German was some unfinished, terrible thing that he had let loose that now had to be corrected. Soon there would be trouble. He did not know what would happen but he knew that these things would be part of the answer, the only answer.

Chapter 17

Jacob made his way to the diner and walked in on the pilot sitting at the counter. He was nursing a cup of coffee, the ever-present cigarette hanging in its position in the corner of his mouth. He sat there like a man alone in his own thoughts. He had seen the expression before, like many pilots who had come in from a long mission, their nerves rubbed raw from stress and fear, minds still whirling with steep turns and jumpy with a thousand thoughts that had spun round in split second decisions, now slowly unwinding and second guessing each error, each lapse, reliving every moment searching for something that could have been done differently.

Jacob circled around behind him, like a boxer would circle a knowing opponent, his mind filled with what he had seen and what Gabe had told him.

"You know now don't you boy? The old man let you see it…?" the pilot asked calmly without looking up from his cup.

"I saw it, but I still don't believe it. That German, those ghosts out there… Tell me what you know." Jacob demanded irritated.

"People have to do things on their own accord son. That's the way things are. They do it on their own and suffer on their own." the pilot responded as if it were something he had said many times to many others who had passed through there before.

"They're all here boy, all the folks who came her same way."

"Don't give me any of that homespun crap! You're my old man, we both know that! You're dead! We both know that too. Who is that German and what does he want?" Jacob demanded.

The pilot took a drag from the butt smoldering between his lips then dropped it down into his coffee cup with a sizzle.

Jacob pressed him. "I know who you are now. I saw you and me together in those pictures. I knew it was you before. You looked like him but I didn't want to believe it. You weren't there when I needed you…I've made it this far on my own. I don't need an alcoholic to get me out of this! You're dead old man, dead and gone! There's nothing you can do for me!"

The pilot spoke to him without looking up, "You've got to know that I didn't want things to go this way…I didn't want to leave you… That was an accident."

"I don't buy it. You could have done a lot of things different, you could have but you didn't. Nobody blamed you for the things that happened in the war. Nobody put the bottle in your hand or told you to fly low over a wire with a stomach full of corn whisky!"

"You're right. Nobody made me do those things, I did all that myself. I'll give you that. But I was stone sober when it happened. It was an accident. I didn't mean to do it; it was just one of those things. You ought to know about accidents?" The pilot paused and looked at him, looked into his eyes as if he knew about the second pass over the target and his mistake.

Jacob thought about that. He thought about the pass and the flash of the memory, the girl, his fear and the image again of himself cowering in the darkness of the pit as the soldiers went about their business with her and killed the people in the village.

"This place, it's all about mistakes son. Things we did, decisions we made, things we should have done but didn't. That's what this is all about. Everyone here is here because of mistakes like that." The pilot rubbed his face with his hands as he worked out an explanation.

"I guess it's because pilots are different from other folks. They're different because they aren't supposed to make mistakes. They aren't allowed to."

"That's a load of crap! Who is the German?" Jacob asked his voice filled with rage and frustration.

"He's a shadow…" The pilot replied.

"Everyone here is a shadow. Who is he?" He asked again.

"He's your shadow." The pilot replied, his voice calm, as if he had waited until that moment to reveal it.

"What the hell are you talking about? I wasn't there! You were there! You were the cause of it, not me!"

"I did what I did a long time ago son. I made my own mistakes and have learned to accept them. You on the other hand, you have a chance now, a chance to change things before it's too late to make changes."

"I don't know what you mean?"

"The girl, she's dead, we are all dead…But you…You are somewhere else, somewhere in between. You have a chance to change things before you are left without any options, before you are consigned to an eternity here!"

"Wait a minute old man!" Jacob shouted, his voice belying the fear rising up in him, "I am not dead or anywhere near it! I am right here, with you and everyone else. The rest of you may be ghosts, but I'm not!"

"You are not dead, yet…" The pilot replied, "You are in between things. You have been around here for some time sport. You've been trying to run from him but the time for running is over. The girl, she deserves more than that. More than a man who runs from the truth."

"You're a great judge of the truth!" Jacob replied, "You left me! You left me with the old man…."

Suddenly a memory became clear to him. He realized in that moment who the old man was, that the pilot had left him there long ago, when he was but a child. He remembered it now, the old man and a child in an apple tree. A lost child, who grew to a young man, a young pilot who stepped into the world of living things to protect them, to fly high over them in the darkness and then, low over targets in some virtuous moment of protection and justice. He had stepped over an unseen barrier, become something that he was never meant to be. He had stepped into a mortal world where emotion and impulsive acts drove men to fatality. He knew that he was right. Other people, earth-bound people went about their lives living day to day with estimations and miscalculations that may make them late for meetings, or bankrupt them, destroy marriages and relations with others or cause accidents but pilots, pilots pay with their lives for their mistakes. They cannot make missteps, they have to make decisions that are right, decisions that keep them straight and level and bring them out of things with their wheels down on the pavement at the end of the flight.

"It's like the old man said, this is the last stop." The

pilot said, knowingly.

"That girl in the jungle…?"

"You know what has to be done."

The pilot looked over at him, his eyes tired and his face gaunt with age, "You've been trying to run from who you are, why you are…You can't run anymore son. You have to get this right. It's who you are. This is home for you. You made that last pass, you did what I did. You made a mistake and you've tried to walk it off but you couldn't shake it. Now you're here, with the rest of us and well, you've got to turn things around. It's the only way." the pilot sighed in resignation, a realization that he too had figured out the answer.

The pilot suddenly roused from the seat and stood in front of him, "We've been given a gift, a way of seeing things, a part of us that has to be up there."

The pilot looked up as he spoke, his eyes closing slightly as if thinking about a distant place, his face quiet as if in prayer.

"Folks fly around all the time, they sit in those big tin can liners that shoot off into space they sip their sodas and read or sleep through it. They don't give it a second thought. But us, we don't see it that way. For us, every moment up there... For us it's not about getting from one place to another. For us it's about being up there, in the clouds. "

The pilot, his face now older searched for another cigarette in his pocket then put it between his lips and searched for a match.

Jacob pulled the Zippo from his pocket and lit it for him.

"Thanks…" he said as he blew out a blue cloud of smoke, "…when you touch the stick, when the engine is running up and you turn into the wind. Its that feeling you get when you feel the wind lifting you up, taking you up there."

Jacob thought about what he was saying and about the feeling. He thought about his own life and everything he had done washed over him again. He understood it. He could feel it, the ground giving way, the wheels rolling over in the slipstream as he gained altitude. He thought about the providence that lifted his heart and made him different from other men.

"You're right about one thing, I wasn't there for you boy. I let it get to me too. I let a few seconds catch me and I let him in on them. That was my fault. I let him take that bomber and then I tried for a time to get it out of my head. I tried to forget about it. I even lied about what happened. Oh, I was sorry, I was so sorry for it!" the pilot said his words bit off with anger as he recounted what had happened.

"I told them that I had engine trouble and was too busy to help them. That's what I told them. I knew they didn't believe me but I told them anyway. They couldn't prove it though, too much cloud, too many other things for the other guys in my flight to worry about. They didn't see that I let him in on them."

The pilot pulled his hand through his hair with a long lingering, painful sigh, "They sent me home, sent me back. They told me that I had had enough and that I should go home and let the younger guys finish the job."

"Then when I got home I tried to find you, I looked up your mother. She was there, still traveling around with that two bit circus, scrounging up as much gas and spare parts as she could lay hands on to keep that moth flying. We were together for a while, you were just a kid.

I should have kept her out of it. I could've gotten a job I guess, I should have but I didn't. No I decided to let her keep things going, while I boozed and let the thing eat at me. Let it take the gift from me."

He looked over at Jacob, "I let her put that Moth into the ground. I killed her too."

Jacob looked over at him, his mind searching to remember the details of the story.

"Then you were all that was left. I had a little boy that needed his mother, needed shoes and books and things. I went back to what I knew. War was over and I spent the rest of my life somewhere between the bottle and dusters flying around, moving from one farm town to the next until one day, a job came along that I couldn't pass up, a town like the one down the road where a half crazy, played out pilot could earn some steady dollars and fly over fields all day. I flew low, kept low over the fields. I wanted to go higher, I wanted it to be like it had been but by then too much time had passed and I was too afraid of it to make it like it was before."

"Like what?"

The pilot didn't answer but pressed on.

"There aren't many of us…only lets a few of us have a chance. Some of us, we don't handle it very well."

Jacob thought about this. He thought about how for as long as he could remember the great wish had been with him. Even when he was killing, he had thought about it, reveled in the joy of being up there in the clouds.

"What about me? I don't remember any town?"

"You weren't there. I let you go…The old man took you in when I couldn't help you any more. He offered so I let him have you."

"That's bullshit! You're telling me you just handed

me over to him?"

"Yeah, some cash and enough gas to get me as far away as I could go. Seemed to me to be a bargain. I mean I was no good for you. Then it came for me again…"

"What do you mean?"

"I mean the wire, I should have seen it. Hell, I'd been over that field a hundred times before, I should have known it was there but, I was too tired, too much work, too much time in the cockpit, let myself get over-extended and well, I caught that wire and ended up here."

The pilot slipped his arm around Jacob's shoulder, "You've got to believe me when I tell you that I didn't want things to work out this way son. I didn't want you to end up here."

Jacob looked at him, looked into his face, the tired face of his memory. He thought again about the moments of tired, desperation, of selfish lust and un-controlled anger that drove indecision, doubt and fear. The things that take men's eyes away from the instruments and sends them, tumbling to earth.

"What can I do?"

"You have to get into that plane out there. You have to get it out of the hangar and off the ground."

Jacob thought about the Mustang again and the fear.

"I'm not enough of a pilot for that. I might have been once but…" A thought came to him, the thought of miles on highways and years on the road. He suddenly could recall a man, himself an old man and another life, a life far from the open sky. He felt his blood run cold with the realization.

"As long as you are here it's no good for you." the pilot answered then walked over to a crumbling cardboard box that lay on a corner of the counter. He rested on a stool and sifted quietly through a box filled with log books.

"Where is it?" the pilot mumbled to himself distracted as he selected a log book from the box.

"Here, here's your log book." He handed it to him casually, "Take a look son; you've got thousands of hours to sift through there, hundreds of flights, every kind of plane you can imagine, its all there."

Jacob looked down at the book and thumbed through its yellowed pages. Dates and times, aircraft and tail numbers, types written there, written in his handwriting, passing over the months and years.

"Where did you get this?"

"The old man, he's kept it for you." the pilot responded.

"What are you saying?" he asked as he continued to pick through the entries.

"What you already know boy. You've been here for a long time. Like all the rest, you keep coming back son, you're circling son you and me and all the rest, trying to get down."

He read the bits and pieces, the Beech, the Stearman, other planes hours all from different departure points but all ending with the same destination, not written as a three character field identifier, but simply as 'HOME' in the logbook.

"Where did all of these come from?" he asked looking up from the pages.

"From all of them, they leave them here. They know they'll be back and that Gabe will keep them safe."

The pilot's eyes grew distant as he spoke, as if an eternity had passed and he could suddenly feel the weight of many years pressing down on him.

The pilot turned him to the mirror behind the counter, "Look at yourself boy, you're just a youngster. Now we both know that can't be now don't we?"

Jacob looked up at the reflection cast into the glass that covered a large picture hanging on the wall of the diner. It was the picture of him standing in front of the Mustang. He looked at his image then at the picture. The young man was gone, the young man that he had been. He was older now, much older. His hair a receding grey crop on his head, his eyes and features weathered with age. He looked at himself, there in the twilight at the edge of a long field of grass peering along a lonely strip of asphalt, watching, listening, and waiting for the passing of planes in the evening sky.

Then like a curtain lifted from the recesses of his memory, the thoughts of years of flying, of silver arrows streaking through the skies defending the lumbering giants as they made their way through the clouds of leaden flack and tracers arching from the guns of enemy aircraft.

He had been there, many years ago in that distant history practically forgotten. He had been there when the jets had been born, when the sky was a frozen landscape of snow over the barren wastes of Korea and later when the jungles of Indo-China crawled with young marines. Flying jet fighters and watching as heavy jet bombers traced silent white lines in the sky. Faces and names, so many that he could not remember lost in so many terrible falls. There had been many falls and failures, many moments of hesitation and miscalculation, so many men with ghosts wandering the deep recesses of his memories. There had been his moment of indecision, the one instant of miscalculation the opening that all pilots feared.

His father broke Jacob's silence, "I know son. It's been a long road."

"So where is the thing now?" Jacob asked.

"You don't need to know everything son. He'll be along directly, when the time comes." The pilot put his hand on Jacob's shoulder.

"I have got to go kid, got things to take care of, you go on out and walk around your aircraft, son. It will tell you all you need to know."

The radio again came to life and the sound of an old spiritual song rang out in a rough field hand harmony.

"We are climbing Jacob's ladder…" it called out over the speaker the chorus echoing out over the airfield, the stinging irony of the moment and the song made Jacob smile briefly and shake his head in resignation. He turned to speak to the pilot but the room was empty and he was alone. He walked over to the door and stared out at the field. It stood there resting on its undercarriage, the silver Mustang now out of the hangar, its gleaming skin shining in the sun.

They finished it, he thought to himself, it doesn't seem possible but they did it.

"Dad…!" Jacob called to him expecting him to answer from the back room. There was only silence. He was gone. There was only the Mustang.

He walked across the field to the waiting aircraft, now sitting alone on the tarmac, its intake smiling, and its nose turned up to the sky. It was inviting him to come closer, to take a good look at it. He walked to it and put his hand on the wing's leading edge, trailing to the tip, walking round it in a way that was familiar to him, familiar to all pilots. They all learn it from the beginning, like one learns to tie a necktie. A series of motions that practiced so often soon become second nature, the routine of walking round the plane, looking for things out of place. Searching for loose rivets, bolts, leaks or wrinkles from metal fatigue or hangar rash. He had done it a thousand times, done it more times than he could remember. Like walking round one's horse before a cavalry charge, looking at the flanks and hooves, making sure all was in order and that the animal would respond when the time came. He made his way to the cowling, and produced a small screwdriver from his pocket. It was with him always, a tool that he carried for just such an inspection. He popped the screws and retaining clips that held down the cowl and opened it. The engine, the 'Merlin' lay exposed before him, its great complex of twisting tubes and screws clear to him. A clean engine, a perfect power plant as new as if it had just been rolled from the factory floor, no leaks no signs of wear or frayed wires.

He climbed up on to the wing and checked the fuel tanks. They were topped off. He could smell the perfume of aviation fuel as the vapors rose from the open tanks. The smell of the fuel reminded him of the old crop duster, who stared casually into the tanks with his cigarette burning between his lips as he leaned over the open tanks in careless disregard.

An odd old scarecrow, Jacob thought with a smile.

He then opened the ammunition bays. Fifty caliber rounds, clean, oiled and belted into position in their retainers, fully armed. Every seventh round marked as a tracer, he recalled as he looked down into the compartment.

He slipped back the canopy and looked down into the cockpit. He saw a parachute sitting in the metal bucket seat. He pulled it from the seat by a strap and held it for a moment, thinking of the silk parachute inside and of memories of chutes billowing from the bellies of dying aircraft. He remembered his ejection from the Phantom, the pain in his leg as he was ripped from the cockpit, low over the jungle and the tumbling fall through the trees to the jungle floor below. He slipped down into the cockpit and before he could find the master, the panel instantly lit up, glowing with yellow incandescent backlighting, as if his very presence there had brought power to the machine. He switched on the radio, tuned it to the broadcast and let the gospel music wash over him. He closed his eyes and gripped the stick, his hand fitting with a familiar grasp about it as the music played.

The sun washed down rays of warmth and the warm breeze wafted about the cockpit. He knew the plane, it was his. He loved it, loved it like the girl, like the old man, like the child he did not know, like his father, his mother and the great wish.

They were all alike, he thought, all these things were together, they were what he was, a great web of souls and wishes, pinned like stars in the night sky, drifting on the wind.

It came to him, the thought of all the times he had looked up to the sky to catch a fleeting glimpse of a passing aircraft. He wondered how many of them were up there, in the dark of night or in the cold, lonely mist of clouds probing the ground, looking for a place to land.

Chapter 18

He had lost track of time. The sun had begun to set and Jacob had become concerned. There had been few instances when Gabe had not been close at hand and he had not seen the old man for some time.

Gabe was like that old rusting tower, he thought. He had always been there, guarding the field, protecting him. He had been a pathfinder in a sky filled with clouds and distant memories.

Suddenly he could hear the sound of an approaching car. An old faded brown Cadillac Deville, well worn from thousands of miles on dusty country roads pulled onto the lot in front of the diner and parked. It sat there idling when suddenly the driver's side window slid down with a hum. Jacob climbed from the cockpit of the Mustang.

"Well, my boy that's quite an aircraft you've got there." the old bear moaned as he shut off the engine and then labored to open the door and pull his frame from behind the wheel.

Charlie brushed off his slacks and held out a fleshy hand.

"You remember me don't ya? Charles Beauchamp... Bo?"

Jacob didn't take his hand but looked around with suspicion.

"Yeah I remember. What do you want?"

The salesman did not respond right away but slipped past Jacob and ambled forward, walking around the Mustang, inspecting it, looking at the skin and sliding his hand along the leading edge of the wing as he walked. He stopped in front of one wing and fingered one of the openings that contained the muzzle of a 50-caliber machine gun.

"Hey son, these guns loaded?" He smiled, and then chuckled coyly.

Jacob did not answer but stood there slowly simmering with anger at his evasiveness.

"I'll bet your quite the pilot aren't you son? I'll have to admit, I underestimated you a little, first impressions and all. I didn't take you for a man of Gabe's caliber or that old drunk for that matter. But, I guess it was an honest mistake. Hell even offered you a whole pile of money to leave. But no, no you had to come back didn't ya."

"Cut the bullshit and answer my question." Jacob replied.

"In due time son, the first rule of a good business transaction is trust and I want you to know that above all else my boy, that Charles Beauchamp can be trusted. Why, I recall a deal, what was it now, 10 no maybe 20 years ago, time gets hazy around here… Yeah 20 years I'd say, I was in this very spot, talk' in to a young pup… A young man just like you…I remember saying to him, 'Take the money son, go on now.' I remember pull-in his plane out of the hangar and even hand propped it for him. Yeah he took that satchel and was off like a shot." Bo chuckled and made a zooming motion with his hand to add emphasis. He then brushed his palm on his trousers self-consciously and looked out toward the tower with envy.

"Never thought I'd be working this hard to close a deal. I tell you that damn tower has been more trouble than it's worth."

Jacob moved toward him, "Where is the old man?" he asked, menacingly.

"Now why do you want to go and push off old Bo without even an offer of a cup of coffee? Never know, I might have something important for you?"

"I swear to God Beauchamp, if you have done something to that old man, I'll kill you!" Jacob grabbed him by the collar of his suit.

"Now, now son, God ain't got anything to do with this and your old Bo's got no fight with you. Why I got no idea where old Gabe is. He and I are old friends. I'm here to help. Besides, it's a little late for kill' in wouldn't you say?" The salesman chuckled as he lifted a shock of hair from his neatly slicked back pate, exposing the blood stained bullet hole in one side of his head.

"What say you have me in for a spell and we'll discuss this like two gentlemen? I mean you're a smart fella...smarter than your old man I'd say."

Bo slipped past him and waddled into the diner. He stood at the counter as Jacob entered behind him, then the old salesman waved his hand and a plate of stew and a cup of coffee materialized suddenly on the counter top. The old bear sat up on a stool at the counter and made him self comfortable.

"Well, my boy like I said, don't know nothing bout ole Gabe, but yer Pa God rest his soul, had to step out for a while. Decided to go speak to my client in person you might say. You want some of this son?"

Before Jacob could answer, the old bear sat down at the counter and tucked a napkin under his chin. He picked up the fork and shoveled some stew into his mouth then glanced at Jacob out of the corner of his eye. Satisfied that he had gotten the reaction from him that he wanted, he returned his attention to the plate of food.

"Listen sonny, I know where he is. Matter of fact, your old Pa asked me to have you take my caddy out that way to meet with him."

"And what about you, what are you going to do?"

"Me? Son, I'm going to finish this delicious meal, smoke a panatela, then I'll probably take a nap in that chair over there and wait for you all to come back."

Jacob struggled with the situation. He could feel the suspicion rise up in him.

"What say we both go see him?"

The salesman wiped his mouth, then used the fork as a pointer as he spoke, "My work is done boy. I set up the meeting. That was my part of the transaction. Besides what would happen if you missed your old man or he decided to have a few drinks with my client? Say he overstays his welcome and my friend decides to take him? Or say he comes back and sees that plane out there, an empty plate and nobody here? Why don't you just let me wait here and you go? Go on now. You've been out on that road before, am I right?" the old bear chuckled as he rubbed his knuckles and returned to his plate.

"I'll keep an eye on things. You go now, go fetch'em and I'll be here when you get back."

Reluctantly, Jacob's concern overrode his suspicion and he headed for the car.

"If anything has happened to him, I'm coming back for

you, you got that?" he called back as the door slammed.

The salesman, almost choking on a mouthful, coughed then waved after him dispassionately as Jacob walked out to the car.

"Keys are in the vehicle son, don't worry bout the gas, got plenty."

"This whole thing stinks." Jacob said to himself as he climbed into the car and started the engine.

"That old drunk should have known better than to go out there alone."

He switched on the radio, "He'll have to meet him out there far out where the tower can't reach. It's one thing in town or close to the road or the fields but, way out there, off beyond the tree line and the woods, it's too far away." Jacob said, talking to himself as he reached into his holster. He still had the gun along with the fresh clip of ammunition.

He drove through the growing darkness as the evening sun receded and twinkling stars lit up the night sky. The evening had become blustery and the wind warned of an approaching thunderstorm, the sky in the distance lit up with the reports of thunder and lightning and heavy rain clouds drifted toward him in the darkness as he made his way further from the road and the sounds of the gospel radio. The grass was illuminated by the remaining moonlight that shone down through an open crack between converging clouds. The blades had turned over and showed their undersides now in preparation for the coming rain. It reminded him of the storm he had fought through when he had first arrived, a cold, heavy storm. He had no idea where he was going but felt that he would know the place when he found it, that the road would tell him.

Then at a threshold where the asphalt ended and a rough dirt road began he stopped the car. Cautiously he got out and stood peering out into the darkness of an open field. The first drops of rain began to fall on the windshield and then without warning, a lightning bolt flashed a neon blue crack in the black sky and was followed shortly thereafter by a severe clap of thunder.

"Its close now." he said to himself, "When the thunder comes soon after the lightning flash that means its close."

He pushed strands of hair back from his face as the wind picked up and began to blow field trash and loose flotsam about in steep gusts. He tried to listen intently through the noise of the approaching storm as another stroke of lightning flashed followed quickly by another sudden crack of thunder. He strained to hear something coming from out over the field and the cracks of illumination rumbling along the edges of the storm clouds building in the distance.

"There. There it is. It's up there. …trying to find a place to land." He said this with a sense of urgency as if it were a scene he had witnessed many times before and he knew that he must find something there in the darkening sky, see it before it could see him.

The cold wind blew stronger still and the rain began to come down, large, cold drops in increasing numbers.

"Yes, there they are."

At that instant the lightning flashed only yards from where he was standing. An enormous thunderclap immediately followed and then another longer strike came that illuminated the sky and the surrounding fields.

He could see it, the lumbering giant, again coursing in and out of the low hanging clouds. He could see it, the machine laboring through the torrents of wind and rain.

"Captain…!" A voice called out as another bolt cracked overhead.

Jacob looked out over the field and could see not more than thirty yards in the distance, the form of an aircraft sitting at attention in a field off to one side of the road. Leaning against the wing stood the young German. He was in uniform, a long trench coat and peaked officers cap, his pale white face and hair standing out in the darkness.

"I see that you have come after all. I had almost given up hope that a fool like Beauchamp would be able to persuade you. I must say, you have reinstated my faith in humanity." He stood there defiant in the pouring rain, the edges of his open trench coat billowing in the wind.

"Where the hell is my father?" Jacob shouted as the wind blew and lightning flashed hysterically overhead.

"Why Captain, whatever do you mean? Surely you don't believe that I would have your father? Indeed, he does not travel this far from his precious bottle. Come, come closer you have nothing to fear. We are old friends you and I." He motioned to him.

The officer bowed slightly as he approached. "I am so glad that you have come. I must say that I have been following you for some time now. It has been very difficult for me Captain. Yes quite difficult to follow you for so long…" The German let the words trail off as if he were remembering something from the past. Then he changed the subject.

"I have someone else who is here as well… Come, come my dear." He motioned at a figure lurking, crouched beneath a wing. A young boy emerged, the small boy who had been with the girl, the child that he never knew, smiling, his eyes shining trance-like in the lightning flash. Jacob could see that the child had changed, he was now clearly both children, he was the child on the road, he was as Jacob had been once, a small frightened child on a lonely road, but he was also another child, a small Asian child, a child that Jacob had never known, a child who had not lived to be born.

"Well…it would appear that your comrade has come over to the other side…" he sighed and placed his gloved hands on the boy's shoulders and then patted him on the head.

"You know such fraternization is very unbecoming, especially for your lady… But then it is my understanding that fraternization is something that she finds particularly to her liking?"

Jacob lashed out with a right that smashed into the pilots jaw and sent him reeling back against the aircraft wing.

"No…no… Don't!" the boy cried out.

"No. No worries my dear. Run along now…" the officer responded, breathing heavily.

"The Captain was merely defending her honor." He held a gloved hand to his mouth, tasting the trickle of blood from the blow, "Indeed, quite stimulating actually…"

He then regained his composure as the engines of the struggling B17 rumbled past in another pass over the field.

"Now, enough with these pleasantries… Let us parley Captain. You see the aircraft overhead, yes?"

"Yeah what about it…?" Jacob replied, suspiciously.

"It is mine Captain. Its crew. They are mine also. Everything here is mine, your father, your mother, that idiot salesman, my little soldier here and of course, the girl."

"There is but a single item that remains and I want it Captain. Heretofore, your Colonel has been unwilling to negotiate, indeed one might say that he has been quite adversarial regarding the subject ignoring the proposals of my solicitor and has made it quite impossible for me to take what is mine! I have asked you here Captain, because I am growing weary of this game and I wish to end it."

"As long as Gabe has that field it will never end."

"This is true, very true Captain." the officer yelled as a gust of wind and a thunderclap punctuated his words.

"However I also know that you Captain, you would like to return to your life! Is this not so?"

Suddenly Jacob could feel a chill run through him.

"I can make this so Captain. I can return you to your reality. I will do so if you would be willing to wager?"

"What sort of wager are you talking about?" Jacob asked with frustration and contempt.

"You and I Captain. We are both fighter pilots. It is our passion. It is who we are. You are the best Captain, or so it is said. I? I am the best. Obviously there cannot be two superlatives."

The lightning again crashed and the thunder growled in an angry report at his words.

"If you win, I shall leave. I will surrender my many trophies except for the girl and the child and you Captain, you will be returned to your reality."

"And if I lose what then?"

"If you lose Captain, I will retain you, the tower and all of those worthless souls wandering the road and the town."

"And Gabe too I suppose?"

"Why of course Captain... Do we have a deal?"

"What makes you think Gabe will go for this?"

"Oh Captain, have you looked at the man? Have you seen our Gabriel? He is tired. He is weary of wrestling with me. I do not believe that you have much choice my friend."

"Why do you think Gabe will have me do this?"

"Why, do you think you have been asked to this party my boy? You are not here by accident you know?" the officer replied.

"Now do we have a deal or not?" The officer asked stiffly.

Jacob thought of his own life, and of the crew in the aircraft passing endlessly overhead, the girl and the child and all the others. In that moment, he knew the answer. He felt suddenly that he had the upper hand.

"I want them all freed, those people in the town, the girl, the child, the old man and my father!"

"Nein…!" the officer clipped angrily.

"I want them or there is no deal!" Jacob stood holding his ground in the rain and wind that blew violently about them.

"Captain, as I said before, the girl is mine, she is a trophy that I will take with me. The child, I have grown quite fond of. Indeed, we all should have someone, to whom we can bestow our legacy, someone, shall we say to carry on one's work? As for the girl, well, it is quite a lonesome place where I will be going, I will need her. Besides, you showed little compassion for her in the past. As for your father, well, let us say that a higher power has already decided his fate. I cannot undo that decision my friend."

"Like I said no girl, no kid, no deal…! Besides, you said yourself, there cannot be two superlatives. Looks to me like you're not much of a gambler…! You sound like somebody who's going to get his tail shot off!" Jacob yelled the words over the thunderclaps and howling wind. He felt confident, sensing a small crack, an opening that might offer some advantage.

The officer's face changed suddenly, it grew tepid with frustration. He paced several steps, considering the offer, and then looked up at Jacob, his face contorted in an angry expression and howled in a painful, plaintive moan, "Very well, Captain. You shall have them all." He then extended a gloved hand.

Jacob took it and a shock of cold sweat rose in him as he clenched his hand around that of the dark specter.

"I shall meet you within the hour."

"How will I find you? I'll need more time." Jacob asked.

The specter responded, "Do not worry Captain, I shall find you…as for time, it is of no consequence…"

With these words the officer picked up the child and sat him down in his lap as he climbed into his aircraft. The little boy waved and smiled innocently from the cockpit as the propeller blades whirred and the prop wash forced a sheet of rain over Jacob and a final lightning bolt flashed. In the next instant they disappeared.

With their departure the rain and wind suddenly stopped and the air grew silent and thick with moisture. A clean scent of green grass wafted like spring perfume from the ground. Jacob turned and walked back to the car.

He thought about the wager. I'm not going to have much time…got to get back to the field.

Then he thought about Beauchamp alone at the airfield, the tower and the broadcast holding the thing at bay. Beauchamp was the salesman, the go between.

Suddenly a thought came to him, the thought of Beauchamp and what he would do.

"Damnit…! I can't believe that I was so stupid!"

"I have to get there before he does something to that airplane!"

Quickly he climbed into the car and turned onto the road, simmering in anger with himself.

How stupid…! I should have known better than to leave that bastard there alone! I should have known that things weren't right!

The Deville swerved and weaved around potholes as he raced furiously over the rough roadbed.

Jacob turned on the AM radio and began tuning in an effort to pick up the station while his eyes remained focused on the dark road that was illuminated by the headlights. Driving frantically in an effort to get to the airfield, he continued searching for the station, tuning around the frequency, struggling to control the car and to find the broadcast. The airwaves howled and clicked in protest as he thumbed the tuner. Screaming phantom voices slipped in and out as he moved it, the cries of desperate lonely shadows drifting in despair.

"There's nothing, I can't pick up anything." He said, panicked and frustrated.

Then he looked up and in the distance could see the glow of a huge fire. As he approached it and pulled onto the gravel drive he could see that the hangar had been set a blaze and was burning furiously. He swung open the door and jumped out of the car before it came to a stop, then at a dead run rushed to the burning structure.

"God help me!" He could hear screams and cries of pain coming from within the hangar.

"Lord…Help me, someone help… I'm burning!"

"Beauchamp…!" Jacob called out to the voice over the roaring fire, coughing on the smoke and hot cinders flying in the wind.

"Beauchamp, where are you?!"

"I'm in here boy! Help me! I'm burn' in up in here!" Jacob could hear his desperate calls, the coughing and choking as he struggled to breathe in the heat and smoke.

Quickly he ran to the service bay that stood nearby and grabbed the roll of hose that was kept coiled next to the well pump. He grabbed the handle and began pumping frantically as he tried to get water on the burning hangar. Water squirted from the hose in short bursts then began to spray in a heavy stream as the pressure increased. The fire had a good deal of time to build and was burning hotter with each passing moment.

"Boy! Come on son! I'm burn' in!" the voice choked out as Jacob soaked the structure. He reached down and grabbed a heavy piece of scrap that looked like an old rusted piece of angle iron and threw it through one of the windows. Heavy smoke poured from the open window as he forced the end of the hose into the opening in a vain attempt to check the fire's progress.

He felt that it was a trap set for him and that he was risking a lot by trying to make his way into the burning building. However he could not stand there and do nothing while the hangar was destroyed.

"Damn it! Where the hell are you?" he yelled in through the window.

"I'm pinned down son! I'm stuck here!"

"I'm coming!" Jacob pulled the sleeve of his shirt over his hand and grabbed the hot door. The handle sizzled in his hand, as he pulled to slide it open and was almost immediately knocked down by the raging ball of flame that jumped forth from the open doorway. He got to his feet, then grabbed the hose and soaked his head and clothes with water. He then soaked the doorway and fought back the angry flames. He crouched down as low as he could and slowly made his way into the burning building.

"I'm over here boy!"

The salesman lay under a pile of rubble from the partially collapsed ceiling that had fallen when the building caught fire and burned.

His face was red and sweating from the heat, his hair singed and blackened with soot, his clothes burned. He labored with breath and words, under the weight of a ceiling beam.

"Well, I guess I screwed this deal good." He said, as he looked over at Jacob and smiled weakly.

"Just shut up and lay still while I try to get this beam off of you." Jacob yelled as he dropped the hose on the floor next to him then looked under the beam for a handhold. He reached his arms around it in an effort to pull it off and struggled with the beam for several moments as the flames continued to burn relentlessly.

"Look, I can't budge this thing! I'm going to try and get this fire under control! You're going to have to sit tight while I douse everything down!" Jacob yelled over the roaring flames.

The salesman grabbed Jacob's arm with a free hand. "I'm screwed son. That bastard tricked me good. You gotta believe me boy, I didn't do this thing! Lightning! He got to the hangar; I tried to put it out son, to get the plane out. I didn't know about the planes boy, all the planes, I couldn't get your old plane out boy, it's burned up. You ain't gonna be able to get this fire put out. It's a good one and there's just too much gas and oil on the floor and everything else."

He looked into Jacob's eyes, "I guess I'm overdue for this anyhow." He looked away and stared into his memory for a moment, "Look, get out of here boy! Get to the Mustang. It's all that's left!"

Jacob looked around, "Where is it?"

"Over behind the hangar out of sight." The salesman smiled again weakly, "I guess I expected something might happen. That it might turn out this way. You're gonna need that plane boy. You got to go. Get as far away as you can before he comes back!"

"I'm going to end this." Jacob said as he looked into the old salesman's eyes.

"If you don't leave now son, you're a bigger fool then your old man."

The salesman looked again into his memory and Jacob could sense that the salesman too had been bound to a debt, a debt that only now would be repaid.

"I'm sorry, Beauchamp." Jacob looked down at him one last time as he laid his head back on some rubble and let go of Jacob's arm."

"It's OK son. Hell, I'm already getting used to it." the salesman chuckled and then, coughing waved him away.

As he made his way to the door and stumbled outside, the entire roof collapsed and the flames engulfed all that remained. Jacob stood there exhausted, helplessly watching the burning pyre.

The station… His thoughts quickly turned to the tower, shut down and no longer spreading its protective broadcast out over the airfield, not much time…!

Jacob took a last look at the burning hangar. He could not help but feel pity for the salesman and the eternity that he had chosen and now had to endure. He turned his back on the fire and ran to the diner. He rushed through the door and looked around the room.

"Gabe? Gabe, you in here…?" He looked behind the counter and ran to the back room. Everything was as it should be, all the photos, the medals, all quietly sitting in place undisturbed.

He stopped and changed his direction, running outside and then around the building with the hope that he would find it. As he turned the corner and walked behind the diner he could see its form, covered with a broad canvas tarp. He didn't need to look under it to know that it was there, waiting for him. Relieved he ran back into the diner and to the back room and found his things on the shelf. As he turned, he heard the sounds of shuffling in the other room, the garbled growl and a loud thumping on the floor. He pulled the pistol from its holster, held the weapon up and walked cautiously to the source of the sound, a closed cupboard door behind the counter. The sound continued with thumping and banging against the door as if something was trying to break out. Jacob braced, then pointed the gun in the direction of the sound, clasped the door latch with his other hand and pulled it open with one quick motion.

"Damn!" He was quickly knocked off of his feet as the trapped form leapt forward at him in the semi-darkness. The gun went off as he slipped back against the floor, and a bullet shot through the ceiling, the report ringing in his ears, his eyes temporarily blinded by the muzzle flash. The form was on him in an instant and Jacob could feel the warm tongue lapping at his face, whining and sniffing with fear.

"Damnit Hop, I nearly shot you! How the hell did you get back here anyway…?"

His anger quickly turned to sympathy and he rubbed the dog on the back of the neck in an effort to calm him, "I know boy, ole Beauchamp put you in there didn't he? Well, everything is going to be alright now, don't you worry boy, we'll find your old man and put an end to this soon."

The dog looked at him through his one eye and satisfied with the answer trotted over to the couch and curled up into a ball on a cushion. Jacob regained his composure, got up from the floor and returned to the aircraft. After managing to get it onto the edge of the runway, he moved quickly with the pre-flight. He fought with the fear rising in his stomach and his hands shook as he moved around the airframe and checked the control surfaces and engine oil. He knew that he would have but a single opportunity to take him down. He did not know if Gabe would ever return. He didn't know if he would be able to save anyone. He was angry with himself for not controlling the fear better. He touched the wings and flaps and rudder and walked around the airframe. He had flown thousands of hours and hundreds of flights with the sky so thick with flack and machine gun fire a fly couldn't have survived it. Now he was gripped with fear, fear unlike any he had ever known. He finished and climbed up on the wing then stepped up into the cockpit.

"Hopefully I won't need this." Jacob said to himself as he pulled the pack of the parachute up and slipped into the harness. He then slid down into the seat and buckled in, pulling the straps as tightly as he could stand them, exhaling and pulling them up to hold him in position and restrain him against the severe maneuvers that he knew that he would be making. He walked down through the pre-start checklist then fired the starter and thumbed the throttle and propeller as the machine rumbled to life. The engine roared and strained against its mounts and threatened to pull the airplane down the runway as soon as he allowed the propeller to take its first bite of air. The instruments spun up and the artificial horizon snapped up parallel to the horizontal and bobbed cheerfully against the spinning gyros.

Jacob checked the altimeter, setting it to zero. He would disregard the barometer setting. He would not be airborne long and would not have the time to fool with it once the engagement started. He double-checked the oil pressure, fuel flow, and all other indicators then gingerly teasing the brakes rolled out square to the runway centerline and waited for the moment. The moment that he had come so far for, over so many roads, so many long, lonely horizons.

Chapter 19

He turned on the radio, the ADF was already tuned and the sounds of scratching and hissing static blasted his headset. The deafening engine noise, the windblast and vibrations forced a chill up his spine as he sat back in the seat staring out of the windscreen. He could see the whirling propeller blades disappear as the throttle advanced slightly and the airframe began to slip forward. Resting on the tail wheel with nose up, he could not see the runway in front of him, only the thick grey sky and the nose pointed like the index finger of a giant directing his attention to a crease in the clouds above him. It seemed as though time had slowed to a crawl and the minutes moved slowly by, like honey dripping from the rim of a mason jar.

Jacob sat there nervously watching the cylinder head temperature rise as the aircraft idled. The engine was not built to sit for long periods idling and he worried about it. He thought that maybe in his haste he had decided to start the engine too soon. He was ready to shut the engine down when like an invisible hand touching him on the shoulder, he realized that the time had come.

He squared both feet on the rudder pedals, right hand gripping the stick and left fingering the throttle and propeller pitch, he worked both forward and let off of the brakes. The engine bellowed in response and the biting propeller pushed him back in his seat as the aircraft almost immediately lifted its tail wheel and began to sprint down the runway. With the tail up he now had an immediate visual sight path down the centerline. The plane picked up speed like a wild stallion and the torque of the engine caused it to pull hard to the left. The beast drank deep from the fuel tanks and wrestled with the propeller cutting through the air in an effort to flip the entire airframe over. Hard right rudder, some right aileron and the nose responded and re-centered. The tires whined and he could see that he had already gotten behind the airplane and was well past his takeoff speed. He cursed himself, relaxed his hand slightly on the stick, thought about a nose up attitude and the airplane responded immediately lifting off in one leap from the pavement. The nose pointed skyward, the propeller clawed at the air and pulled the aircraft like a toy, racing through the clouds. Jacob moved quickly, adjusted throttle, mixture, and pitch and got the canopy closed. The rushing air subsided slightly as the canopy sealed shut. Pressed against the seat, his mind raced to keep up.

"Damn, the landing gear." he cursed himself and his inattention realizing that he was still behind the aircraft.

The silver body shot forward like a hungry shark homing in on a helpless prey gaining speed with every passing second, threatening to rip the landing gear off in the slipstream. He fought the controls and managed to raise them, working the lever and watching the attitude and airspeed as he worked. He had only been airborne a few moments and already he could feel himself sweating with the work needed to keep the plane flying. With the undercarriage out of the slipstream, the aircraft gained more speed climbing faster into the clouds, pushing itself further out in front of him.

Then within seconds he was on the instruments, buried in the heavy overcast and cloud, busy bringing up flaps, cleaning up the airplane in an effort to transition it. The billowing mist covered the canopy in opaque white. He pushed the nose over in an effort to remain within the cloud cover and invisible to other aircraft while he turned on the radio and tuned to the tower. The radio howled in protest and filled his earphones with a constant haze of static. There was no sign of a signal.

"He'll be here soon." Jacob whispered to himself, "I'll be on my own without that tower…"

The airspeed continued to climb and in the climb was well in the yellow band, teasing the red line and the plane protested. He retarded the throttle slightly more and looked at his altimeter. It read 3500 feet and continued winding up, rate of climb 4000 ft per minute. He pushed the nose over harder, retarded the throttle more.

He maintained a close scan of all of the instruments, the attitude, airspeed, and compass. He was still climbing; straight and true though he could not see anything outside the cockpit, the canopy opaque with the white mist of clouds. He knew that if he did not stop the climb he would be out within the next few moments.

A quick bump, a dip, a rough patch of jagged cloud tops, and then he broke out. He was above the cloud layer now; the sky was deep dark blue, darkening to black, then to infinity and all the unknown that lay above him, the vast expanse of an eternal abyss, the stars, the planets in their courses, drifting silently above him, around him. The sun was gone, only the moon shown bright like a blue-white florescent light on the horizon illuminating the cloud layer that stretched out before him like a frozen prairie of snow.

He pulled the throttle back and tuned the prop pitch. The engine responded and the aircraft settled to a level attitude, grumbling like a tiger on a leash, looking for an opportunity to leap free.

Well, so much for keeping a low profile, he thought.

Now out in the clear the aircraft instantly became a part of him again. He had only to think of bank or turn or climb and with almost imperceptible movement of the controls the beast jumped in response. He rolled over and split S at the bottom of his roll trailing off in the opposite direction. He climbed with full power, pointing the nose higher and higher until the aircraft hung on the propeller and rumbled in protest. Near a stall at the top he kicked the rudder pedals and the aircraft rolled over into a dive. Airspeed indicator in the red, the altimeter unwound and he felt himself lifted from the seat as the engine whined and the airframe shook and buffeted in the building shockwave in front of him. Racing down to the cloud deck, he nudged the stick back and drew back the power. The nose bobbed up in response and the engine whine receded as the plane once again took on level flight.

He felt his nerves begin to settle and his confidence returned. Long forgotten reflexes, actions that he had not practiced for a lifetime returned and he felt the sense of control come over him, and his aggression reduced to a firm, dispassionate ember that burned within him. It was the one discriminating thing that above everything separated fighter pilots from the rest, the ability to calculate and remain calm under fire, to control fear and anger and channel aggression into precise control of the weapon.

After a few more minutes he felt ready to meet the fighter waiting for him in the clear sky off somewhere on the horizon. He advanced the throttle and directed the aircraft to climb.

It was so beautiful, the open clear sky around him, too beautiful a place for such an ugly thing. It had always been ugly in his mind no matter how he tried to drown it or wipe it from his memory, he could not fool himself with glory or duty or honor it was an ugly business.

He held the Mustang in the climb and flew out away from the field toward the waiting specter. He wanted the advantage of altitude and without the sun at his back he knew he would need any other advantage that he could get. He remembered his training but knew that there would be little to help him in the darkness. This would require eyes that could see in the dark. I'll have to let him come to me. This was the plan. There would be so little margin for error, so little time to recover, everything in an encounter happened so fast and with such chaos that every edge and every advantage was needed.

He scanned the darkness, making wide turns, being careful now not to fly straight and level at any time for more than a few seconds. Now at altitude he stepped the throttle down and banked into a left turn when in the distance, he saw a flash, nothing more than a tiny glistening flake of light hanging below him off on the horizon. His altitude and the cloud layer below had provided a backdrop for the bright light of the moon. The white prairie of cloud revealed the contrasting form that was racing up to meet him. At first he discounted it as a star or maybe an illusion from the moon shining on the canopy. Then as he turned again, the flash materialized and took the form of a small cross of wings and fuselage. He was not entirely certain that the aircraft was approaching him.

Maybe I drifted too far from the field. Maybe he is over it now circling and waiting for me off there in the distance?

Then a third turn and he could clearly see the dark black of the form as the aircraft closed on him almost before he could react. He was still looking at it almost mesmerized at the sight of it closing on him when it lit up with muzzle flashes.

"That son of a bitch is shooting!" He yelled and immediately pulled hard right and dove past him.

It seemed unbelievable, the aircraft had climbed up to meet him and had been on him in only moments, firing on him even though he had positioned himself well above him. Now he had to dive away and had given up both surprise as well as the advantage of altitude that could be traded for speed and attack. It was not expected, it was not a natural thing for a pilot to do what this one had done. It occurred to Jacob that this had been the pilot's great advantage, a willingness to bring the fight forward regardless of the apparent advantage that his adversary might think that he had, and use it against him.

"Can't let that happen again."

He turned hard and glanced at a rear view mirror that Gabe had installed on the upper lip of the canopy overhead. He thought it a little silly when he first saw it, but now, could see why he had done so. The grey FW190 appeared right behind him in the mirror and was lining up for another shot. Jacob broke hard left and dipped the wing to a 90-degree turn. He strained and groaned as the force of gravity pulled him down into his seat and tried to squeeze the blood from his head. He could feel his senses tingling and his field of vision narrowed with the darkening walls closing in on his peripheral vision. He had felt it many times before, on the very edge of consciousness. He was at his limit and almost blacked out when the black shadow of the fighter's tail suddenly bobbed into view. He struggled for another instant and held down the trigger. Instantly the guns responded and yellow scratches of light flashed forward as the tracer bullets sailed under the target as it bucked and weaved in front of him.

"Lead him you dumb ass!" he grunted under his breath, his chest compressed with the weight of the turn. He pulled harder on the turn, pulled back harder on the elevator to compensate for lift and led just for an instant, the nose of the opposing fighter. Several of the flashes disappeared into its fuselage as he broke out of the turn, leveled the aircraft and climbed in an effort to catch a few moments of altitude before the enemy was on him a second time. He then rolled over and looked through the top of the canopy down at the aircraft below. It looked to be undamaged by the burst and was again climbing up to meet him however, this time he was prepared and pulled back hard on the stick. Instantly they were nose to nose closing at over 700 miles per hour. Jacob fired and managed to put a group into the nose and left wing of the approaching fighter as it screamed past him.

Again the advantage was lost and the German fighter raced down on him as he broke to the left a second time in an attempt to avoid the oncoming fire from its guns. He could feel several rounds hit the airplane as it dove through the middle of the circle of his turn. Suddenly seeing an opening he rolled over and followed in an effort to vector roll in behind him. He weaved back and forth in Jacob's sights as he tried desperately to center him for a shot in the darkness. Jacob fired a burst and again thought that he had inflicted some damage to the rudder and tail of his target. He then leveled for an instant and the German pulled up sharply and allowed him to slip past. Now the mirror was again filled with the fighter, pouring fire into the Mustang from behind.

"Shit! Gotta get out of this…!" Jacob yelled to himself as he broke hard right and split-S again under his opponent. He then dove straight down to the deck of clouds below.

I have to get to the clouds before he cuts me to pieces! He thought, as he ran to the clouds that enveloped the aircraft in the cover.

He thought for a moment that he had lost him, that the fighter had slipped past him and was now lost in the clouds as well. He looked quickly at his altimeter. It indicated 200 feet.

Too low, he thought. It was apparent that the weather had gotten worse down below; the cloud cover now was lower over the ground.

He looked up at the windscreen and in an instant saw the looming tail of the fighter ahead of him in the cover, an image like a ghost through a silk screen of white vapor tearing through the clouds. Jacob fired and broke again to the left in an effort to avoid a collision. They both probed the clouds repeatedly, each trying to gain the advantage, firing, turning then lost again in the mist.

Then it happened. Without warning the oil pressure gauge began to fall and Jacob could feel the weight of the nose as the engine began to struggle. Immediately he pulled back the throttle and tried to enrich the fuel mixture in an effort to cool the engine and avoid an immediate failure. It responded with a rough growling protest.

Here it comes… He must have gotten to the crankcase or the oil cooler. I'm not going to have much time. It's going to come apart here real soon. Didn't think it would take him this long. I'm only going to have one chance, he thought.

Then the voice of the German came to him through the radio. "Captain, I don't think you can keep up this game of hide and seek much longer? I can see your smoke through the clouds; I know you are there. Hold still now, it won't be much longer."

"Keep coming boy, that's it boy come on now, fly right up my ass!" Jacob said to himself as he continued to fight the Mustang and the last of the oil drained from the engine and the red-hot pistons and crank began to fuse. He now recognized the scene; it was as it had been that first night. He had tried before. Tried and failed.

"Not today boy! Not today!" Jacob yelled as he braced for the final salvo and the engine seized with a series of loud heavy reports.

It was a distinctive sound, a sound of heavy iron and steel breaking, jagged steel rods driving piston shafts into a crankcase like pile drivers. The nose of his aircraft dropped immediately in the drag and sent him diving through the clouds.

I'm going to take him down with me, he thought, I'm going to lead him right down into the ground!

He didn't care; he was filled again with the desire to kill, to bring down an enemy at any cost. What happened to him, no longer mattered, it was about the others now. It was about Gabe, the girl, the boy, his father…

Suddenly the radio was filled with sound. It blared forth without warning and Jacob flinched in spite of the panic he was already immersed in and then laughed out loud at his good fortune.

"And I say unto you, get thee behind me Satan! I will not succumb to the ravages of temptation and sin! For man was cast in the image of God Almighty! Can I get an Amen?" The preacher bellowed out the words and picked up the pace bringing in the help of a hymn.

"Now folks, sing along as the Sons of Glory sing that 'Ole Rugged Cross'!"

The radio blasted out the sound of the four-part harmony accompanied by a poorly out of tune piano. The ADF needle swung immediately to a position directly off of the nose of his aircraft. He dove through the cloud layer and broke out at 150 feet. He could see the tower again looming like a great giant, its structure less than a few hundred yards from him. He turned with the last of the airspeed he had remaining and popped the canopy in anticipation of a crash landing. He looked out of the canopy of the Mustang as it lumbered along on its final glide to the ground and could see the German streak past him and slam headlong into the tower. One of its wings sheared off and the fuselage exploded in a vicious ball of fire that engulfed the entire structure.

Within seconds his Mustang side slipped and then floated on rapidly bleeding airspeed as it neared the ground and stalled over a cornfield. The field had been plowed under for the coming winter and the aircraft slammed hard into the soft earth then slid along the ground, pulling on the metal skin, driving the propeller into the earth, bending it and bending the airframe. It slid for what seemed an eternity, metal folding and tearing under the strain until it finally came to a stop.

Jacob turned off the fuel and master switch and sat there for a long time. He pulled off his helmet and laid his head back against the seat.

"I have got to stop landing like this!" he said to himself as he crawled gingerly out of the cockpit and slid down onto the wing. He laid on it exhausted and tried to catch his breath.

He suddenly felt very tired, so tired that he wanted to sleep, sleep for a long time. His eyes grew heavy and his surroundings dimmed. He could hear the sound of a truck approaching from the distance, hear it stop and the familiar sound of the door slam. He rolled slowly on to one side and could see Gabe hobbling toward him from the edge of the open field, then others from a lone giant, sitting quietly in the adjacent field. They were there now, all of them, they were down.

He rolled back again and looked up at the sky. He could see now the crease in the clouds, breaking open and the shining light of the moon illuminating the edges as the clouds parted. The overcast was moving off; the light came down in thick beams from the sky above. He lay there and smiled letting its rays wash over him.

For the first time since his arrival he was at peace. He had saved more than the 'great wish'. He knew that he had saved much more and in doing so, had saved himself, the girl, the child, his father, all of them. The evil had been put down and defeated, not by his bullets but by the same power that had saved him long ago, on a cold cloudy day over a forgotten country road.

Chapter 20

"Are you alright son?" Gabe asked with a worried look, his chest heaving as he tried to catch his breath.

Jacob looked over at him with a sigh and a slow grin, "Oh yeah, I'm okay."

"Well I got to admit son, I'm not much good with radios and such and well, that old radio tower is a little temperamental. I wasn't sure I'd get it back up in time but I guess it worked out alright." Gabe smiled.

Jacob looked over at the burning structure of the tower and the remains of the aircraft as it slowly fell to pieces in the flames.

"Well I guess that fixes it?" Jacob asked.

"Yeah it looks like you fixed it good son." Gabe said as he looked over his shoulder at the smoldering ruins of the tower and the burning airframe.

"Wish I could say something better about the Mustang." Jacob said through his breath.

"Don't worry none about it son, I'll take care of it, you just lie there for a minute."

"I want to see them. Take me to them Gabe." He tried to prop himself up on an elbow but sagged back.

"Now just lie still there son, we got time now, all the time in the world."

"No, get me to the truck. I have to see for myself."

Jacob made another feeble attempt to get to his feet and fell back on Gabe's shoulder as the old man worked to help him up. Gabe pulled the truck onto the field and then helped Jacob onto the rough metal bed of the truck, covered him with a heavy blanket, threw another one under his head and sped away bouncing along the rutted field, to the airfield.

They pulled up to it standing there in the open field, its drab green skin, dulled and weary from weather and wind. Men stood around it, the café men, once spent and drifting in lonely solitude, together now loitered about it. Some seemed confused, scratching their heads or looking to each other quizzically. Others stood shaking hands, talking, offering each other cigarettes and laughing; a lot of schoolboys on holiday.

A lone figure stood apart from them, his flight suit hanging loose on him, the signature smoke between his lips, he pushed his hat back from his forehead and Jacob could see his father there, standing at the nose of the aircraft looking up at it, his bare hand touching the image painted on it.

Gabe brought the truck to a stop and got out, pulling Jacob's arm round his neck and helping him out. Slowly he took the several steps to meet him.

"She's fine now son." Gabe said panting under Jacob's weight.

He looked at the nose of the aircraft, its artwork showed the image of the young girl, an exact image as if painted by the hand of a portrait artist. The image was clear, and the countenance unmistakable.

"It's the lady who flies..." a small voice called, giggling as the child ran across the field and approached them. He ran up to Jacob then ran off playfully.

"The lady who flies..." Gabe said as he looked over at Jacob.

He could see it now, the woman, his love, the great wish, the wish shared by all who fly.

She was not his, not one man's but for all men, the shining brave thing that all men dream to hold, all men wish for in the depths of their hearts, the clear smooth air above the cloud deck that cradles them, suspends them above time and the grinding compromise that fights to pull them down. He knew this now, the answers to questions, so many that he had struggled to know.

One of the crewmen walked up to them, "Colonel Sir?"

Gabe turned to him, "Yes Lieutenant."

"Well Sir, the boys and I we were talking and well we were wondering if it would be all right we'd like to go home now."

Gabe looked into his eyes and looked across the years. He looked at Gabe, looked deeply into him and could see that he too was one of them.

Gabe snapped up as best he could with Jacob still clinging to him, "You have my permission to go son. You're long overdue."

He then extended a hand to Jacob, "I guess I'll see you on the other side kid."

Jacob clenched his hand, "Sure, I'll see you."

The men made their way to the giant, talking to one another then in turn, kicked their legs up, through the hatch and into its belly.

Within several moments, he appeared at the side window of the aircraft, slid it open and called out to Gabe.

"You best get back now and Gabe, keep that dog clear. He's only got one eye left!"

Gabe pulled Jacob around and the two of them made their way to the truck. Gabe slid him into the cab.

"Think you can take the ride over to the diner son?"

Gabe motioned to the giant and could see the men waving to them through the open windows and gunner's position. The engines in turn started to come to life as Gabe pulled the truck away and moved off to a spot off of the field. They sat there in the truck cab waiting as the giant's engines spun up and came to life, bellowing like a roaring blast furnace. The ground shook as they roared, the vibration shaking the truck and making the window buzz in the doorframe. Jacob could feel her life in the rumbling engines and whirring propeller blades as they passed in spinning revolutions.

She was alive, always alive now, he thought.

The giant began to roll, slowly almost imperceptibly at first, then faster, as it crossed the open field. Its tail came up the tail wheel spinning, and then bouncing on the main gear, flaps down for maximum lift, it met the horizon and lifted free from the earth. Up it went, the props spinning so fast they appeared as wheels within wheels pulling the giant up into the heavens. Then slowly, like a tightrope walker on a wire, it turned on a wing, then leveled itself and passed low overhead. The sound was deafening, almost too much to bear as the giant passed.

He could see her face as it passed them; see her face shining her eyes looking down on him as it passed. She was smiling, smiling at him, saying to him that he had closed the circle, made it right, that he had fixed it. They sat there for a long time, watching as the giant climbed and then receded into the distance. It became no more then a small speck on the horizon, then finally it was gone.

They sat in silence, listening to it as it receded, until there was no longer a sound of engines but only the sound of the wind in the grass. He thought of the Mustang, lying again in a heap on the field.

"Gabe, Where is she?" Jacob asked.

"She's gone son."

"What do you mean gone?"

"Her and the boy, they had to leave. It was the only way."

"Leave? What is this? I don't get it, she loves me, and she wouldn't just go?"

"Don't worry you'll see her again…"

"What do you mean?"

"You know son, you ask a lot of questions. Just be still for a spell."

"Well when will I see her?"

"You will soon, but first, we'll need to get you squared away then get to work on that plane." he said with a sigh.

"I got an old bottle of scotch whisky a friend of mine brought back from England a long time ago. Been saving it... Figure now is a good time to see if it's any good. You up for it…?"

"Sounds good to me Colonel..." Jacob replied as he laid his head back on the blanket, "Just as long as I don't have to make any more forced landings, I think my luck has just about run out."

"Oh, I don't know boy, you might be surprised… there could be a few more lucky pennies in your pocket yet…"

Jacob smiled slightly then grimaced as a pain shot through his left arm and up through his chest.

"Oh damn, that isn't good." He gasped suddenly.

"You just lie there for a few minutes son, I'll get you home."

Suddenly he began to feel numbness, as if he were not himself but a disembodied spirit floating aimlessly about the scene, not in it, no longer a part of it, but like a dispassionate observer who was watching it from a distance. He could not move, he could not reply to Gabe's words, he could feel himself slipping away. Gabe's voice became a distant sound, the sound of muffled conversation like a radio voice in the background. He could hear them there in the background, the voices the scratching reverberations and buzzing of the receiver, wind blowing in the cockpit, a cold wind, so cold that he could not breathe, he could not catch his breath, he could not feel, but only watch as the truck pulled away and the field drew out of focus.

Again he was dreaming, dreaming in darkness, the airfield, the tower, like pylons passing as he sped round them, the pursuer now behind him, the pressure on his chest, forcing him deep into the seat as he turned, fighting the controls, the slipstream of the planes in front of him, buffeting him as he forced his way past, faster now, the contrails, tracers marching toward him.

Again he was in the Phantom, flying fast and low over the jungle, the sudden hail of tracers, the lights in the cockpit, the rush of the wind slamming him into his seat as he ejected.

A throbbing sound, black whirling blades overhead, throbbing pain in his leg and the blades whirling, as he was lifted up and into the belly of the helicopter.

His eyes closed, the world went black.

Chapter 21

The room was a cold, sterile place with lime green, aqua cinderblock walls scrubbed clean with disinfectant, the floors shining like wet glass. The gurneys stood in attentive rows along the walls, their stainless steel, cold and gleaming. Situated in the basement of the hospital it had no windows to let in sunlight or heat to warm its occupants. Double doors stood mute, their windows painted over, closing the room off from the hallway on the other side.

Outside the room, people passed; doctors, nurses, visitors, orderlies walking to meetings, or other duties. Their comings and goings threw faint shadows under the florescent lights and the sounds of passing shoes on the clean linoleum mixed with their conversations and laughter. But in the room, all was quiet and still, no sound, no light only the rows of gurneys and the silent sleep of people for whom the passing of footsteps and chatter on the other side of the door meant nothing. They were lying on the gurneys. Silent, sullen, their blood settled and pooled in the lowest parts of their bodies, their fingers cold and blue and their faces ashen.

Jacob laid there, a new arrival to the room. He had been brought in only moments before. A young orderly had wheeled him in and found an opening in the rows for him, then without a word or second thought about him left him lying there, shut off the light and walked out into the hallway to his next errand.

He laid there a large tag with a wire tie twisted around the big toe on his foot, an aqua green sheet draped over him. The tag contained vital information, name, rank, serial number and so on. His nude body was still and lifeless.

Beyond his body, the eyes of his soul lifted and he could see the room and the darkness all around him.

Where am I? He asked himself. He looked at the rows of bare feet lined up for inspection each one with the same tag and wire tie on the same toe of the foot. He thought he could see his own foot and the tag.

What do I do? I am afraid, the words drifted into his mind.

Then it came to him, he could see clearly now, a destination at the end of a long road. It shone like the morning sun on the horizon and he began to remember.

He could hear voices in the room with him. Impatient, urgent voices that began to fill his consciousness with orders of measured doses, actions and requests for information, responses given in tight intervals, vital signs, responses measured and reported in quick precise words.

The room became bright; he was lying on a bed, the mattress was hard and the sheets taught and fresh with the smell of bleach and alcohol.

"He's not going to make it doctor." a voice rose up from the foot of the bed.

"Keep the epinephrine coming and be ready with those paddles."

He could hear the voices, smell the medicinal, sanitary smells and hear the sounds of equipment and the hydraulic action of instruments and compressed gas. He could feel increased pain and pressure throughout his body.

Then, without warning, he was there within himself. He was no longer away drifting on the wind. He was there in the moment with the world and in the present.

He opened his eyes in an effort to focus on the image hovering over him. The warm, inviting face of a woman, dressed in a nurses uniform stood over him, looking down at his face with concern, then nothing, only blackness.

"We're losing him again doctor." the nurse's voice urgent and yet moderated as she moved in the hazy light above him. He could still hear their voices and their movement as they fought again to recover him from the edge. His mind drifted and he was filled with the cold black darkness as death again rode toward him in an effort to carry him away.

In the next instant, Jacob could feel the dry air rush into his body and he shivered on the cold steel surface. He sat up suddenly gasping for breath the pain of the sutures pulling at him. Cautiously he sat up and slid round to the side of the gurney letting his feet hang over the side. He shivered with cold in the dark room and looked around at the rows of bodies that lay quietly around him. The shadows that had been there only moments before were gone and the room was silent. Only the sounds of passing footsteps from the hallway outside could be heard in the darkness of the morgue.

In the darkness he could not see that there were not

two feet dangling over the edge of the gurney. He could not feel the loss of his limb. It was as if the leg was still there, the knee, the calf, the foot still attached to him.

He slid from the table in an effort to stand and took the sheet with him in a motion to wrap it around his torso. His arm prick from the earlier IV bag bled slightly and stained it as he slid down and prepared to land on the floor. His remaining foot gave way as he attempted to balance himself on a leg that was no longer there. He fell to the floor; his face slapped the linoleum with a crack. It came to him then, the realization that his leg had been amputated.

Its gone! The thought rushed into his brain like ice in his veins. He felt sick, sweating, in a cold panic, paralyzed with fear at the realization.

I must get out of here. He thought as he began to crawl forward and approached the door and swung it open pushing his body against it as he dragged himself along. He entered the hallway shivering with cold against the shining linoleum, his eyes blinded by the brightness of the florescent lights overhead. His body ached and protested as he struggled to pull himself along, sliding painfully along the floor.

He felt the great age that had come upon him, a weight that came to his body as if he had climbed from a long swim in the sea and was now struggling against an overwhelming fatigue in an effort to make his way to the beach.

Several nurses and an orderly who were engaged in a lively conversation walked down the hallway and stopped as Jacob looked up at them his naked body under the sheet, the toe tag still attached to his remaining foot.

Noticing the tag on his toe, one of the nurses put her

hand to her mouth and fainted to the floor. The second bent over her, then looked up over at Jacob again and yelled at the orderly who was standing there his mouth open in shock.

"Go get the doctor on call! Do it now!" One of the nurses called out.

The boy snapped to and began running down the hallway, disappearing around the corner.

The nurse turned her attention to him, then looked around and produced a wheel chair that was folded at an entrance at the end of the hall.

"Let me get you in here." she commanded in a businesslike tone. We are going to get you to the ER." She began to wheel him away as the nurse on the floor groaned and began to regain consciousness.

"You alright…?" the nurse asked her companion.

"Yes, I think so."

"Good, tell the doctor when he gets here that we are on our way to the ER with a 'sleeper'!" she yelled over her shoulder as she hurried him away.

"Ok. I'm sorry, I…"

"Forget it. Just tell him!" the other nurse ordered as she moved him down the hallway toward the emergency room.

Chapter 22

The room, starched white with the antiseptic precision of clear alcohol and glazed porcelain sat quietly in its place among an orderly row of rooms. It was one among many, nondescript, cells that made up a long hall of hospital rooms that held the old, the sick, the dying and the demented.

Jacob laid there, his stump a long dead reminder of a limb, scarred and shriveled with age. There had been many years that had passed since a war and a low pass over a jungle had taken it.

He lay there in the hospital bed, sheets tightly fitted around him, his head and back propped up by several pillows behind him. He looked around the room, his eyes shifting slightly. He looked over to the window, straining slightly in an effort to see outside. He could hear the traffic passing below, the sounds of cars and trucks, of work going on in the street below his window, sounds like the electro-mechanical rumbling of machinery moving on a carrier deck far out at sea.

He was an old man now, old and alone in the stark reality of hard hospital mattresses and the pain of bedsores and old memories that would not heal.

A young doctor and a nurse entered the room. Jacob in his age looked upon the young man and found it difficult to believe that the man was old enough to be in high school, let alone be a physician.

The doctor looked down at the chart.

"Good morning, ah, Captain…Captain…" he said as he scanned the chart to find a name.

"Jacob doctor." the nurse spoke in tired exhaustion.

"Yes so it is. Good morning Mr. Ah…" the doctor again looked at the chart, "There is no last name on the chart, nurse?"

"Sorry doctor but there was no other information. We tried to find more but that's all they had."

"No last name?"

"The serial number showed up but, no last name." she responded.

"Probably some foul up at the VA, in any event… and how are we feeling today?" the doctor asked as he thumbed through the chart and records.

There were several seconds without a response.

Jacob tried to speak. He could hear the words. He could understand, but when he tried to form words his brain would not respond. He tried to move his mouth, his lips quivered as he worked the words over in his mind, trying to form a sentence. He tried to move his arm, tried to raise his hand but the limb would not respond.

"What's the matter, Captain?" the doctor asked.

"He's unable to speak, doctor." the nurse interrupted.

"Yes, I can see that, nurse, what is the matter with him."

The nurse, slipped her hand to the chart that he was holding turned a page and pointed to the notes.

"Oh I see we had a stroke recently. That explains it."

the young doctor responded dispassionately drawing the stethoscope from around his neck, "Your chart says that you've had a pretty serious stroke, had a heart attack, triple bypass, a year ago and oh and a visit to the morgue I see… You a smoker…?" he asked again forgetting Jacob's condition.

He placed the cold steel of the stethoscope to Jacob's chest and probed for signs of life.

"He has very limited movement in his right side, doctor and no longer walks with the prosthesis." she interjected in an effort to answer his question.

"Really, well then, no, I suppose you gave up smoking a long time ago, along with several other things I'd imagine." the doctor mused.

"Good. That's good Captain. Now breathe please…" The doctor said apathetically as he pulled the instrument from his ears, took up Jacob's wrist and looked down at his watch.

"Well everything seems to be in order here, your heart is stable, your rhythm normal. You know Captain we thought we'd lost you the other day, scared the hell out of the nurses. I have to admit you surprised us." the doctor said as he continued monitoring for a moment, and leaned toward the nurse, "How long has he been in here?"

The nurse looked again at the chart, "He was brought in a few days ago, the people at the retirement home said that he collapsed during the evening meal."

The doctor acted as though Jacob could not hear their conversation, "Well we are feeling better aren't we?" he said as he made notations on the chart.

"It looks as though, we could have you out of here in say, the next day or so…"

He turned again to the nurse, “Any next of kin or maybe a friend that we can call?”

Jacob thought about the question. He could recall no one. There was no family. He had business associates, acquaintances, but they were only faces, people who’s names he had long forgotten, not friends. He had been alone.

“Not that I am aware of doctor.” the nurse responded, “We are to call the service and they’ll come and get him when he is ready to be released.”

The doctor finished writing, clicking his pen closed with a thumb and snapping the chart closed with a brisk, well practiced movement of his hand.

“This kind of thing is a real shame. No family, no friends, a person in this shape. Sometimes I wonder…” The doctor stopped himself in mid-sentence and returned the chart to its place at the foot of the bed.

The nurse pushed past the doctor and began working the pillows behind Jacob’s head as she spoke, “If you are finished doctor, we’d like to get the Captain into his wheelchair?” the nurse asked. She knew where the doctor was going and wanted no part of the conversation.

“What, oh yes that’s fine, I’m finished.” the doctor replied quickly and walked toward the door, “Take care now, we will have you out of here and back to your own bed very soon.”

The nurse then moved over to a call button and rang for an orderly who brought a wheelchair and helped him to the seat and then to the bathroom.

Jacob sat on the toilet, in glum humiliation with the orderly standing over him, watching him relieve himself. He stared into the mirror that hung facing the toilet on the back of the door.

Is that me? He thought and tried to lean closer to the reflection in an effort to peer into his own eyes and inspect the face of the old man staring back at him.

My God, how long has it been? How many years? It seems like only yesterday when I…? He caught himself suddenly urinating on the floor.

"Damnit! Now look what you've done." the orderly said under his breath as he picked a towel from the sink and began mopping up the flow.

"Now you'll need some dry pajamas." the orderly sighed impatiently as he left him sitting there in search of clean clothes.

I can't even take a piss by myself, Jacob thought.

The orderly moved with dispassionate efficiency, his strong hands lifting the old man from the seat and methodically dressing him in clean pajamas, then sitting him down in the wheelchair.

"Where would you like to go?" the orderly asked as he moved behind the chair and grabbed the handles.

Jacob could not respond but thought that the young man could not take him where he wanted to go. The man pushed him over to the window and left him sitting in the chair.

Jacob looked down at the satchel that had been left sitting on a low nightstand beside the bed. He could see the faded gold block lettering, 'Beauchamp Products' etched on the side. He remembered the miles, the compromises.

It must have been a dream, he thought as the sounds of traffic, the noise of the world passing made its way through the window panes and filled him with the reality of the moment. It was a somber grey reality, one that left him drawn down and doubting that any of it had ever happened. It was like many small things, the kind of thing that pushed him into a depression and made him recall the many years that had rolled by. He was reminded of a man too busy to do things right, to check things. Moments of indecision and impatience that had changed everything. He had worn these things like a heavy overcoat, the lapse in judgment and a second pass over the target, a girl who long ago had died when he could not bring himself to risk death, that moment and the pain that he had carried in his chest, like a knotted fist that had brought him back again to the hospital and nearly killed him. All of these things pressed down on him. He had tried so many things to find refuge, to start again. Things he had tried without success.

He thought again of the dream, of himself on the steel gurney with the eye of his soul looking down upon him and wished again the great wish, the wish of all pilots, to be up there, away from the earth. Somewhere there in the heavens there was relief, he thought. He wished harder and prayed, prayed that what had happened had not been a dream, that somehow he had mended what had been broken and that there could be something more than this glum reality before him, something more than a weary obituary.

He recalled how every time he heard the sound of an aircraft he was compelled to look up, to look for it, to find it in the sky. He thought of the long roads, the towers that on occasion he would see. He would travel far off the road to track them down, and then find nothing. He had spent a lifetime searching, the years had rolled onward and the years turned to decades in the blink of an eye.

They were all dead now…all of them dead. It was a dream, just a crazy illusion; rationalizing that which in a sudden sweep of emotion he had momentarily prayed had been true.

He drifted off to sleep in the chair and the business of the hospital wound down as he slept. Orderlies, nurses moved in scheduled shifts outside his closed door. He sat alone sleeping as they passed by tending to other patients. The afternoon turned to night and the hospital wound down further to quiet echoed footsteps in empty hallways and the muted voices of television announcers calling a basketball game on a small portable set as the night watchman dozed in front of it at the front desk. As the hours grew later, the sounds receded still further and along with the sounds from the street below faded to stillness as the halls of the hospital fell silent.

Then in the quiet of the late night, there came a faint tapping on the linoleum floor, a quiet almost imperceptible sound like the beads of a rosary shifting in someone's fingers. Slowly the sound grew though only by a faint measure and became a rhythmic tapping that progressed along the hallway. The sound joined with the sound of footsteps, several sets of footsteps, also quiet and a low panting as two forms quietly slipped past the front desk and made their way to Jacob's door.

Jacob opened his eyes as the sound approached him. He did not know how long he had been sleeping, nor why the faint sound had caused him to wake. He looked down and was startled by the image of Hop's single-eyed stare looking up at him, panting from the walk down the hall, looking as always forlorn and exhausted.

How the hell did you get in here ole boy? Jacob thought.

The dog acted as though he had heard what he was thinking and stood up bracing his paw on Jacobs's leg, lightly licking his motionless hand with his tongue.

"We slipped in while the guard was sleeping, son."

"We have a surprise for you!" the young boy blurted out, too filled with excitement to hold it in any longer.

Jacob heard the voice, the sound of the old man who had materialized from the darkness and stood behind him. Next to him, the small boy stood by, the son he had never known, holding a small model airplane, quietly playing with it.

Gabe looked over at the boy and put his index finger to his lips, "Let's be real quiet now son, don't want to wake the sick folks…"

The boy smiled, his eyes twinkling with a cherub's delight.

Jacob could not speak, but could gasp a weak smile as Gabe reached down and took the handles of the wheelchair. He bent low to Jacob's ear, "It's time to go son…"

They slipped past the sleeping guard and made their way down the ramp to the old pickup truck that sat at the curb. He looked up as they approached and could see the grill the rusted hood and broken headlight of the vehicle as it sat there.

He remembered how he had thought that he had seen it many times before. There had been many times over the years when he thought that he had seen it, many instances when, in passing through he caught a glimpse of something familiar in a cracked windshield or a squeaking break lining. He had been fooled many times and had convinced himself that it was only his imagination and not the object of his memory.

He felt suddenly as if a weight had been lifted from him, knowing now that he had not been dreaming that it had been true or that he had lapsed into a dream and wanted to remain there.

Gabe helped him into the truck and struggled with the wheelchair, sliding it into the bed.

"Won't be need'n this much longer." he said as he, the boy and Hop climbed in and together they pulled out on to the road. The street lights passed along the windshield in rapid succession as they made their way down the sleeping city streets. The tires hummed, rumbling over rough spots in the pavement and the breeze from the open cab blew warm air that coursed over them as they drove off into the night.

Jacob closed his eyes and let his head fall back against the door frame. He prayed that if it were not true, that if he were again dreaming that he would sleep for eternity.

Chapter 23

A tiny shard of glass etched a contrail of white across a vast open field of frozen azure sky. Its progress seemed almost imperceptibly slow, its engines silent at such an altitude.

He sat there in the truck and watched its progress through the windshield. He could see that it was moving, and had traced its path in a straight diagonal on the glass first from one smudged insect then to another as it passed through his field of vision.

They had driven through the night and now the hot summer sun beat down on the roof and turned the inside into a simmering steel box. He sat there cooking slowly in his own sweat, his eyes tired with sleep and his mind adrift as they made their way along a desolate stretch of country road. Gabe had not spoken since they left the hospital, his eyes fixed on the road ahead. He did not need to speak.

Jacob thought about the people up there as they passed above him. He imagined them, sipping drinks, working, napping, a mother quieting a cranky infant, faces peaking occasionally over the seat backs as the airliner slipped through an ethereal slipstream on its way to some destination. They were oblivious to him, to the comings and goings of those who earthbound below made their way along like so many ants. He thought about these things, the great sea of people with connections, with homes and families all thrown together to ride a white pencil line that the aircraft so small and far away burned into the sky. He remembered what his father had said about them, and how pilots saw these things differently.

He peered over the dashboard at the road. It stretched out to the horizon as it always had, in the illusion of converging lines. He sat in silence wondering about his destination and if he again were not just dreaming. There had been many occasions to think about this over the many lonely roads that he had traveled over the years.

He was far from the city now, far from the hot, bustling mass of humanity, the crowded sidewalks and boiling snarls of endless traffic. He had driven so far along two lane back roads, far from the pavement, and the homogenous series of stops on highway exits and endless replays of common towns sterilized by discount stores and fast food chains.

There had been so many small towns. They were like islands in the great ocean of fields that stretched out over the years in a hazy mirage of distant horizons, tired overworked plant managers and jobless rural people. Like him, they wanted only to get away, to escape the grinding boredom, the unrelenting sameness that throbbed like a dull painful toothache that never went away, never subsided but held on somehow and grew with every passing year. He could see it in their eyes, the tired painful desperation that had come from a slow insidious process of husbandry and domestication. Each compromise, each bit of indecision and fear each small reward added to a diet that slowly reduced them to the herd. He knew that he had been like them, beyond the days of youthful ambition, too far into the mistakes and carelessness of a thousand missteps, living in a dull routine without respite or escape.

He thought again about the pass over the target. Like a thousand times before he thought about it, about the girl and his fear. He thought about how those things had weighed upon him and how a man with one leg had struggled along, carrying the memories of those things with him like a millstone about his neck.

There had been only the road and the dream. The single thing that until now seemed only to have been the fantasy of an old man's dying brain, starving for oxygen in a hospital morgue.

He had tried many times over the years to find the place, to return to the dream. A newspaper ad would catch his attention as if it had been left open for him to read. He would look down casually at it and the ad would look back at him, like a quiet pleading. He would travel miles to properties far out of his way fitting them in between business meetings.

There had been many meetings, many quiet smoldering sessions, dates and times that he had dutifully made. He thought of them now as a solid mass of time, of a summed total of life experience that read like a telephone book. All of it seemed, hopeless, a meaningless string of colorless pages that said little. He had had little to live for. There had been some exceptions, moments when he was distracted by an occasional small plane flying low over a field in the middle of open country. He had chased many a small, single engine plane with his gaze.

He would drive for as far as possible in parallel with it, watching first it then the road as it passed overhead, wondering if possibly that plane had been one of them.

He felt that he could not resist the desire to see them and to make certain that these places and things were not simply the result of idle dreaming. He wanted to see them himself, walk out onto the tarmacs and look down range of the runways, even if they were nothing more than cow pastures or abandoned shacks and his wooden leg, nothing more than a reminder that he would not fly again and that the great wish was no longer something for him.

Gabe thumbed through the range of AM radio stations that faded in and out. He continued twisting the knob and Jacob's thoughts faded as Gabe searched for the next station broadcasting its faint signal from some remote corner of an old building or from a shack set back off the road. As Gabe worked the knob Jacob caught the faint sound of a familiar voice ringing out through the static hum, a strong, confident, soothing voice that spoke in the marked cadence of a radio evangelist, singing words in measured phrases about, hell, damnation and redemption.

He remembered that he had heard it said that if one could reach out far enough and had a receiver capable of picking up the faintest of signals, that every sound no matter how ancient or insignificant could be intercepted. This notion entered Jacob's mind as he listened and the sound got stronger and a litany of gospel songs, Bible readings and personal testimony grew in clarity and intensity over the airwaves.

The sounds soothed the headache that throbbed in his temples and the numbness in his arm, again like a hundred times before in spite of his denials, his futile attempts to distract himself with work. The numbness that would not go away, would not be silenced, numbness that eventually made itself known by pinning him to a hospital bed.

He could imagine the place. He could see it emerging from off the edge of the road as he came to the end of a cornfield. It was there, alone, in an empty expanse of closely cropped grass, the low cinderblock buildings that he had imagined over the miles, their tired, dilapidated structures abandoned and long forgotten. He could see it all, the building and the place. It had been there a long time, the cheery sign on the front now faded and worn to the point that it could barely be read.

He imagined what the place had been like when it first opened, about the occasional salesman or truck driver who might've stopped for a sandwich and seeing the pictures on the walls would ask if the owner was in the service or had once been a pilot. He imagined Gabe giving them conversation and the litany of stories. He could see them on the weekends as well, people from town coming by on sunny Sunday afternoons after church to watch the planes take off and land. They came as modern day barnstormers who might fly in with an old relic and offer to take a brave soul up for a flight. He could see all of this and the place was alive with the colorful banter and adolescent exchanges of pilots and mechanics, the smell of av-gas and motor oil, low droning aircraft engines and the bark of tires as planes touched down and trundled their way to the tarmac. He could see all of this in the place.

He could see an old picnic table there in the shade of an apple tree away from the heat. He could see the lit cigarette in his hand looking down at it he could see it glowing amber, orange and the smoke rising like pencil lines in the tiny thermals. He could see the remains of a windsock, frayed and hanging from a pole next to the building limp in the burning sun. He listened to the radio and dreamt of the place and of summer.

He had lost track of time in traveling and the signals from dozens of stations had in succession become weak, drifted then died to nothing, only the static hum of distant broadcasts that struggled to cast their message across the chasm of remote open country.

He sat there, sweltering in the unrelenting glare of the sun, watching the small silver sliver drift in lonesome anonymity, thankful that it had not been a dream, or if it had, that there would be an eternity of dreaming ahead.

Then Gabe stopped the truck and Jacob once again saw what had been in his heart. A great field of low cropped green grass blew in the sunshine, a field that was wide and clear with only the surface of black asphalt runway and the buildings long since gone, reduced to memories.

A large white tent had been erected on the site; it sat like a huge circus tent its open flaps blowing in the gentle breeze. About the tent in the grass, a multitude of aircraft stood parked in casual rows. Their owners sat about under wings or stood leaning on fuselages with rags wiping shining metal or fabric skins and talking with lively anticipation. It looked as though hundreds had come, though he could not imagine why.

Gabe helped him out, and then into the wheelchair.

"Don't you worry bout this son, soon you'll be home." He said as he pushed Jacob toward the tent.

The others followed as the little boy, Gabe and Jacob crossed over the threshold of the makeshift church, a congregation turning toward them, looking at them warmly as they entered. As Gabe wheeled him up the aisle he could hear the sound of a choir of voices and the loud chiming of an old piano coming from the stage. When he reached the front, the singing stopped. Jacob could see the people crammed into the tent seated on old wooden folding chairs set out in rows from front to back or standing in the back of the tent near the entrance. Fathers and sons had relinquished seats for mothers and daughters, young mothers held fussy infants or quieted small children who were squirming impatiently. The floor was bare grass and the heat from the day continued to hang in the air. It was thick in the tent and people sat wilting in their Sunday clothes some quietly fanning themselves as they waited for the preacher to begin.

The preacher sat quietly with several others at the front of the room on a large wooden platform that elevated the group above the audience. He was a young man, very young, almost a boy. He was plainly dressed; simple, his features thin and quiet. Of the group on the platform he seemed the least likely to be the preacher but rather more like a child who might bring ice water or turn the sheet music for the pianist. He sat and waited calmly for the crowd to settle and for the room to quiet to silence. It became still, quiet except for an infant in the back of the room and the insects singing outside in the grass.

The young man rose to his feet and walked slowly and confidently to a pulpit that had been fashioned from several discarded peach crates. He held cradled in his hand a black leather Bible that he opened and with practiced grace turned to a marked page and began to read aloud first in a calm, quiet tone then, louder and stronger, gathering strength with each word,

"And Jacob was left alone; and a man wrestled with him until the breaking of the day. When the man saw that he did not prevail against Jacob, he touched the hollow of his thigh; and Jacob's thigh was put out of joint as he wrestled with him. Then he said, "Let me go, for the day is breaking." But Jacob said, "I will not let you go, unless you bless me." And he said to him, "What is your name?" And he said, "Jacob." Then he said, "Your name shall no more be called Jacob, but Israel, for you have striven with God and with men, and have prevailed." Then Jacob asked him, "Tell me, I pray, your name." But he said, "Why is it that you ask my name?" And there he blessed him."

Then the preacher looked out over the silent crowd and turned the pages over to another section. His eyes searched the room and for a moment, locked onto Jacob's as he read again,

"…Then he fell asleep in that place and had a dream. He saw a stairway erected on the earth with its top reaching to the heavens. The angels of God were going up and coming down it and the Lord stood at its top…."

The preacher lowered the Bible and looked out then at the crowd and again looked at Jacob. The preacher opened his hand resting the Bible on a palm and then pointed with the index finger of his other hand,

"…For the Lord himself, with a word of command, with the voice of an archangel and with the trumpet of God, will come down from heaven and the dead in Christ will rise first. Then we, who are alive, who are left, will be caught up together with them in the clouds to meet the Lord in the air…"

Then suddenly with the words, he heard it, the crackling staccato of an idling radial engine churning, its pistons sucking hard to get just enough fuel to stay alive. The sound of it flooded his mind with familiar images of an old aircraft, an old friend from a long time ago. He could feel it through the steel wheels of the chair, vibrating the ground as it spun the propeller in endless revolutions.

The congregation turned to him then to the entrance of the tent.

Gabe looked down at him in the chair, his eyes quiet, filled with emotion.

"It's time to go son."

Jacob could feel his body grow stronger now, he felt himself lifted from the chair, the eye of his spirit looking at the congregation and at his remains sitting there in the chair, old and tired, a worn shell.

He emerged from the tent, again the young man, strong and true and saw it standing there, waiting patiently for him on the tarmac, its bright yellow wings and tail, its royal blue fuselage shining in the sun.

"Jay-kob?" the voice came up from behind him. She stood there behind him, her arms crossed in front of her with a playful impatience.

"It's like a dream, the most beautiful dream I could have." He spoke without looking back at her but only at the aircraft idling, vibrating with impatience.

He looked back and saw her now; the face was again the face he remembered. She was there again in front of him the woman in the jungle, barefoot on the pavement of the runway, she was the personification of all of them, her eyes and comely shape the prop wash blowing her hair and the hem of her dress in billowing folds, the image of the woman the olive face of his dream.

She stood there smiling, holding the hand of the little

boy, the son he had never known, the child standing next to her, in the billowing of her hem, smiling.

She took his hand and suddenly they were sprinting together to the aircraft. He could feel his legs, strong and supple under him, his body once again filled with youth.

He climbed onto the wing, took her hand and in turn lifted her and then the boy up to the cockpit as well. She looked back at him and smiled with excitement as he slipped a foot into the step on the fuselage and climbed in behind her.

The afternoon sun had crept lower on the horizon now and the heat of midday faded. Jacob could feel the cooling breeze of the prop wash and no longer felt the fist in his chest or the sweat of the hot summer day, only the wind in his face, the wind of the prop as it spun up and pulled the tail in behind it on the centerline of the crumbling remains of the runway.

She looked back again at him smiling now, her face flushed by the sun, her eyes bright.

He looked at her, then down at his hands on the stick and the throttle, young hands, strong and confident on the controls.

He slipped the throttle forward and the aircraft rolled, picked up pace and raced to the end of the runway. He was with the airplane now, they were one and the endless horizon beckoned them on, on to the great cathedral, its limitless rafters reaching ever upward to the outstretched angel wings of cumulus that reached out to him from the cotton landscape above to cradle them as they drifted with the wind.

He thought of them all now, Gabe, Hop, his mother and father and all of the nameless faces in town. He knew that he would see them again, that there would be an airfield out there somewhere waiting for him when he was ready to land.

I'll be home soon, he thought as he pointed the nose upward and gained altitude. He switched on the radio and turned the volume as high as it would go. Over the blast of the wind and drumming growl of the engine, a gospel song rang out,

"You have to walk that lonesome valley all by your self..." the song began.

Not today...Not today, he thought as the aircraft grew smaller, and then slowly faded from view.

The sound of the engine remained for several moments more, and then it faded leaving only the sound of the breeze over the grass. The tent faded and disappeared too. The planes that lined the runway also took up positions and in turn lifted, rose into the sky and faded away, climbing too into the great sea of stars as day became night. There remained only the grass, waving green and tall in an empty field, empty except for the remains of an asphalt strip that faced the southwest into the wind, where the horizon met the setting sun and a lone tower stood like a sentinel guarding the lonely remains of a rural mythology.

An owl sat high on the tower overlooking the field as an old three-legged mongrel dog, stepped out onto the asphalt and sat quietly waiting, waiting for the sound of an approaching aircraft.

Printed in the United States
81004LV00001B/1-6